Flip My Heart

Elizabeth Seckman

This is a work of fiction. Names, characters, places, and incidents are products of the author's imagination or are used fictitiously and are not to be construed as real. Any resemblance to actual events, locations, organizations, or persons, living or dead, is entirely coincidental.

World Castle Publishing, LLC
Pensacola, Florida
Copyright © Elizabeth Seckman 2020
Paperback ISBN: 9781953271204
eBook ISBN: 9781953271211
First Edition World Castle Publishing, LLC, October 12, 2020
http://www.worldcastlepublishing.com

Licensing Notes

Cover: Alex M. Diaz
Editor: Maxine Bringenberg

Chapter 1

Danni checked her make-up in the bathroom mirror one more time. It had been adequate in the hotel this morning, but under the harsh scrutiny of past acquaintances, it suddenly failed miserably. The fresh coat of foundation did nothing to conceal puffy eyes or dark circles…did she suddenly have a furrowed brow, crow's feet, and frown lines? Wasn't twenty-eight too young to be a wrinkled old crone? She fumbled through her purse, ashamed of herself for even caring at a time like this. The funeral home had done its best to make the bathroom look homey, with pots of silk flowers and scatterings of sponge-painted fleur-de-lis, but it was still a shitty place no one wanted to visit.

She held the tube of mascara in the palm of her hand, staring at it as if it were a drug, and she was the junkie on the verge of surrender. It really didn't matter how she looked. This day was about saying goodbye and paying her respects to the woman who had raised her. Taking a deep breath, she held it, willing the tears not to fall. Max had raised her to be strong—or tried, at least. Danni didn't feel strong. Nothing was more tempting than curling up in a ball and crying until she could cry no more. The stifled sobs raised her body temperature, and she suddenly felt too hot, her clothes too tight. What cruel bastard invented funerals?

The bathroom door opened. The sound of high heels clicking on tile got Danni's attention like the blast from a siren. Fully aware she looked like a horrendously old raccoon, she groaned. She grabbed her purse from the sink, hugged it to her chest, and slipped inside a stall. Silently she turned the lock, then settled herself on a toilet seat with her feet tucked under her. She sat as still as granite.

Through the crack, Danni could see two sets of heels. Black, sling-back sandals. The voices of the feet whined as they did their business and touched up hair and make-up. Danni heard hair spray and frowned. She rolled her eyes and felt the beginnings of leg cramps.

Then she smelled smoke. Someone lit a cigarette? Who did that in a public bathroom? And why was Danni hiding from hair-spritzing smokers? She should stand up and walk out of the stall, allow her legs some blood flow and her pride some breathing room. But she didn't. As much as she willed her body to move, it flat out ignored her... wouldn't so much as twitch.

"Tori! I thought you stopped smoking."

Danni closed her eyes and groaned inwardly. Tori Smith.

"Oh, I had. But I gained three pounds. And quite frankly, I'd rather take my chances with cancer than let my ass get huge."

Laughter.

Hilarious joke at a cancer victim's funeral, bitch. Danni imagined screaming the words, but her jaw clamped shut so tight she worried she'd chip a molar.

"Speaking of big asses. Have you seen Danni yet?" Tori asked.

Danni felt the heat rise from her heart to her face. Her stomach churned. "No. Do you seriously think she'll show? I mean, when was the last time she crossed the Oregon Inlet?"

"I heard Max begged her to come home — from her deathbed — and Danni ignored her. Can you believe that?"

"No way. I know Danni hates coming home, but she'd never dodge Max."

"So, where is she, Tina?"

Tina Barrick. Tori's shadow. In Tina's defense, Danni had also walked in the beautiful dynamo's shadow. But she'd grown out of it. Tina obviously hadn't.

"Maybe she couldn't make it. I heard Max never told anyone she had cancer, not even Darby."

"If she lied, it's only because perfect little Danni's life has gone straight down the toilet since she left to 'conquer the world.' I heard her husband left her *after* he squandered her entire inheritance and *after* he moved in with a woman in Florida. I hear Danni offered to go to counseling, and he suggested fat camp instead." Tori laughed.

"What a prick. Did he really?"

"Oh, for crying out loud, Tina, don't tell me you feel sorry for her?"

"Danni was always nice. I swear, Tor, I think you hate her because her and Fisher —"

"I suggest you shut your mouth. Fisher pitied her. He told me himself there was nothing between them."

Danni's breath caught in her throat. She covered her mouth with her hand to stifle the gasp.

"Hah. I think he's lying, or sincerely underexaggerating. I dropped her off at his house in the middle of the night. I'm not an idiot."

"Underexaggerated? Is that even a word, Tina?" Someone punched the hand blower with some force. Tori said, in a voice loud enough to be heard over the dryer and possibly out into the hallway, "Fisher feels nothing for Danni but pity." There was a pause. Then, "Don't shrug your shoulders at me." Tori's words echoed off the walls, sharp as edged steel. "I know Fisher. He's told me all about the pathetic Rodanthe Luna Lowry. Fisher thinks her mother did too many drugs while she was pregnant with her. Screwed up Danni's brain."

"Well, all I know is there are ten minutes till start. I hope, for Max's sake, that she makes it."

"Max is dead." Danni heard the sizzle of the cigarette being doused by running water. "But we had better get a seat. Maxine Lowry was crazy as a bedbug, but she sure as hell was popular."

The heels clicked across the tiles and out the door.

Danni stepped out of the stall and wished beyond all wishes she could skip all of this and go home — if a one-bedroom apartment where she lived out of boxes could be called home. Instead, she wished she was away from here — maybe on an airplane flying to another country where she could start a new life.

A new life. That was the answer. She could walk out of this room and disappear, never see any of these people again. Who the hell would miss her? All the loving people who thought she abandoned her aunt in her time of suffering? She could say goodbye to Max from anywhere. It didn't have to be in this claustrophobic tomb that reeked of mums, ferns, and expired perfumes.

Danni tucked her purse under her arm and slinked out of the bathroom. Midway to the exit, she heard her name called. The voice stopped her in her tracks. She turned slowly and smiled as if by instinct. A tear rolled down her cheek. "Fisher."

"Where are you headed? You all right?"

He was bigger than she remembered. The navy had filled out his six-foot frame with muscles. His hair was still dark as midnight, especially now that it was longer with waves and curls.

"I was, um, getting a breath of air."

"Well, it's past time to start. I told them to wait; you'd show up."

"I...." Danni bit her lip. "I've been here a while." She blinked back the tears.

Fisher closed the gap between them and wrapped an arm around her. "I understand." He gave her a hug and held her for several minutes. "You're not alone, Loonie."

She nodded. For now, she would accept that lie.

He kept an arm around her waist as he escorted her into the sanctuary of the church. She heard whispers as she walked past row after row of packed pews. Fisher seated her in the front row and sat next to her, her hand gripped in his. There was a poster-sized picture of her aunt on the altar, surrounded by flowers and collages pieced together from snapshots of her aunt's life. Danni's life. Danni sat and looked over the pictures as the minister's words droned in her ear like the buzz from the highway.

Eyes closed, she blocked out all the sounds. None of it mattered—not the words of the eulogy or the coughs and sniffles of the people behind her. Her mind wasn't in this dreary place. It was relaxing in her happy place—a place in time where Max was alive and available in the flesh. An image so real, she could feel Max's hand in hers, hear the cry of a whipping wind, smell the salt from the sea.

Together they walked along the shore. It was night. Her aunt stopped and looked to the sky and said, "When I come here and look out at the moon, I feel closer to my sister. I miss her laugh, her sense of humor, her kindness." Max sighed. "But looking at that moon, I think of her pregnant with you looking out over that black sky and saying, 'Max, at times like this, I'm not afraid. My child will never live in fear. Maybe it's the old island magic in me, but I know my baby will be a girl, and her name will be Rodanthe Luna. It will protect her. Her first blessing.' And so, she named you Rodanthe Luna that night."

A name Danni hated. It was ridiculous. Max should never have let a schizophrenic teenager name her bastard child. Max had always told her she would appreciate the name one day. That day still hadn't come, especially not after marrying Rick Cee. Max was the first to point out with a hoot and a thigh slap. "Danni, if you marry this fella, you'll be Rodanthe Luna Cee. Luna Cee? Get it, lunacy?"

Danni ignored the hint the universe shoved in her face and married Rick Cee anyhow. And it had turned out to be lunacy. *Oh, Max, why didn't I listen to you?*

"'Cause you're as stubborn as a mule," a voice spoke behind her. Danni opened her eyes and spun in her chair, scanning the guests behind her. She startled a thin man with even thinner hair with her accusing stare.

"Sorry," Danni mumbled. "I thought I, uh, heard a bee."

She turned back around. Fisher gave her hand a squeeze and smiled down at her.

Danni concentrated on the minister's words. She couldn't allow her mind to stray.

"Max was a friend to all, a stranger to none," Pastor Philip said.

A flash of light from the corner of her eye caught Danni's attention. The light seemed to come in from the window. Danni squinted, trying to see past the glow. In the glow, there was a shadow. Something—no, someone—stared from the window. Danni shielded her eyes with her hand to get a good look. It waved at her. The glow from the window dimmed for just a moment, and Danni could make out the figure.

It was Max! Curly hair poking out from under her straw hat. Ornery grin on her face.

She jerked on Fisher's hand and pointed to the window. Fisher looked, then patted her leg with his free hand. "I'm sorry, Danni. Seems like the lawn crew could have waited till after the service to get to work. That's rude."

"Lawn crew?" Danni looked again. A guy in a ball cap looked in the window, then disappeared.

Danni chewed the side of her cheek and decided grief was causing her to hear and see things. Must be the stress. She returned her attention to the service. A girl dressed in all black stepped to the podium. "Max saved my life," she said. Danni tried to listen intently to the story of how her aunt had befriended the homeless girl and her dying mother. Danni smiled a little. This must be Darby. Max had wanted her to come home to meet the girl, but she never had the time...or the money. Danni felt her heart squeeze at the realization that the bitches in the bathroom were right. She was a horrible person. She had let Max down. How could she ever forgive herself?

Max taught her everything. There wasn't a single part of her life that wasn't a credit to Max, from being able to drive to advanced calculus. It was all Max. Max Lowry took the time for all things. Danni never took time for anything. Danni bit her lip. Her chest hurt. Her cheeks blazed.

Then the voice spoke to her again. "Danni."

Danni looked for the voice, then looked to the people sitting next to her. No one else was looking. No one else heard voices. Just her. She looked at Fisher. He smiled down at her and brushed a roughened thumb across her cheek, giving it an at-a-girl pinch. She leaned close to him and whispered, "Did you hear that?"

"Hear what?" he whispered back.

Danni bit her lip. "Nothing. Never mind." Danni tried to concentrate on Darby's words.

"Danni. Look right," the voice said.

Danni looked right. She saw her aunt's head bob up from behind a spray of funeral flowers.

"Look left."

Danni snapped her head left. Max waved from behind the minister. Danni blinked hard to clear her vision. She covered her eyes with her hand and rubbed before looking up again. The minster had bunny ears behind his head.

Danni covered her mouth and looked at the people around her. There were tear stained faces and looks of mourning, but no one, absolutely no one, acted like they saw Max bouncing from place to place at her own funeral service. Danni rubbed her eyes harder. Evidently, guilt was making her see things. She looked across at the minister again, and he was alone.

Max was gone. Danni wiped away a tear, which was followed by another. Then another. Suddenly there was a flood of them. There was no stopping them. This was the emotional onslaught she'd hoped to avoid, or at least save for her pillow. Fisher pulled her close and held her against him. He was warm and still smelled like Dial soap and fresh cut cedar. She gladly buried her face in his chest, gripping his suit jacket, and decided to stay there until the service ended. So what if everyone thought she was a big baby? She didn't give a damn about any of them. After today, she would never see another one of these people again. She was leaving this island for good.

Darby finished speaking. The minister asked for others. A parade of people spoke, but Danni didn't care who they were, didn't listen to what they said. Her aunt was amazing. Her aunt was perfect. She didn't need anyone to tell her that.

Finally, there was no one left who wanted to speak.

Danni peeled herself away from Fisher, blew her nose, and dried her eyes. The minister gave his final prayer, ending with the assurance that all could trust in God, have faith in his plan. Danni snorted and rolled her eyes. A few heads turned to her, but she offered no explanation. She followed the procession out of the building into the harsh afternoon sun.

As the herd of people went east to the beach for a final prayer,

Danni bolted to the west. She heard Fisher call her name, but she didn't look back. She would send him a nice thank-you note when she got...wherever she was going. Nearly running to her car, she almost turned an ankle, but she made it. Half her skirt was still hanging out of the car door when she slammed it shut, but she didn't care. She put the key in the ignition and tromped the gas.

As she approached Highway 12, she suddenly had company in her car. The once empty passenger seat was filled. Her aunt looked at her and clucked her tongue. "Why, Danni, you ain't even gonna stick around? I have a keg of your favorite beer and a fish fry for tonight."

"What the — ?"

These were the only words Danni could formulate on her tongue before she heard the blare of a horn and the squeal of tires. Bam! Loud as a gunshot, her car collided with an oncoming truck.

Chapter 2

Crap. How will I pay for a rental?

That was Danni's first thought as she looked out over the mangled front of her Prius. Fisher pounded on her window, but she ignored him. If she didn't roll it down, she didn't have to answer whether or not she was okay. Obviously, she wasn't. And a glance in her rearview mirror told her it was about to get even worse. They were coming for her—the funeral attendees. Gaping and gawking, they lurched toward her like creatures-of-the-damned coming to devour her soul. To her left, the guy in the truck who hit her, or more precisely who she hit, swung shaking legs to the ground and hobbled toward her, evidently determined to join the circus of sympathy.

She hit the auto lock button, closed her eyes, and rested her cheek against the airbag like a sharkskin pillow. Fisher pounded harder and called her name. He sounded panicked, but she knew he was built to worry. And rescue. Fisher saved people. That was really a nice quality, but she wasn't ready to be saved yet.

Sirens blared in the distance. They were coming for her. The bumped-up blast of a fire engine horn got her attention. If she stayed in the car, they'd use the jaws of life and saw her little car open, pull her out, and strap her on a gurney. Climbing out, offering a mea culpa to the crowd was the least humiliating option.

"Why in such a hurry to run away? Good lord, you act like this place is filled with alien zombies out to suck your blood."

Danni turned to the voice and found Max sitting beside her, adjusting her bucket hat in the rearview mirror.

"Aliens. Zombies? Bloodsuckers? Could you have possibly come up with a more random assortment of beasts?"

"How 'bout ghost alien zombie bloodsuckers?" Max's chubby face wrinkled as she winked.

Danni touched her forehead. It felt tender. It was probably bruised. She was obviously hallucinating from head trauma.

"Oh, bull." Max snorted. "You saw me before you ever crashed your silly little car into that truck." Max looked around. "So, when did you get this? Thought you had the Jeep. Now, that was a beach vehicle."

"Rick traded it in. He wanted to be more environmentally conscious."

Max let out a guffaw and slapped her knee. "Why, I ain't heard nothin' more stupid than that."

"The environment was important to us."

"Sure. Sure, it was. Is that why you bought that huge house? For two people?"

Danni shook her head, her lips pressed together. "If it makes you feel better, it's sold. I'm...I'm in the middle of downsizing."

"Mmm hmm. Is that what the kids are calling it these days?" Max asked.

"I'm working on my finances and things—"

"Ah, Danni. Don't you know it's just plum crazy to try and lie to me? I'm your aunt. I can see right through you." Max laughed. "Ghost pun intended."

Danni groaned. "Oh lord, I have gone crazy. How are you here? Did you lie to me about being dead? Is this some sort of joke? Is everybody in on it?"

Max never answered the question. She faded from solid to fog, and said as she disappeared, "Heads up, darlin'; he's comin' in."

Before Danni could say, "Huh?" the passenger side window shattered. Danni saw the base of a concrete porch urn come closer and closer, and then it was through her window. *Rock shatters glass, bitch.* Danni laughed at the thought and allowed her head to relax against the seat.

Fisher climbed into the car. "Danni?" She didn't answer.

How could she explain? He cradled her cheeks in his hands. "It's all right, Loonie; you'll be okay. The ambulance is almost here." He took her hand and held it, caressing the skin with his thumb.

"I don't need an ambulance. I'm fine. I just need to go home."

"Danni, you have to see a doctor."

A fireman dressed in his yellow coat approached. Danni looked at Fisher. "They sent Big Bird to rescue me." She laughed at her own joke, then rolled her eyes with regret when she realized Fisher didn't get it. His brows furrowed together, and worry clouded his eyes.

"I'm joking, Fish. Just joking, for God's sake. Doesn't that prove I'm fine?"

Fisher leaned across her and pressed the unlock button to let the fireman in. Danni relocked it. Fisher shook his head. "Come on. They have to check you."

"I'm fine."

"Please? Do this for me, Danni. I have never asked anything of you. Ever. You owe me."

He slid out of the car, allowing the paramedic to take his spot. Standing in the lot, he looked as nervous and wretched as a mom with a kid in daycare. His eyes remained glued on what was happening inside the car as they checked her over and prepared her for transport to the hospital.

Danni thought about arguing and refusing care, but she figured that would draw more attention than going peacefully. She certainly didn't do it because Fisher had played a trump card in the game of guilt. Besides, maybe she did need a doctor to help her get rid of the hallucinations. She was pretty certain she spied Max standing behind Fisher, her hand on his shoulder, whispering in his ear.

Chapter 3

Fisher followed the ambulance to the hospital. The blinking lights and the wail of the siren made his palms sweat against the steering wheel. If Danni died —

She'll be all right, he told himself. But only by the grace of God. "Damn tiny clown car," he said to the empty car. She could have been squashed with the weight of the truck. He couldn't imagine a world without Danni in it. Even though he had hardly seen her more than a handful of times in the last six years, he still knew she was alive and well, and as her friend, that was enough.

The ambulance pulled into the emergency bay. The double doors swung open and out jumped the medics who pulled out the gurney that held her, its folded legs dropped to the ground. Fisher parked his car and hurried to the ER front desk, practically jogging across the parking lot. Eager to see her, he wasn't happy to hear he had to wait. He took a seat and tried to stay calm. He grabbed a sports magazine from the stack but didn't read it. Instead, he absentmindedly rolled it into a baton and slapped it against the palm of his hand.

"Mr. Cee?"

Fisher opened his mouth to correct her but closed it. If she made the assumption he was Danni's husband, he wouldn't correct her. As Mr. Cee, he was being escorted to her without question.

Down a wide hallway, through double doors, there was Danni. She looked fragile, lying there looking pale and shaken. When she spotted him, her eyes lit up. "Fisher."

"Hey, Loonie. How you doin'?"

"Couldn't be better."

"Ah, sarcasm. At least you didn't lose that."

Danni smiled. "I never lose that."

He pulled a chair next to the bed. Resting his elbows on his knees, he leaned toward her. "You scared the hell out of me, little lady. I saw you pull out, saw that truck coming, and...shit, I thought it was going to be bad. You must have a guardian angel."

"Maybe I do."

A large welt ran across her forehead. She probably hit her head on the steering wheel. "Whatever kept you safe, I'm grateful for it."

Danni nodded. "Max was there. Taking care of me."

"She was?"

"Mmm, hmm." Her eyes fluttered closed. "She protected me."

Fisher knew from boxing in the navy that a concussion could cause drowsiness and confusion. And death. "Wake up, Danni."

"I'm tired."

He needed to talk to a doctor. "I'll be right back."

"Okay," she said without opening her eyes.

He hurried to the nurse's station. "Excuse me. When will Danni—um, Rodanthe—get the results of her CT scan? She's drowsy and—"

"There is no CT scan. She refused it."

"That doesn't really seem like a decision the patient, especially one with head trauma, should make, is it?"

"She doesn't have insurance, either. I'd say the doctor doesn't want to give her unnecessary tests she'd have to pay for later."

Fisher frowned. Danni wouldn't get subpar care because of money. He wasn't rich, but he wasn't too poor to pay a hospital bill. "I'll pay for it. I want her to have the test."

"I can ask the doctor. But I assure you, it's unnecessary."

"Humor me."

A woman in a white coat stepped out of an exam room.

"Dr. Marz," the nurse called across the hall. The doctor walked toward them. The nurse explained as the doctor approached. "This gentleman is here for the car wreck. He's concerned there wasn't a CT scan ordered."

The doctor nodded. "Mr...?"

"Cooper. Danni is a friend. She's here alone for a funeral, and—"

"Mr. Cooper, your friend is the one refusing medical care. I can't force her to have tests or even stay here for observation. If you were her husband or her next of kin, we could assume that after the crash, she was disoriented and you could request the tests, but even with that, if she flat out refuses, we can't force care on her."

Fisher's jaw felt tight. He should've known. Damn woman, always was stubborn. "I'll talk to her." He thanked the doctor and made his way back to Danni. He sat in the chair beside her and grabbed her hand, waking her up.

"I'm cold, Fisher. I want to go."

"I need you to listen, Danni."

She nodded, rolled onto her side, and faced him. Her eyes were heavy, her lips parted. The desire to kiss her was so strong, it made his throat feel tight. He reminded himself that she was married, and even though he was feeling a strong disgust for a man who would send his wife driving across the country to her beloved aunt's funeral alone, knowing she didn't have insurance, married was still married.

He leaned close and rubbed her arms. They were like ice. She was freezing. He pulled her closer; she snuggled in. He couldn't help but think how right this felt. Without thinking, he kissed her temple.

"I want you to do me a favor," he said.

"Yeah?"

"I talked to the doctor and asked her to give you a CT scan." She shook her head.

"Come on, Danni. For me."

"I—"

"The hospital will cover it. And an overnight stay."

Danni pulled back. "I don't want to stay overnight. I want to go now."

"Look, your car is definitely totaled. You can't get a rental tonight. You could stay with me, and I'd enjoy that, but I'd feel better knowing you were somewhere where people knew what they were looking for—in case of head trauma."

"Is it because I told you I saw Max there with me?"

He shook his head. "It's because I saw the crash. You're lucky to be alive. And I'm afraid there could be something wrong, and they could miss it—"

"I'm fine."

"Don't make me call your husband. Ask him to force—"

Danni jerked in his arms. "Don't bother Rick. I'll stay. Just to make you happy."

"And you'll get the scan?"

"Yes, I'll get whatever they need to prove I'm fine. But I'm only staying one night. I need to get...home."

"Good girl, thank you." He rested his cheek on the top of her head and held her. After a few seconds, her body went limp against him. He gave her a shake. "Danni?"

Her eyes fluttered open, and she looked up at him. "I'm just tired. I drove for two days without sleep and had the worst hotel last night. I swear, there was a frat party or something going on." She yawned. "I just need some sleep. That's all."

The door opened and closed. A nurse so thin she could have passed as a skeleton walked in. "No making out," she said. "We run a respectable hospital here."

Danni pulled away. "I...I was cold."

"It's seventy-two degrees in here. That's not cold."

"Maybe you could get her a blanket instead of a lecture."

The nurse gave him an eye roll but grabbed a blanket out of a cabinet and laid it over Danni.

"See? That wasn't so hard." Fisher's scolding sent the nurse out of the room with a sniff.

"Fisher," Danni scolded.

"What? She was being a bitch."

Danni snuggled herself into the pillow deeper and pulled the blanket up around her neck.

"I told you not to sleep."

"Then you shouldn't have worked so hard to make me

toasty."

"That's pretty rotten. Blaming my good deed."

Danni smiled at him. It was a good smile, a natural curve that eased some stress from her face. Since he'd seen her this afternoon, her face had looked pinched. He kept telling himself it was because of Max, but he couldn't help but think there was more. She sure didn't want him calling her husband. Could there be problems in paradise?

A small pang of guilt hit him in the gut. Did he really hope Danni's marriage would fail? Sure, it would be nice to have her back home, but logically, he knew that would cause him some serious problems.

Danni had hurt him worse than any human being ever could. He should still be furious with her, but when she was this close, all that mattered was that she was here. When he hugged her at the funeral, it was like an electric current rushed through him. When they were kids, they never went more than a few hours without contacting each other. After she left for college and met Rick, that ended.

Why do you lie to yourself? The thought flashed through his head and made him squirm in his seat. The silence started right after that night...his best memory was his worst.

"I'm just messing with you, Fisher." Danni poked his arm. "I'll stay awake if you tell me what you're thinking about."

I was thinking about making love to you, wondering why you didn't love me back....

He'd never say that. He cleared his throat and wiped his suddenly sweaty hands on his dress pants. "I was just thinking you're back for a shitty reason, but I'm still glad you're back."

Danni never got to respond to his answer. The door swung open, and the nurse from the front desk came in. An orderly came with her. "Ready for some tests, sweetie?"

Danni nodded. "I guess I'm ready as I'll ever be."

The nurse turned to Fisher. "If you want to give her a kiss, you better grab your chance—she'll be tied up for the next hour or so."

Danni's eyes grew wide. Fisher shook his head. Hell yeah,

he'd love to kiss her. But he wouldn't. He laughed off the suggestion with a chuckle and made his way back to rows of chairs in the waiting room. The place was empty, except for the lady mopping the hallway. Fisher nodded at her, and she smiled, then went on her way, dragging her rolling bucket.

His phone rang. Tori's face grinned at him on the screen. He sighed but tapped answer. "Hey," he said.

"Hey yourself. How's it going there?"

"They're taking her in for some tests. But she seems fine."

"Good. I was worried. Are you staying there long? I was thinking I should go stay with Darby. She really shouldn't be alone, not tonight."

Fisher rubbed his eyes. Tori was right. Darby was just a kid. Today had to be hard on her too. He could send Tori, but Darby couldn't stand her, even on a good day, and today was the worst kind of days. "Don't bother going over. Maureen is taking her to dinner, and I'll be home tonight." He made a mental note to call Max's friend, Maureen, and ask her to grab Darby, and he'd pick her up later. Maureen was probably waiting on an update on Danni anyhow. He should've called her an hour ago.

"Well, is there anything I can do to help?" Tori sounded worried. He'd forgotten Tori and Danni were friends too.

"I can't think of anything. I talked to Milo at the garage, and he got all of Danni's stuff out of her car before it went to the impound. He's dropping it off at my house."

"It sounds like you've taken care of everything. She's lucky to have a friend like you."

Fisher rubbed the back of his neck. Danni was his friend. That was all. He'd been enjoying taking care of her like she belonged to him, but she didn't. She was someone else's wife, and he was being a selfish ass, not telling her husband. If she was his wife, he'd want to know, to be there with her. "I suppose…," he took a deep breath, "I should call her husband."

"That's a good idea. Danni probably won't want you to, but only because she's so stubborn and hates to have anyone know she ever screws up. I swear, if I've told her once, I've told her a hundred times, she's human — she needs to lighten up on herself."

"She asked me not to call him."

"You're not listening to her, are you?"

"No." His spine stiffened; he sat straighter in his chair. "But I don't have his number."

"I think I have it." There was silence. "There. I texted it to you."

"Why do you have her husband's number?"

"Danni and I are friends, you know. And she's horrible about keeping in touch. When she ignores me for too long, I text Rick, and he makes her make contact."

"Oh." He sighed and ran a hand through his hair. "That sounds like Danni."

"I know...frustrating." Tori sighed. "All right, sweets, you take care of yourself. Don't stay too late. I know you haven't gotten much sleep lately, and I don't want you crashing on the way home."

He assured her he'd be fine. Nothing could hurt him. Although, with Danni in the mix, he was probably lying.

Chapter 4

It was a dream, a common one for Danni. In this version, Fisher sat by her bedside and leaned close...so close she could feel the heat from his body. He brushed back her hair ever so gently, slowly, as if he was relishing the feel of her skin on his hand. After a moment, he leaned forward and kissed her forehead. His lips lingered there, and he said, "I love you."

Normally Danni would wake up alone. Reality and depression would seep in as she remembered how little was right in her world. This time, the dream ended with beeps and cold, soft hands touching her arm. Danni jerked away.

"I'm sorry, girlie. I didn't mean to wake you. I was trying to readjust this blood pressure cuff." The cold hands belonged to the nurse messing with the cords and monitors stuck to Danni. "The doggone thing just won't stay up. I think I need a smaller cuff. Why they put such a big one on a little thing like yourself is a mystery."

The nurse was tall, broad-shouldered, and athletic. Danni figured she probably looked like an over-fed Hobbit next to her.

"Let's see if I can get this tight enough to stay on...just need a few more BPs to round out the night's readings."

Danni rubbed her eyes. "What time is it?"

"Around three."

The last thing Danni remembered was going in for the CT scan or MRI, or whatever in the hell the test was.

"You feeling all right? Headache?"

"No, just piecing things together. The last thing I remember is going for the MRI...."

"CT scan. And I figure that is the last thing you remember. You gave everyone quite the scare. They gave you a mild sedative, and you went out like a light. We couldn't rouse you, no matter what we tried. Fortunately, the scan was good, and your vitals were strong. Your boyfriend said you hadn't slept well in days, so we let you sleep it off while we monitored. Hence the need for the cuff."

"I was tired," Danni admitted. Then she thought of the boyfriend comment. "Fisher isn't my boyfriend. He's just a friend."

"Really? Well, he might be wanting to be more than a friend. I've heard of men picking up bar tabs to impress a lady, but this is the first I've seen a man pick up a hospital tab."

"He what?" Danni tried to sit up in the bed, but the sheets were tangled around her. "He can't do that."

"Gotcha. You got the husband, too, right?"

Danni's cheeks burned. "Divorced."

"So, why isn't that tall piece of sweetness your boyfriend?"

"Because we're better as friends."

"I don't know, sweetheart. He sure seemed like he'd be a great boyfriend."

"For someone else. Not for me."

Danni settled back in bed, Tori's words echoing in her head, *Fisher pities her.* Danni's spine stiffened. Pity was bullshit, and Fisher knew how she hated it. She'd deal with him tomorrow.

The nurse tested the cuff. It stayed on, so she stopped fussing with it. "Too bad for Fisher. You're probably breaking his heart. I've never seen a man so worried. He's got to be head over heels."

Danni didn't even dare to wish for such a thing. That was dangerous thinking. She licked suddenly dry lips.

"He stayed right in this chair until you woke up enough to tell him you were all right. He kissed you goodnight, left his number with me for emergencies, and promised he'd be back in the morning."

"I'm sure he will be. Where there's tragedy, Fisher is there to help. Which is sweet, but hardly love."

Chapter 5

Danni gazed at crystal blue skies through the sealed hospital window. It was beautiful but offered no warmth. The nurse's chatter about Fisher being crazy about her made her feel out of sorts. She'd spent the last few years refusing to think of Fisher at all, but now with tragedy and stupidity redirecting her life, he was once again front and center. And she wasn't sure that was good for her.

Fisher didn't *love her*. She was his friend. His dipshit little hanger-on that he watched out for, and she didn't need that. Even now, at her most pathetic, she could still take care of herself.

"You're up and moving. That's a good sign," Fisher said from the doorway.

She jumped, holding a hand over her heart as she turned. "Fisher." Her surprise was replaced with annoyance. "I need to talk to you. The nurse told me you paid—"

"I have a friend who runs a foundation. Don't go freaking out on me."

"I wasn't freaking out. I just didn't—are you telling me the truth? What kind of foundation? Give me the name."

"No. You're going to trust me."

"I trust you. But I know you'd lie to shut me up."

Fisher grinned. "You say that like it's a bad thing."

Danni sighed. To Fisher, honesty didn't apply in every situation. Maybe he was right. If Danni had lied to him ten years ago, she wouldn't have lost her best friend. But Danni went with honesty, not because she was some sort of moralistic idealist, but mostly because she had a big mouth and blurted the truth before her brain evaluated the information she shared.

"Fisher, seriously, I don't want you paying my bills."

"You wanting to leave here or argue? I already told you I've got everything covered."

Danni dropped it, for now. He was right. It was past time to get out of there. "Am I allowed to leave?"

"You most certainly are," a peppy nurse said from the doorway as she maneuvered a wheelchair around Fisher.

Fisher was a handsome guy, with broad shoulders and an imposing height. The nurse gave him a double take as she passed. A look of recognition lit up her face. "Fisher Cooper," the nurse said. "What in the world are you doing here?" She turned her gaze to Danni as she asked the question.

"I'm picking up Danni."

"Oh, so you're Danni." The nurse nodded her head. "I should have known no one would actually go by Rodanthe."

"You know Danni?" Fisher asked.

The nurse laughed. "No, no. I know Tori, and she's mentioned Danni a time or two. Odd name for a girl, so, of course, I remembered it."

"I see." Fisher nodded.

"Tori is my bridezilla bestie. We go to all the bridal shows together, waiting ever so patiently for our cold-footed men to buy rings." The nurse gave Fisher an elbow to the ribs. Then she turned to Danni, practically shoving a wheelchair into her legs. "Your chariot awaits, ma'am."

Danni's heart dropped, and her mouth went dry. Fisher frowned and grabbed the plastic bag full of her clothes from the bed. "Does she need to sign out or anything?"

"Nope. She's free to leave."

Danni sat in the wheelchair, suddenly grateful to not be standing. It was insane to think a guy like Fisher wouldn't have someone, but Tori Smith? Of all the available women in this world, he was with her? Her chest hurt so bad, she wasn't sure she could breathe properly.

In the car, she watched as Fisher walked around the front of the hood to the driver's door. She wished she had somewhere, anywhere else to be right now. Fisher was consorting with the enemy.

"You want some lunch?" Fisher asked as he maneuvered the car from the hospital parking lot.

Danni shook her head and stared out the window.

"You all right?"

It looked like it might storm. Clear blue skies were being absorbed by spreading dark clouds. Danni hoped there was thunder and lightning. A good atmosphere cleanser.

Fisher took her hand and gave it a squeeze. She pulled it away. She didn't need his pity.

Fisher cleared his throat. "I was going to tell you about Tori. We dated for a while, but it's—"

"None of my business. That's what it is."

"Danni—"

She shook her head. "I'm fine. It's just...my aunt just died. I don't have to be okay."

He pulled over at a public beach access as the first splatter of rain hit the windshield. Tourists continued walking up the boardwalk toward the beach. Danni thought about rolling down her window and telling them if the wind picked up, they'd regret being surrounded by sand. But then she thought the hell with it, let them figure it out on their own.

Fisher brushed a loose hair from her cheek. "It will be all right. I know Max wore some damned big shoes, but you'll get through this."

"You're right. I'm fine. Death is part of life. I don't know why I'm being so melodramatic about it."

"Danni, it's okay to hurt, and you have—"

She held her hand up to stop him from offering platitudes. "I don't want to talk about this right now. I just want to get off this island."

"You're leaving?"

"I have to."

"What about Max?"

"What about her? She's dead. I can wish all I want—"

"She made me promise her you'd take care of her personal

affairs."

"Really? You've seen her too?"

"I saw her almost every day of my life, but we never talked about you until she was in the hospital. Max predicted you'd run off and told me to stop you. She wanted you to take care of her personal affairs, not some stranger. And there's Darby—she's waiting to meet you. She needs someone right now as much as you do."

"Look." Her voice was sharp. "I have enough of my own problems. I don't need to pile on someone else's."

"Whatever."

Fisher put the car in gear and turned it north, tires squealing on the asphalt. He drove up the road in silence, the vehicle lurching to a stop at each red light. Fisher's jaw clenched and unclenched.

Danni cleared her throat to speak but could think of no words that would explain how it felt to be back. Home for Danni wasn't a comfort. It was a place to put her life under a microscope and judge her every flaw. Add in the heart-wrenching knowledge that Fisher was with Tori, and she seriously needed to get the hell out of there. Her life wasn't perfect anywhere, but it was better than here.

But it sucked to have him this mad at her. She hadn't seen him this mad since he found out about her and Renzo Colo. Danni's cheeks flamed, and her heart fluttered. The Fisher she knew was often judgmental, hard-headed, and held high standards she never could meet. Obviously, that hadn't changed. If she wasn't doing exactly what he thought was right, he was pissed. Well, he'd just have to get over it. She didn't have to prove anything to him or anyone else. The realities and memories of this place sucked, and she didn't want to be here. That was no one's business but hers.

They arrived at the rental car place. Fisher didn't move from behind the wheel—didn't even bother to stop the engine. He rolled the window down as Danni stepped out in the now pouring rain. "Don't forget your suitcase in the back seat. I had Milo get your stuff out of your car. You're welcome."

Rain soaked Danni's back as she leaned into the car to collect her suitcase, the hospital bag, and her purse. Fisher didn't move a muscle to help. This was probably his idea of tough love. She mumbled a thanks.

He looked straight ahead, his stare fixed on the rain hitting the windshield. "So, what do I do with Max?" he asked. "Should I mail her out to you, or take care of her myself?"

"What do you mean?"

"Her ashes, Danni. We didn't spread her ashes after the service because I figured you'd want to be there for that."

"Seriously? Why didn't you just—?"

"Really?" He turned and glared at her. "You really don't give a damn, do you?"

"Me? Not give a damn...about Max?"

Fisher nodded.

Danni dropped her suitcase in a puddle. "How can you say that?"

"Because that's what it seems like," he said. "So far, you haven't put yourself out at all. I've never known you to be this selfish."

Danni grabbed her suitcase, yanking on it so hard she pulled a muscle in her shoulder. She ignored the pain and headed toward the rental office.

Fisher jumped out of the car and grabbed her by the arm. "You're going to let strangers take care of Max's things? All her stuff, her life? Hell, Max herself can be scattered by just anybody. I suppose nothing is your problem. Nice Danni, real nice."

"You don't know what this is doing to me," Danni shouted, tears rolling down her cheeks. "I can't do this right now. Everything is falling apart. I have nothing going right in my life at all. And now, you say I don't care? How can you of all people accuse me of not caring?"

"Because, Danni, when you care about someone, you do the hard thing. You owe it to Max to take care of her affairs. She didn't want anyone but you in her personal stuff."

Danni took a deep breath. "I can't."

Fisher shook his head. "Bullshit, you can't. You won't. There's a big difference."

He let go of her arm and walked away. Danni ran after him, grabbed him by the back of his shirt, and pulled until he stopped walking. "Why are you being so mean?"

Fisher shrugged. "I'm not being mean. Max wanted you to stick around a while."

Danni gasped. "Do you think that's why she was haunting me?"

Fisher looked at her as if she'd asked him if he'd seen any pink whales.

"Oh, never mind." Danni looked beyond the parking lot to the gray shingled beach homes and a clearing sky. The sun chased away the clouds like it was hell-bent on erasing the rain. A woman who looked like Max waved to her from the other side of the road. Danni waved back.

Fisher looked over his shoulder, then to Danni. "What is it?"

"It's Max." Danni moved quickly around Fisher toward the woman. But after taking a few steps to the east, there was no one there. Nothing but cars. She slowed to a stop. Was Max telling her goodbye? No more ghost Max? Danni felt panic like she was suddenly surrounded by quicksand and had nowhere to go.

Then there was Fisher. He squeezed her close and kissed the top of her head. "It's okay, Danni. Come back with me. You shouldn't be alone right now." He tipped her chin until she was looking at him. His thumb brushed away a tear. "You can stay at my place. I have an extra bedroom. You need to deal with Max's will, her property. You have to do this. You owe it to her. You know how she loved that place. It's offensive to walk away from it like it's nothing."

He was right, and she knew it. "I suppose I could spare a couple of days."

"Good girl. It'll be all right. I'll be right there. I won't leave you."

Danni nodded. He held her for a few minutes longer, his hands firm and strong against her back. She allowed her cheek to rest against his chest. When he said things were going to be all right, she believed he had the power to make it happen. Was it dangerous to trust in any human that much?

They drove toward her homeplace — the little town of Salvo, North Carolina.

Danni pulled at her lip as she considered the visions of Max. Was she losing her mind? Going crazy like her mother?

"Fish...," she said, turning toward him in her seat. "You know my mom was crazy. Do you think—?"

"You're not crazy."

"But...I keep seeing Max."

"I don't think you're crazy. I think," he answered slowly, "and mind you, I only had basic psychology, but I'd guess these visions are a manifestation of your grief."

"You had psychology? I never guessed you for a college kind of guy. But then I guess I don't really know you anymore."

"Of course you do." He reached for her again, but she tucked her hands under her thighs. If he was with Tori, the traitor, they needed to keep clear lines.

He looked disappointed.

"What?" Danni asked. "Why are you looking at me like that?"

He looked back out the windshield. "I'm not looking at you in any way. I was just trying to make you feel better. You act like I'll bite you."

"I'm sorry. I'm out of sorts. Everything is just...wrong."

"I understand."

They arrived at his house and pulled into the driveway. It was the same single-story cottage he'd grown up in. It looked freshly painted, with white clapboard siding and the same blue porch and matching shutters. The brick columns that held the house above flood level were left their natural clay color, but there was new white latticework running between each column for the underpinning. As kids, the porch had been fully open. They played under the house for hours and hours building sand cities.

Fisher interrupted her walk down memory lane. "Darby's here," he said. "She's undoubtedly hungry. The kid eats like a longshoreman. If you'd like, we could order something or go out and grab something."

"She's here?"

Fisher nodded. "Has been since Max went into the hospital."

"Is she staying with your mom?"

"No, with me. I bought the house from Mom when her and Bill moved to Oklahoma."

"Really?" Danni asked. "I didn't realize she moved." Danni felt even more out of touch. She took a deep breath. "Is Darby okay?"

"She's holding up."

"Poor kid. What will happen to her?"

Fisher shut off the engine and took a deep breath. "Max was all Darby had, and now you will be her only family. She needs you, Loonie."

Danni swallowed hard and shook her head. "Surely there's someone else. Max knows I'm the last person to be trusted with a human being." Danni blinked away unwanted tears. "I haven't made a single good decision in my entire life."

"True. Your track record sucks, Bugs Killer, but she's a resilient kid. She might teach you a thing or two." He chuckled and gave her hand a squeeze.

"Bugs Killer." Danni frowned. "That's a low blow. You realize Bugs's death wasn't even my fault. It was that damn Tori. She's the one who left the lid off the snake cage, not me."

"You admitted to it. Mrs. Schiff must have asked you a hundred times if it was really you."

"Because she knew I was lying."

"Tsk, tsk, Danni. You know better than to lie."

"Yeah, I know. Tori said she'd get whipped, and I knew she wasn't lying about that. And I thought it was a no-big-deal fib. I didn't know admitting to leaving the lid off the snake cage also meant I was admitting to helping the damn thing escape and eat the bunny. Poor Bugs. I had nightmares for years about that."

"Do you realize that's the first time you told me the truth about that? You lied to me for years to protect Tori."

"I suppose I've carried the guilt for her long enough. Do you know how many people signed my yearbook 'To Bugs Killer'? It was scarring."

His warm brown eyes were so full of tenderness...or pity. He fixed a strand of her hair that fell across her cheek, brushing it behind her ear. Her eyes slowly closed. It was such a simple thing, but it made her heart do a flutter beat. When she opened them, Fisher stared down at her. He looked pale like he'd been caught cheating.

"I shouldn't—" He pulled his hand back and shut off the car engine. "Come on. We'll get some lunch."

With that, he hurried out of the car, and another weight was added to her soul.

Chapter 6

Fisher seemed to have a hard time remembering she was married whenever she was close. For most of his life, being with Danni had been as natural and as familiar to him as his own self. Even after years of separation, being with her felt right, like nothing had changed.

But everything was changed. She was married—a fact he needed to keep in mind.

As they walked up the drive to the porch, Danni asked, "Why did your mom move to Oklahoma?"

"Bill insisted, and you know Mom—what Bill wants, Bill gets."

"He still a jerk?"

"Crankier every year. It's probably for the best they moved. Bill and I were a few arguments away from a fistfight."

Danni patted his arm. He knew he didn't have to explain it to her. Danni had seen the fights, often offering him refuge in the middle of the night when he couldn't listen to them anymore.

"I never understood why your mom put up with him."

"Max said she was afraid to be alone."

Danni shook her head. "I'd much rather be alone than miserable. I used to think Max was odd for never marrying, but I'm beginning to see the upside of the single life."

Fisher's feet stopped. More evidence of trouble in paradise? The thought made his heart race. He wanted to ask, but couldn't form the right words, or trust himself to sound solemn and sincere in his phony concern. The truth was, he had no interest in advising her through the rocky waters of marriage. He wanted her to abandon ship.

His mother would be ashamed of his lack of devotion to lifelong vows made before the Almighty. They mattered to him. But sometimes, wasn't it better to cut your losses?

"You all right?" She turned to him. "I'm sorry if I offended you. I wasn't trying to insinuate your mother is an idiot."

Fisher grinned. "But she is?"

Danni chuckled. "She is. Bill is such an ass. Discard that losing hand and draw another one." She placed her hand on his forearm. When he turned to her, she pulled him in for a hug. "I'm sorry, Fish. I've been a shitty friend. We could get together later—we won't even have to sneak the beer out of Max's stash—and have a 'we hate Bill' session."

Fisher smiled and held her tighter. "I'd enjoy that." He'd think this moment was a dream, but a mosquito was trying to make a snack out of his neck. He nuzzled his face in her hair. "I've missed you, Loonie."

"I've missed you too. You're the best of us, Fisher. You really, truly are."

~*~

Danni wanted to sink into him and stay there forever. Nothing in her world ever did or ever would feel as good and natural as being close to Fisher. Compared to her ex-husband, Fisher was a giant. Rick was a tiny man with small, soft hands. Last year, Danni officially tipped the scales and weighed in heavier than Rick. He was a svelte 145; Danni a chubby 150. It was this revelation that put the final nail in their marriage coffin.

Part of Rick's resentment was Danni's weight, so Danni agreed to join a gym if he agreed to see a marriage counselor. After two weeks of sweating her ass off, she weighed more than when she'd started. When she did her weekly weigh-in at the gym with Rick watching over her shoulder, he'd been so pissed at her weight gain he'd yelled that they didn't need counseling, she needed fat camp. Her trainer gave Danni a headshake and a friendly word of advice. "Girl, you need to get yourself a divorce. Mmm hmm. That is what you should do."

So, she did—seven years of her life and nothing to show for

it.

If she'd married a guy like Fisher, she'd have had to go well over two-hundred pounds before he could tease her for being the heavyweight in the relationship.

Danni shook off that thought. Fisher was her friend. She'd not risk mixing flesh and friendship ever again. But she had to admit, being here, wrapped in strong arms with her cheek resting against a heart so powerful she could feel it reverberate against her skin, felt good.

He stroked her hair, brushing back the loose strands. "It feels good to have you back."

Danni squeezed him tighter. There were so many things in her life she wished had gone differently.

A horn blew, and tires crunched in the gravel drive.

Danni jumped. Fisher let go of her and turned toward the sound. Before her sat a Mustang painted so bright a yellow that it bounced the sun's glare back at Danni, nearly blinding her. When the door opened, and Tori's skinny body slithered out, Danni wished she had gone blind. She didn't need to see how perfect the bitch was. Skinny enough to wear a body-hugging skirt, and not a single blonde hair was out of place.

"You comin', Fish? I found a listing you might be interested in."

"Uh, not today. I told Danni she could stay here while she gets Max's affairs in order."

Tori reached in and shut off the engine. She sashayed toward Fisher, who moved away from Danni and down the steps.

Danni shook off the instant feeling of loneliness. It was ridiculous. She tried not to look, but it was like passing a car wreck, and her eyes stayed glued to the sight even as the sickening pain in her gut grew. This wasn't a casual hug. This was a long, comfortable, they-do-this-often sort of hug.

F-bombs exploded in her head. This was unreal. Fisher couldn't possibly be attached to that. Danni swallowed the bile that crept into her throat and pushed away the urge to vomit. What the hell was Fisher thinking?

"You doing okay, Danni?" Tori asked, keeping an arm

around Fisher's waist.

"Fine and dandy," Danni managed to choke out. Then she directed her gaze to Fisher and said, "I better check on Darby." She barely had the words out of her mouth before Tori slid away from Fisher and wrapped Danni in her skeletal embrace.

"Danni, Danni, Danni," Tori said. Her perfume was so strong, Danni could taste it with every breath. Danni did her best to wiggle out of the hug. "You're not fine or dandy. You poor, poor girl."

Danni broke away. She took a step back and grabbed a fresh suck of air.

Tori shook her finger at her. "You had us worried to pieces. Why, Fisher would barely eat a bite last night." Tori returned to pawing Fisher, wrapping an arm around his bicep.

"Well, I'm fine," Danni said. "I should've been smart enough to look both ways."

"I swear, a part of me worried that you'd lost your mind and were doing your own version of the bridge jump."

Bitch. Horrible, awful, soulless demon from hell. Tori knew how much Danni hated to talk about her mother's suicide. Danni wanted to punch her in the face, but instead, she smiled. "Thank you, Tor. For your concern and for all your kind words at the funeral. How a person handles themselves in a tragedy shows a lot about their character."

"Words? At the funeral?" Tori looked seriously confused.

"In the bathroom? You and Tina? It was before the service — the things you had to say were so — enlightening."

Tori looked from Danni to Fisher. She looked nervous, like a boxer against the ropes. Maybe Danni was a true heavyweight, after all. Danni felt a surge of glee. She'd stuck it to the evil bitch, and it felt great.

But Tori recovered. She flashed Danni her sickeningly sweet smile, and said, "Ah, Danni. It was the least I could do."

Bested again, Danni spun around, not sure if she should go through Fisher's front door or take off down the narrow sand path that connected Fisher's land with Max's. Before she could decide, the front door swung open and a skinny teen with long, dark hair and a bit too much eye shadow hurried across the wide porch and grabbed Danni by the arm and pulled her to her. She whispered, "Take me home before I have to deal with that bitch one more day. You gotta. Max said you'd take care of me. Start doing it."

"What?" Danni sputtered.

"I need some stuff," Darby yelled over Danni's shoulder toward Fisher. "Danni said she'll take me home. I'm sure Tori will appreciate the privacy." Darby whispered to Danni, "Bitch told me often enough what a nuisance I was."

"Seriously?"

Darby nodded. "Not in so many words, but I got the point."

Danni understood. She'd been on the receiving end of Tori's evil most of her life. Danni gave Darby's arm a squeeze and turned to Fisher. "Darby's right. I need to take her home. I think she's homesick."

"Yeah, homesick," Darby parroted.

"I'll go with you." Fisher pulled himself away from Tori and took a step toward them. "You're supposed to be monitored tonight."

"Darby can do it."

Fisher looked worried. "Ten minutes ago, you weren't sure you wanted to—"

"You said I could do it, and you were right. High time to man up."

"I'll come with you."

Danni bit her lip. Of course, she'd love to have Fisher with her, but the troll might follow. Danni would rather chew glass than watch them be a couple. Her brain scrolled through plausible excuses. "Darby and I need to become acquainted. What better way than cold turkey?"

"Don't be ridiculous," Fisher said. "Just give me a second, and I'll go with you."

"Yes," Tori said sweetly. "We—"

"You've done enough. Trust me." Touching Fisher's arm, she said, "I have Darby. Like you were saying, we are like—like sisters. We have to do this."

Darby nodded her jet-black head. "Yeah, we hafta do this. Alone."

The pair squeezed passed them on the porch and nearly ran down the narrow path, across the wooden bridge that arched over the narrow canal, and through the thicket of pines that lead to Lowry land. Arm in arm, they laughed like naughty school kids who'd bested a bitch teacher.

Once they were out of earshot, they slowed. Danni cleared her throat. "Are they...dating? Like seriously?"

"They were, but they broke up. From what I hear, she gave Fisher the shit-or-get-off-the-pot ultimatum, and he dumped her. Never tell a guy with commitment issues to marry you or else — he will always pick the 'or else.'"

"Why is she back?"

"Like any bad case of herpes, she's tough to get rid of, and there's always the risk of new flare-ups. She leaves town for a few weeks at a time but always comes back. One time, she was gone for almost a year once, and I thought we were rid of her for good, but she showed back up with the new knockers and the fancy Mustang. Max said she probably fleeced some poor bastard only to leave him when he was out of money."

Danni gasped. Too busy trying not to vomit, she'd missed the huge boobs. And they were mighty big. Way bigger than you'd expect on a gal as skinny as her. Danni's mouth dropped. She didn't know what to say...on either count.

Fisher, how could you fall for that augmented bitch?

Darby adjusted her backpack on her shoulder. "She's horrible. When Fisher first made the offer to let me stay at his place, I was all for it. Fisher's great and has high speed Internet. My other choice was Mrs. Maureen. She's sweet and all, but she doesn't have Wi-Fi, and I'd had to sit on her back porch and steal the signal from her son's house across the street." Darby let out a long sigh. "I hadn't figured Tori into the equation. My God, since Max died, she practically lives there. She would be soooo nice to me when Fisher was around. As soon as we were alone, she'd make bitch comments about me getting under foot and say rude things about my mom. Like she ever met her."

"That must be one of her specialties. My entire childhood, I could expect at least a monthly reminder that my mom committed suicide and had mental problems. Tori Smith is evil. Pure evil."

"I used to respect Fisher," Darby said. "But it seems he thinks with his penis like all other men."

Danni cringed at the words. *How could Fisher be so stupid?*

Their conversation quieted as the Sun Shiner Inn—the yellow brick hotel these two "sisters" had grown up in under the loving hand of Max—came into view. They sobered and slowed to a stop, then stood side-by-side, staring at their home.

Chapter 7

The Sun Shiner Inn was no longer radiant. In Danni's memories, it always stayed the same as the last time she saw it—a static perfection that was a lie. The place was in a state of disrepair, with faded and chipped paint. The planters on the concrete porch were empty, save for a beer can balanced on the edge of one. Danni remembered it as it had been, with sunny yellow paint and crisp white shutters and railings. Petunias always grew to overflowing in the pots. It was all so changed. It had only been—what? Five years since she came home. What happened?

Darby was quiet too. She looked up at Danni, her eyes filled with tears. "Max would always hear me coming. She'd be at that door waiting on me, and she's not there now."

Danni put an arm around Darby. She was right. Max always sat in the front office and always knew when someone stepped onto the property.

There was no more Max, but Max did teach her a thing or two. Danni looked at Darby. The girl looked scared and probably felt as lost as Danni did. Only Darby was a child, and Danni was now the adult in the room or parking lot. Danni slung an arm across Darby's shoulder and gave her a squeeze. "We'll be all right, Darby."

They approached the door together. As Darby pulled a key from her pocket, her face puckered, and tears spilled over dark lashes. "I have had this for a year, and I have never had to use it. Not once." She wiped at her eyes. "This isn't fair, Danni."

Danni hugged her tight. "No, it isn't. But it'll be okay. I promise. We'll make it through this, together."

Darby looked up at her and smiled. "Max said I'd like you."

Danni took the key from her. Her conscience stuck her with guilt as she realized she should have taken the time to meet this child a year ago.

She stuck the key in the lock and swung the door open. The office looked like it usually did—in serious need of a decorator, cluttered, but tidy. Danni stepped into a room still cloaked in seventies-era brown and gold. The lamps on the table had owl bases. Owl. Like the bird. Danni touched the creature's wings and smiled. Max never got rid of things, even when they were ugly and well past their time. Max loved what she loved.

Darby paused a moment. "You okay?"

"Fine," Danni said. She cleared her throat. "Just wondering how Max got anyone to return to the hotel after they saw the décor."

Darby shrugged. "People liked her. And she kept the rates cheap."

Danni touched the worn register on the desk. Max never did get the hang of computers. All of the reservations at the Sun Shiner had to be made over the phone and logged into the reservation book. Max's sweater hung off the back of the chair. Her coffee mug was turned upside down on a folded napkin. It was as if Max had run to the store and would be right back.

She couldn't be gone. So much of her was still here.

Danni fought the tears. If she let them roll, she'd probably not stop.

Fortunately, Darby's phone rang, interrupting her thoughts. Danni overheard Darby tell her friend on the phone that she couldn't go out. Danni blurted without thinking, "You should go. You need to be with your friends."

Danni shocked herself so much by her words she blushed. She looked at a recent picture of Max. It wasn't even framed yet but taped to the wall. It was a shot of a smiling Max holding a sand shark in one hand and a fishing pole in the other. Danni could have sworn the image winked at her. Danni shook her head to clear her mind.

"You really think I should go?" Darby asked.

"Do you want to?"

Darby shrugged. "I don't know. Maybe."

"Then go."

"What about you? I should help you do stuff here."

"I'll be fine. I think Max has been haunting me. She'll keep me company."

"Max said you were funny," Darby said. She grabbed a piece of paper from the desk and jotted down a number. "Here's my number. Call me if you need me."

Danni picked it up. "Let me give you mine."

"I've got it. Max gave it to me months ago."

The girl's words piled on more guilt. Darby was obviously a bright, likable kid. How could she have not taken the time to meet her?

"What time should I be back?" Darby asked.

"Whenever."

"Really?" Darby's eyebrows shot up.

"I mean, of course, you need to have a time to be back. What's a reasonable time?"

"One o'clock?"

"I suppose—"

Darby rubbed the back of her neck like she had a sudden cramp. "Max always made me be back by eleven, 'cause I'm only fourteen."

"Well then, eleven-thirty. Since you're so honest."

Darby smiled and turned to leave.

"Hey, Darby," Danni said. Darby turned to her. "Enjoy being young, all right?"

"Uh, okay," she said as she backed out the door.

Danni groaned and said to the empty office, "I am now the creepy adult that says stupid things to kids. Good lord."

She walked through the office to the residence. Everything looked familiar but felt foreign. Same plaid couch. Same navy recliner. As usual, Max's hand sewn lap quilts covered the backs of each. A narrow hallway off the living room led to the bedrooms and bath.

When Max had taken in Darby after the girl's mother died,

Max called Danni for permission to give the girl her room. Danni had thought it was an odd question—she hadn't lived in the little apartment for years. Of course, Darby could have the room. But now that she was back, moving through the apartment, she realized her old room was now filled with posters of heartthrobs that Danni didn't even recognize. Danni was roomless. Suddenly, she felt homeless.

"Well, Max, it looks like I'm taking your room."

Danni moved on down the hallway, past frame after frame of pictures. Danni had walked past these pictures a million times in her life but rarely stopped to look at them. She flipped on the hall light. There was a picture of her and her mother. Vi Lowry had been pretty for a lunatic. Danni sighed and moved on down the wall. There were countless pictures of herself from kindergarten to graduation, and every stage in between. Mixed in with the highlights of her life were pictures of Max and her best friend, Maureen, as teens, holding large-mouthed fish on the beach. They were both skinny and still dark haired, their smiles broad and genuine. A photo of Jake, Maureen's son. Danni never met Jake. He died of liver cancer before Danni was born. Looking into his unlined face, Danni realized he'd died much too young. Maureen's heart had to have been broken. Time after time, these women's hearts were broken, yet they continued to smile—year after year, photo after photo.

Reminded that she came from the same hardy bloodline as her aunt, Danni continued down the hallway perusing the photos until she came to one of herself and Fisher. They were sitting on the dock, facing the water with the hotel behind them. It was a candid shot, taken by Max from her canoe. She'd paddled out to get a picture of the hotel for a newspaper ad. Instead, she captured them as Danni liked to remember them best. As friends. She was wearing Fisher's hat—one she'd stolen off his head minutes before.

Danni pulled the picture off the wall to see it closer. They looked so happy. They'd been the best of friends. Until—

Danni shook her head, placed the picture on the wall, switched off the light, and moved on. She swung open the door of Max's room. She expected to see Max sitting on the bed, but the room was empty. "Where are you, Max? I don't want to be alone."

Danni lay down on the bed and wrapped herself in the quilt. She placed a hand on her chest. It hurt to breathe.

"Is this what heartbreak feels like?"

No one answered. Maybe she should have stayed with Fisher or let him come keep her company. Then she remembered — Tori would have come too. Maybe she could call him in a little bit unless he'd gone with Tori like Tori wanted. Danni couldn't stop herself from imagining their cozy little date. Did Fisher smile at Tori the way he used to smile for her?

Danni pulled a pillow over her head and screamed.

Chapter 8

Danni lay there, finally relaxed and half asleep, snuggled in her quilt when her phone buzzed. She pushed a hand out of her cocoon and pulled the phone to her ear.

"Hey, Danni, baby. I wanted to check and see how you're doing."

It was Rick. Maybe he did care about her. After all the fighting and the year of silence, it felt good to hear his voice, void of the usual irritation. Maybe something good would come out of this.

"I'm holding up. It's weird to be here without Max."

"Then leave."

A ball of pain burned in her chest. She nodded, unable to respond to his statement. Leaving made the most sense, but she couldn't. She had let Max down in life; she wouldn't let her down in death. "I have things I need to do here."

"So, you're out of the hospital?" Rick asked.

"Uh, yeah."

"I take it you're okay?"

"I'm fine. Hardly a scratch." Nothing but a possible concussion and some hallucinations.

"I told that guy you'd be fine."

"That guy?"

"That old boyfriend of yours."

"Fisher?"

"Yeah, him. What a little fag. He was freaking out and expected me to hop on a plane and come there 'cause you had a fender bender."

"I didn't realize he called." *Fisher, you freaking liar. I agreed to those tests to keep Rick from knowing, you shithead.*

"I think he liked to be the boss." There was a pause. She could hear him take a breath. "I was surprised to hear you haven't told him we're divorced."

Danni rubbed the back of her neck. "I've barely spoken two words to him before this week, so no, I've not gotten the chance to tell him."

"Maybe you don't want him to know?"

"Why would I care about that? It just hasn't come up."

"Maybe it's because you don't want to be divorced."

Danni squeezed her eyes closed. Of course, she didn't want to be divorced. Who wanted to be the person kicked to the curb? But still, she didn't know how to answer...it could be a loaded question.

"I've been thinking. You should sell that place and come home."

"Home?"

"Yes, home. This is your home. I know things have been rough between us, but after I heard you were in a wreck, I imagined you gone and.... Well, maybe we could work things out."

Danni took a suck of breath. A year ago, she had wanted nothing more than to work things out—she should be ecstatic right now. But she felt no thrill. It was as if the pain of loss was too sharp to dull, even with words she thought she wanted to hear.

And there was Fisher—which was ridiculous because he had Tori. What was her reason for not wanting to try again?

She thought of Darby. She couldn't sell and run home without at least talking to Darby. "I can't just leave. I have to consider Darby."

"Who the hell is Darby?"

"You remember Darby—the girl Max took in?"

"No, I don't remember." He sounded irritated. "I thought you weren't ready to be a mom. Or has infertility made you instantly maternal?"

Danni wasn't sure if he meant to hurt her with the comment, or if he was simply a natural at slicing at her. Danni took a deep breath. "She's a teenager. I'm hardly playing mommy."

"How can you afford to stay there? Are you going to get a job, or are you going to live on the money you got from the divorce?"

"Money I got from the divorce?" Danni rolled her eyes. The marriage had cost her a fortune. If someone had told her that marrying someone gave them full access to her assets, she would have lived in sin and skipped the trainwreck. Life with Rick Cee had started as a big adventure and ended in a crash.

"I take it you're still blaming me for the business failing?"

It was his idea to invest all of her money in their own real estate business. No matter how much she worked, she could never plug all the holes. Every month, they hemorrhaged cash. When they divorced, they sold the agency and divided what was left of the estate her mother had left her.

"I'm not blaming you," Danni said. "I just find it ironic that I came into the marriage with over two million dollars, and left it with a few thousand, and you act like I benefited."

Rick sighed. "You're right. They say no one benefits from divorce." He was quiet a second. "I feel like we rushed into the divorce. We should have done more counseling."

"I tried—"

"I know you tried. It was me. I was frustrated. I felt like a failure, and I took it out on you. I wanted to at least give you a baby. Do you know how worthless I felt? I failed at the business. I couldn't give you a family."

"That was on me, remember?"

"But if I could have made enough money, I could have afforded the invitro. Maybe one day—"

"I don't want to talk about it."

"I'm sorry," he said. "You sound down."

"I think it goes with the territory. I came here for a funeral."

"At least she was old and got to live a good life."

"I suppose." She was tiring of the conversation.

She could hear his sigh across the phone. "I really miss you, Danni. I wish you'd come home."

"I can't."

"If you change your mind, I put money in your account.

There's enough for a plane ticket home. I'll be waiting for you."

"You put money in my account?" Danni sat up, stunned. "You didn't have to do that."

"I didn't want you to be stranded there."

"I appreciate that. And it's not that I'm not grateful, but I'll send it back to you because I'm not coming back anytime soon. Not yet. I need some time. I need to be here, at least for a little while."

"Is it because of that guy?"

Danni blushed. "Don't be ridiculous. I told you—"

"Are you screwing him?"

Danni almost fell off the bed. "Who? Fisher? Are you insane?" The idea of her and Fisher made her heart skip a beat. "He's just a friend."

"Sounds real friendly. You two have probably been a thing for years."

Danni rolled her eyes. "I think you're thinking of your own infidelities. I never cheated."

Rick took a loud suck of breath. "I'm sorry. I get jealous and a little unreasonable." There was a pause, then he said, "Sometimes you don't realize what you've lost until it's gone."

Danni looked around the cluttered room. The wood paneled walls were covered with her aunt's handiwork—amateur watercolors, sea glass chimes, and dried flowers pressed in shadow boxes. The room was an homage to her aunt's life. A life Danni had taken for granted because she never dreamed her aunt would ever be gone. She was the constant in Danni's life. No matter what fell apart, there was Max to help her piece it back together.

Until now.

Danni took a deep breath. "I do understand. More than you could ever know."

Rick hung up with a promise to call later. A promise Danni doubted he'd keep, but if he did, would it matter after all the strife between them?

Chapter 9

Danni didn't know what to make of Rick's call. He always managed to irritate the hell out of her, then make her feel guilty for being annoyed. He was also a pathological liar, so the idea that he suddenly cared about her felt like a trap. She opened her banking app to see if he had put money in her account. That was sweet, wasn't it? Why did a sweet gesture make her feel like there was no air in the room?

"You here, Max? I could use your advice." Danni looked around the room. If there was a place likely to be haunted, surely it was this room, so full of Max's treasures.

Nothing.

"Max? If you're here, say something—boo—anything."

Silence.

But in that silence, there was peace. Her body relaxed, and she drifted off to sleep with the knowledge that this was where she needed to be. Maybe this place wasn't so bad. Here, she felt Max's strength. Her humor. Her kindness. In this place, Danni wasn't so alone.

When she woke, she felt invigorated, even in the face of a hard truth—she had no idea what her life would be five years or even one year from now. All she had was right here, right now. One day, one problem at a time.

Danni marched from the bedroom to the office and settled herself in the comfy leather swivel chair. She flipped through the papers in the top drawer looking for where to begin. The mechanical ring of a rotary phone cut through the silence and made her jump in her seat. She grabbed the receiver just to make the sound stop.

"Hello?"

"Danni? This is Maureen. You remember me?"

"Of course." Danni smiled. Maureen was Max's oldest, dearest friend.

"Well, I have Punkin here, and Max told me to bring her to you after the funeral."

"Punkin?"

"Yeah, Punkin. Max's dog?"

"I didn't know Max had a dog."

Danni hadn't had a dog in years. Rick hated animals, which should have been a red flag—Max had always told her to never trust someone who hated animals. Or the beach. Rick hated both. Both were messy nuisances that failed to be worth the expense.

"...and that's how Punkin found herself a home. You know Max, she was never one to turn away a stray."

Danni realized she hadn't been listening to a word Maureen said. But she wasn't about to admit it, so she kept her response generic. "That's our Max."

"Max always told me the little dog was a guardian angel. And of course, she wanted you to have her."

"Great. I'll come…. Well, I'll come as soon as I can get a rental car or a ride."

"Oh, I'll bring her up. Been wantin' to visit you anyhow. I would have come to the hospital, but Fisher needed me to stay with Darby so he could stay with you. He was so worried about you. You're special to him, you know."

"He's a good friend."

"Mmm hmm. That he is."

Danni blushed. Maureen was the third person to insinuate there was something between her and Fisher. It made her feel more than a little awkward, especially when she knew he was with Tori. Danni shook off that thought. "Thank you so much, Maureen. I'll be here all day."

Danni hung up the phone.

The office door opened, the little bell jingled. "We're closed," she said before looking up.

Fisher cocked his head sideways and held up a bag of groceries and her suitcase. "Even for a guy who brings you stuff and the keys to a not-so-new, but shiny rental car?"

"Oh, it's you." She squirmed in her seat. Thanks to Maureen's suggestion, Fisher didn't loom over her as her old friend. He was suddenly all man, and he was heating up the air in the tiny room.

"Thanks for sounding thrilled." He closed the door behind him.

"It's not that. I'm just settling in." She waved her hands around the room. "Trying to decide what to do first."

"One day at a time."

She nodded. "I suppose that is the best approach. At least until I get things sorted out."

Fisher set a bag of groceries on the desk and tossed her the keys to the rental car. Danni looked out the window—there sat a blue SUV.

"I told Milo to give you the one that can best withstand an impact."

"Aren't you a smart ass?"

"I wasn't joking. You're my friend. Your well-being is my biggest concern."

Danni bet she was his biggest concern. She probably caused him a crap-ton of problems with his skinny bitch. Tori surely wouldn't want her to stick around here long, much less be friends with him. But Danni didn't care what Tori thought any more than she cared what Rick thought. In the harsh light of loss and mortality, neither seemed to rank as problems.

"Oh yeah, I have a bone to pick with you, buddy." The desk chair squeaked as Danni leaned back. "Rick called. He wants me to hurry home. Seems someone called him. Someone who promised he wouldn't call him?"

"Tori told me I should call, and I decided she was right. He's your husband; he had a right to know."

"Tori suggested it, huh? What the hell kind of game is she playing?"

"Game? She was concerned about you."

Danni laughed. "I bet."

"Is there something I should know about you and Tori?"

"She told you to call my husband knowing full well that my marriage is over."

Fisher's eyebrow popped up like he was pleased and intrigued by the news, but his initial shock was quickly followed with a frown. "What's that mean? Is it that we're-only-married-on-paper bullshit?"

"I mean it's over, literally. No husband. We divorced a year ago."

"Seriously? Like a judge ruled on it and everything?"

"Like it cost thousands of dollars in legal fees, and I have the paper to prove I failed at marriage just like I have failed at just about everything else."

Fisher didn't seem to hear her. He grinned. "How did I not know this?"

Danni shrugged. "I never told Max. I wasn't exactly proud of it."

Fisher grinned. "But you should be. We should celebrate."

Danni frowned. "Is a failed marriage really something to celebrate?"

"It is when it was a huge mistake in the first place," Fisher said. "He never deserved you."

"You never even met him."

Danni shook her head. Fisher was always that kind of friend. He backed her no matter what, even when he didn't know the story. She could make Rick's case for him, but as she ran the particulars through her head, she doubted Fisher would see Rick's side at all.

The excuse of no longer finding her sexually attractive, therefore needing to have affairs, seemed lame. Add in the insult that he'd made that revelation a week after she got the report from the fertility clinic, explaining that she had too many problems to ever hope to conceive a child.

Danni pulled her shirt away from the fat roll, the waistband of her pants created. She didn't blame him for the comment. Rick wasn't the most cerebral of men. In his mind, the right thing to do was to support his infertile wife, but subconsciously, she knew he blamed her for it.

Rick wouldn't win man of the year for wanting to get rid of her, but he was only human.

Danni sighed. "Rick is struggling. There's a lot he resents me for. A lot of things I resent him for."

"Did you cheat on him?"

"Of course not. He was the cheater."

Fisher nodded.

"Today was the first call from him in almost a year. Thanks to you, he says he loves me, he wants me to come home, and he even sent me money. You are a miracle worker, Fish. You accomplished what a year of therapy failed to do."

"So, are you headed home?"

"No. It'll take more than one phone call to fix things. Besides, I'm realizing there's more to my life than Rick. I was so caught up in trying to save my marriage; I didn't notice Max was sick. That this place was getting run down." Danni looked around the office. The light fixtures were dusty, the carpets needed shampooed—thorough cleanings Max never would have skipped, if she hadn't been sick. She had needed help, and Danni never noticed. "No, I'll get things caught up here. Then I'll decide what to do about Rick."

Fisher stuffed his hands in his pockets and stared down at her.

"What?" she asked.

"Nothing." He shrugged.

"Why are you looking at me like that?"

Fisher shook his head. "I'm not looking at you *like that.*"

Danni stood, pacing the small area behind the desk. Fisher always judged her harshly. No matter what she did, she ought to have done better. He probably thought she was being a bitch for not calling Rick or being nice to him when he made an effort, though tiny and in no way enough to make up for all of the hurt he'd caused her.

She locked her gaze on his. "My marriage. My business."

"I never said anything."

"You called him; you started it."

"How was I supposed to know? You never talk to me anymore."

"And why should I? You seem to be quite happy with your life. With Tori and your little dates looking at houses, or whatever it is you two do."

"It wasn't a date. I'm not—"

Danni waved him off. What he did with Tori wasn't something she wanted to know a damn thing about. "What you do is your business. Personally, I don't care one way or another."

His nostrils flared, and he looked grim. "I never figured you did."

He looked downright stony. Danni bit her lip. Had she turned this into a fight? She wasn't trying to pick an argument with him, she just wanted—what did she want?

She covered her face with her hands and groaned. "I'm sorry. I'm being difficult." Tears burned her eyes as she looked around the office. "I'm not sure I can do this. Earlier, I thought I knew what to do, how to go forward. But I'm not sure. I think I'm just lying to myself."

In two steps, he was in front of her, pulling her into him for a hug. He held her tight, saying nothing for a long time, then said softly, "You'll get back up again. You're stronger than you think."

Danni shook her head.

"Yes, you are." His lips were close to her ear. "Stay, Danni. You need time for yourself. Don't go running back to a guy because you're scared or because he makes a half-assed gesture. You can do this on your own. You're stronger than you think."

She shook her head. "I don't think I am."

"Yes, you are. Stay at least until Darby finishes this school year. It's only a couple of months. You know how the kid must feel. She doesn't want to move to a new school at the end of her freshman year."

"I'll talk to her."

"Then for no other reason," he dried her cheeks with his thumb, "you could stay because I asked you as your friend. I've missed you."

She looked up at him. His eyes were such a warm brown. He was always a gorgeous kid. Now, he was a gorgeous man with features so perfect, a complexion so rich, and a body so firm, he could have been carved from island cedar. His Hatterask roots ran deep—from his towering height to his rich black hair. He belonged to this land, like his ancestors before him, who'd inhabited this area since loincloths were in fashion.

The image of Fisher in a loincloth made Danni feel a little flushed. And the feel of his hard form—after years and years of tedious sex and abstinence—was more than she could swallow, literally. Hit with an instant case of dry mouth—perhaps a case of instant dehydration from his heat—she couldn't answer him yes or no. She just stood there, holding onto him.

A car door closed. Danni jumped and pulled away.

Chapter 10

Maureen popped her head in the door. "Knock knock."

Danni nearly fell over the office chair in her attempt to back away from Fisher fast enough.

Fisher, calm as ever, nodded to the older woman. "Maureen." Then to Danni, he said, "I better get going."

"Oh, don't go on my account." Maureen lifted a small animal carrier. "I'm just bringin' the dog."

"I was headed out anyhow. I have to get back to work. I just dropped in to give Danni a few groceries and dropped off her loaner car."

"That was thoughtful of you. But then, you're always so thoughtful. Isn't Fisher thoughtful, Danni?"

"Always." Danni couldn't help but look at Fisher. "You have been the biggest help, Fish. Thank you."

He gave her a nod and a look so intense she couldn't maintain eye contact.

"Think about what I said, Danni."

Danni nodded, trying to swallow past the lump in her throat. How could Fisher be her friend if he made her heart race?

Get yourself under control, Danni thought as her eyes followed Fisher out the door.

Maureen gave her a grin and a wink. Danni wanted to tell Maureen to stop thinking what she was thinking, but then she'd have to admit she was sending off some weird signals.

Maureen mopped beads of sweat from her brow. She was a big woman—about Max's size, only Max was always sturdy and athletic. Maureen was round with a crooked walk from a bad hip.

Maureen set the animal carrier on the desk. It took her some effort, but she managed to unlock the door to the little dog cage and swung it open. Out walked one of the ugliest dogs Danni had ever seen in her life. It was a brown mutt with wiry hair and a face nearly obscured by gray fur. Maureen said sweetly, "This is Punkin."

"That's a dog? It has to be the most hideous looking thing ever."

"Rodanthe Luna, how could you say such a thing?" Maureen scooped the small dog up and looked at Punkin like she had never seen her before. "Well, I suppose she isn't exactly a beauty. But she's a good dog."

Punkin whined and squirmed. Maureen put her down. The dog walked away from them and curled up in a corner. Maureen whispered, "I think you hurt her feelings."

"That's ridiculous," Danni said, looking at the wiry mutt. Punkin looked away. Danni bit the side of her cheek.

Maureen went to the dog and lifted her up and cradled her for a hug. "There, there, girl. Danni didn't mean anything by it." The dog licked Maureen's cheek. Maureen chuckled. "You are the sweetest little thing. Forgive Danni's impertinence. She's just suffering her own loss." Maureen looked at Danni. "How are you holding up, dear?"

Danni nodded. "I'm doing okay. I've had a few moments. It's still so hard to believe she's gone. Sometimes, I feel like she is right here with me."

"And she is."

"No, seriously, I...." Danni didn't want to sound crazy, but it was Maureen. If she couldn't confide in her, then who could she tell? "I saw her, like a ghost, at the funeral. And today, I swear, she was here. I couldn't see her, but I could feel her with me."

Maureen's gray head bobbed. "No doubt she is. Max always said that Lowrys were weed stock."

"Weed stock? Like...." Danni mimicked smoking a joint.

Maureen chortled and slapped her leg. "No, no dear. Weeds, like unwanted plants. You can cut them down, but they keep on living. Especially when they're cut down after they've stored all their energy."

Danni shook her head. "I don't follow."

"You know how if you cut down a tree that's ready to hibernate for winter, it will grow back?"

"I had no clue. I assume you cut down a tree; it's gone for good."

"Ha! Then it's time you learned something. A tree stores all its energy in its roots. And when a tree is prepared and ready at the end of its natural season, it can grow back from the roots."

"So, you're saying Max is stuck here on earth?"

"Not stuck, not stuck at all. Max is certainly yucking it up in Heaven. But I think her soul is so full of energy and is so rooted to this place that a small bit of her, almost like a scent, lingers on."

"Have you...seen her?"

"Oh, no! But she's been leaving me signs. My spring flowers had a second bloom the day she died. And every morning, there is a gray-headed gull sitting on my kitchen windowsill. I tell her, 'Morning Max,' and she caws. I give her a bowl of apple crisp, Max's favorite, and she stays there until I finish my morning cup of coffee."

"I.... Are we insane, Maureen?"

"Not at all. We're islanders. Living on shifting sand reminds us that this world isn't as concrete as some like to think. We also know there is as much mystery to what lies under our feet as there is explanation. That knowledge helps to keep the mind open and clear."

"I doubt many people would call hallucinations clarity of mind."

"Well, now, those people probably think they're too smart to believe in things they can't see."

Danni smiled. "Thank you, Maureen. I was afraid I was going nuts — shades of my mother."

Maureen sighed. "Your momma was a fine girl. No shame in being like her."

"She tried to kill me. She was either totally insane or hated me."

"No, no, of course not. She loved you. But she was troubled.

After you were born, Max thought the postpartum depression amped up her normal depression. Max tried to get her committed from the hospital after she delivered you, but no one would hear of it. Your mother wouldn't eat or sleep. She sat cross-legged in the hospital bed, holding you and rocking back and forth. She'd watch the news and obsess about everything from global warming to nuclear strikes. It was far from normal, but there was nothing Max could do without a court order, and the shrink that saw her said it was typical anxiety. The best Max could get was an order from social services that Vi had to stay with Max for ninety days."

"Was she even home a day before she tried to drown me in the sound?"

Maureen looked a bit like a bobblehead like she couldn't decide between a nod or a shake. "That is a trick question, little lady." Maureen shook her finger at her. "She didn't try to drown you. She wasn't thinking clearly. But yes, it was her first night home that she dropped you in the water." Maureen looked sad. "Poor girl. Once Max got her committed, and they had her on the proper medications, she hated herself for what she almost did to you."

"But not bad enough to stick around."

Maureen sighed. "Did Max never tell you anything about Vi? Anything about her troubles?"

"Talking about my mom made Max sad, so I stopped asking when I was little. Honestly? I didn't even know my mom jumped off the bridge or tried to kill me until I was in the sixth grade, and Tori told me."

Maureen rolled her eyes. "She always was a mean little thing. Max should have talked to you about Vi. You know, she called Max from the bridge. She said it wasn't suicide, it was a sacrifice—her life for yours."

"That's bizarre. But maybe if she knew she was losing her grip on reality and was a danger to me, I can see where she would think she was doing me a favor. Did she ever say what she was thinking when she tossed me in the water?"

Maureen nodded. "Voices in her head told her to baptize the

baby to keep her safe from harm."

"Wow. Good thing Max was right behind her."

Maureen nodded. "I always thought Vi was too sensitive for this world like she psychically couldn't process the evils she encountered. Add in the depression and the voices, and she could barely function."

"Was it schizophrenia?"

"Most likely. Whatever it was, it was nearly impossible to treat. I think they tried every kind of medication imaginable. Nothing ever quite worked."

"That's sad." Danni sighed. "You're right; Max should have told me more about her."

"I wonder what Max did with her artwork. Your mother was a talented artist, you know."

"No, I didn't know." Danni sighed. "Honestly, I don't often think of her. Max raised me, no thanks to my mother."

"Ah, dear," Maureen said. "You've got to forgive your mom. Love her for the good things. She loved to grow flowers and paint. She was a sensitive girl, and she was only nineteen when she died—really just a baby herself."

Danni nodded. She'd never thought of her mother as a teen mom. In Danni's mind, she aged along with Max. "I suppose when I was nineteen, I dropped out of college like a fool and married Rick."

"Young people can be too impulsive for their own good. That's for sure."

"I guess I am more like my mother than I realize."

"Well, now, there are big differences too. You have Max's sensibilities."

"Sure. I was talking to a dead lady yesterday."

Maureen chuckled. "You're fine, Danni. Think of it this way—you are touched, but not touched in the head."

"Is there a difference?"

"I think so. I don't consider me having a new bird friend a problem."

Danni nodded, hoping Maureen was right, but making a mental note that if she kept having visions, she'd call a shrink for some meds. "I suppose if Max were to be inhabiting an animal, it would be a loud-mouthed gull."

Maureen chuckled. "Oh, now, you're gonna pay for that." Maureen looked up at the ceiling. "That was Danni saying that, Max, not your buddy Maureen."

Danni blew her nose, dried her eyes, and enjoyed a good laugh. "Thanks, Maureen. I appreciate the talk. I've had so much going on in my head — guilt over Max piled on top of old mommy issues." Throw in Fisher...Fisher and Tori. Just the usual tortures of home sweet home.

"Max did things her own way, all the time. We were best friends for over sixty years, and I didn't know she was even seeing doctors until last week. Stubborn old fool. I think she tried to deny she was at all weak like Vi and took it to the other extreme."

Danni nodded. "I can see that. And I can understand why she did it. Max was strong for everyone. She prided herself in that. And she certainly only did things how she wanted to do them."

"She was stubborn as a mule. I couldn't believe she hadn't told you." Maureen shook her head. "That reminds me. Max gave me...," Maureen dug through her oversized purse, "a letter for you." Maureen handed her a blue envelope. "She wrote this just in case you didn't get here from the west coast in time."

Danni clutched the letter to her heart. "Thank you, Maureen. I'm so glad you came. It all still sounds crazy, but it makes me feel like I don't need a straitjacket — at least not yet."

"Prayer works too. It will keep you grounded. Never forget that." Maureen gave her a big hug. "Well, dear, I better get going. I get to watch my grandbabies this evening. Would you and Darby want to come down for dinner? You could meet my boys."

"Darby's out with friends. I told her she could go — do you think that was all right?"

"Why, most certainly. It's good to see her behave like a kid. How 'bout you? You gotta eat."

"Thanks, but no. I want to look around here a bit. Maybe go over to the ocean. I haven't seen the Atlantic in years."

"Well, if you change your mind. You remember where I

live?"

Danni nodded. Maureen gave Punkin a kiss on her furry head and handed her to Danni on her way to the door. "Now Punkin, you take good care of Danni. Don't be sore that she called you ugly. She'll see your inner beauty soon enough."

After Maureen left, Danni scooped up the mutt and carried her to the recliner in the living room. Settling her on her lap, she gave her a few apologetic strokes to her fur before she gently opened her aunt's letter.

Chapter 11

Divorced. The word rang through Fisher's head. Danni was single. As in available. For now. She met and married her last husband in a matter of months. Who knew when husband number two would come along. Or when husband number one would show up for round two.

Slamming his truck door closed, he berated himself for being so weak where Danni was concerned. He'd managed to wipe her from his thoughts years ago, at least for the most part. There were times when he was weak, like if he drank or when his dog died. Those were times when memories of her would come rushing in.

And the idea of something other than friendship with Danni was insane. Every attempt to love her failed. He couldn't forget that, no matter how much she made his heart race or his—

"You okay, Fish?" Luke Barrick gave him a punch in the arm.

Fisher pulled on work gloves and dragged a pile of two by fours off the back of his truck. "I'm fine."

"Does this have anything to do with Danni being back?"

Fisher dropped the stack he was holding, and they clattered to the ground. Luke laughed as if that answered his question.

Fisher bent over to pick them up but paused. Why should he lie to Luke? They'd been friends for a long time. And he knew Danni and the situation.

"Danni's divorced. Did you know that?"

Luke nodded. "Tina mentioned it a few months ago."

"And you didn't think to tell me?"

"Tina made me promise not to tell, and she carries my balls in her purse."

"How did Tina find out?"

"Tori, of course."

"Tori knows?"

Fisher thought of Tori playing dumb last night. Giving him Rick's number so he could call him like a fool.

"You've got to give Tori a bit of a pass on this, man. She's crazy about you. Tina says she's been on pins and needles knowing Danni would be back."

"Why should she care if Danni is back?"

Luke laughed. "Seriously? You're seriously going to play dumb with me? We all know, if Danni wants, she'll have you eating out of her hand in no time."

"Bullshit."

"Come on man, it's Danni."

Fisher shrugged.

"Fine. Billy over there is single...hook him up with her."

The idea of another man, any man, having Danni sent irritation up and down his spine.

Luke laughed. "Told ya."

"Fuck you."

"Hey Billy," Luke yelled to the blond-haired guy mudding drywall. "Did you see Danni at Max's funeral?"

"Hell yeah."

"She just got divorced. You want me to hook you up?"

Billy dropped his trowel in the gray "mud" and looked at Fisher. "You okay with that?"

"No, I'm not okay. Her aunt just died. She's my friend, and I won't let you assholes play games with her."

"And that, my friend, is why Tori is nervous. Things haven't exactly been going right with you guys. She has to be thinking this breakup is going to be permanent now that Danni is back in town."

"Danni won't stay. She hates it here."

"That should make Tori feel better. I mean, it is the dream of every gal to win at love by default. Add that to your marriage vows, 'Dearest Tor, you may not be the love of my life, but you win because the other gal forfeited.'"

Fisher flipped him off and went back to work, but Luke's words stuck with him. He hadn't realized he'd made his feelings for Danni so obvious, especially when he wasn't even certain he could ever trust her again. The hard truth was, he'd always love her. There was nothing he could do about that. But he couldn't, wouldn't ever let her close enough to hurt him again.

Danni was best as his friend, nothing more. Besides, if she was his friend, he couldn't lose her again. Relationships failed, but friends were forever.

Look at his relationship with Tori. They'd dated on and off since high school graduation. No matter how hard they tried, fights happened—he'd piss her off, she'd throw shit at him, and then she'd move out in a tantrum.

He sat on an empty paint bucket and tried to sort things out in his head, but there really was nothing to sort. All thoughts turned to Danni. He replayed their last conversation in his head. At what point had Danni gotten pissy with him? Before he could decide what went wrong, his phone rang. He pulled it from his pocket and answered.

"Hey, Mom. What's up?"

"Just checking in. Making sure you're okay."

"I'm fine. Why wouldn't I be okay?"

His mother whispered, "I heard Danni was back."

"Why does everyone act like she's some kind of problem for me? It's ridiculous."

His mom made that noise, the one that was probably meant to be supportive, but to him, it oozed pity. "Come on, Fish, it's Danni. I know how much you loved her."

"We're friends."

"Come on, you're my baby. I know how you feel about her. I don't want to see you hurt. Again."

"I won't be hurt. I'm not you. I won't let myself be anyone's doormat." His mom took a deep breath. He shook his head. "I'm sorry, Mom." He walked to the unfinished window and stared at the cluster of pines. "Maybe all of this is making me a little crazy. I'm glad she's back, but you're right—I don't want the same thing to happen like before. It's in everyone's best interest that we remain friends."

"Maybe you should just be honest with her—tell her how you feel."

Fisher shook his head. Danni knew. She had to. Telling her would only embarrass them and make their friendship awkward.

"Not happening."

His mother sighed. "I won't push. I know how it is to love someone. They have the ability to hurt you like no one else, but still, you love them."

Fisher leaned his head against the open casement. "I know that."

"I never wanted that for you. I always thought Danni would be—well, I never expected Danni to hurt you like she did."

"I didn't either. And trust me, it won't happen twice."

He worked in silence the rest of the day. Fortunately, the sounds of saws and nail guns disguised the turmoil going on in his head. After lunch, he texted Tori and asked her to meet him at his house. He needed to make it up to her. She'd been a big help the last few weeks, helping take care of Darby and helping him and Maureen plan the funeral— all things Danni should have done. Instead, she popped in for the service and tried to sneak out right after it. If she hadn't been hit by a truck, she'd already be gone from his life. Not to mention, she not only cheated on him but married another man three months after she met him. The problem with Danni was that she was emotionally unstable, and when he was with her, he was equally out of control. Danni brought out emotions, both highs and lows, that he'd rather keep under control.

He didn't have that problem with Tori. Life was stable, for the most part. And when it wasn't, when they broke up, it didn't feel like someone had ripped his heart from his chest and driven over it with a semi.

If he was smart, he would reconcile with Tori. They got along well enough. She was a good cook and not hard to look at. But best of all, she didn't have the power to make him insane.

Danni did. How many people pointed out to him how lost he was to Danni? That was proof; she was his kryptonite. On his way home from work, he would stop at a jewelry store and take a look.

If he was committed to Tori, Danni would have no power over him.

Chapter 12

Danni unfolded the letter. She looked at Max's left-handed scrawl, and her heart squeezed. She clutched the letter to her chest and took a deep breath. Punkin whined, and Danni patted her head, wiped her tears, and placed the letter carefully against her knee.

Dear Danni,

If you're reading this, I bet wrong. I fully intended to beat this cancer, but evidently, that wasn't meant to be. Damn. Hope Heaven's warm. I'm tired of winter.

First, forgive this coward for not telling you. I figured I'd be well by Christmas, and this would be nothing more than one more anecdote I could bend ears with, but since you're reading this "back up plan," you know I guessed wrong. Don't be mad at me for being selfish and not telling you. If these are my last days, they will NOT be about cancer. I will live until I die. I won't be a walking dead woman. I'll do this my way, or I won't do it at all.

And doing it all my own way includes the plans for my funeral too. (Maureen will do this. She'll need something to do. Poor girl will miss me. Call and ask her for help occasionally, she lives for that crap.) So anyhow, I also want a wake—a good one with beer and music. Screw it up, and I swear I'll haunt you, even if I have to bribe St. Peter himself.

BTW, no tears at my wake. Loosen up, have fun. Dance. Oh, how I love to dance.

As I write this, I'm thinking—my old knees won't have arthritis in Heaven. I could dance a jig without having to ice the joints for days later. Don't worry, I'm not talking myself into going, just sayin'.

All right…am I rambling? Oh well, I suppose on this occasion, you won't mind.

Before I forget. All you need to know about my estate is in a file labeled *Darby's to-do list*. I didn't want her to find the papers by accident and get her all worried for nothing. I would ask that you take care of her, but I know you will.

Now, I know you probably expect me to tell you what I want you to do for the rest of your life, and honestly, I have considered using my "death bed" to my advantage. But I realize as I have less guaranteed time for looking forward, looking backward is what I do most. I've decided life is what it is. Some things I thought were blessings turned out to be curses. Some things I thought were tragedies sent my life in the most positive directions. So, how can I tell you what choices to make? All I can say is this—

Listen to your heart and, in all things, be dynamic.
I love you, kid. Max.

Danni held the letter to her chest and cried. That question of the ages—the plague of consciousness—why? Why couldn't Max have had more time? She deserved it. Danni needed her. Darby needed her. There were so many evil, worthless people on this planet—why take one of the best ones?

Punkin looked up at her. With her head cocked and ears perked up, Punkin almost looked cute. "I'm sorry, Punkin. You're not really so ugly." Punkin whined and went to work licking at the salty tears.

"Thank you, Punkin. I'm so sorry I called you ugly," Danni said. The dog jumped from her lap and curled under the coffee table. Plagued with guilt, Danni went to the kitchen for a treat. She found a box of dog bones under the kitchen sink and carried one to the little dog. Punkin sniffed it and looked away, head dropped. Danni felt her nose. Warm and dry. She wondered if it was supposed to be cool and dry, or was it always supposed to be wet and cool. She hadn't had a dog in years, so she couldn't remember. Pulling the dog out from under the table, she hugged her as her mind began to spin with worry.

What if Punkin was sick? What if she died? Maybe she was heartbroken over coming home and finding Max gone. Didn't dogs do that sometimes? Danni cradled the dog. The more she worried, the sicker the dog looked and the warmer her little body felt. The dog was obviously fevered.

And it was Friday afternoon. What if Punkin got sicker over the weekend? Danni googled the nearest vet's office on her phone. They were only open tonight until six then closed until Monday morning. If Danni waited that long, it could be too late. She grabbed her purse and the keys to the rental. She'd not make the mistake of hesitation twice. Not where a creature's health was concerned.

She carried Punkin to the car and set her down in the passenger seat. She talked to her softly as she punched the address to the vet into the GPS. She drove off, carefully looking both ways before entering traffic. She drove up the island again, patting Punkin's head. "Do you miss Max?"

No answer.

"I miss her. I bet you miss her too. But I'll take care of you, Punkin." Danni chewed the side of her cheek. "Rick would never like you. You aren't even pedigreed. Rick likes a good pedigree. And money. Rick likes money. You got any money, Punkin?"

Punkin's ears twitched, and she closed her eyes.

"I didn't think so." Danni turned toward Nags Head. "Almost there, little girl."

She arrived at the vet's office and waited her turn with the dog cradled on her shoulder like a baby. A half-hour later, Punkin was called, checked, and sent away with a clean bill of health. The only thing the vet recommended was exercise since Punkin was a bit on the plump side.

Danni carried the dog back to the car and set her on the passenger seat. Punkin laid her head down on her paws and stared up at Danni. "He called you fat, didn't he? Why, I don't think you're fat. But a walk is a good idea. I could use one myself."

Punkin looked at her, her head cocked as if she was listening.

"I don't know why people think they need to tell us we've

gained weight. We're smart girls; we can figure out what size we are. We don't need doctors or bitches at funerals to point it out. Or jerk ex-husbands. It's not like I got fat overnight. I was there the whole time."

Slowly, a thought occurred to her—how did Tori know she was divorced? And that her weight was an issue? Danni must have told Max and forgotten. There were a few post-divorce nights where a bottle of wine was her only companion. Maybe she drunk-dialed Max and didn't remember doing it.

Maybe if she did stay here a while, she could work on getting in shape, then when she got home, Rick would be so shocked. Then *she* could decide if there was a future for them on a more even field. Maybe there was, maybe there wasn't. Maybe she would reject him. Then she could go from dumped to dumper.

That would be pretty sweet—a small bit of vengeance for all the hurtful things he'd said and done to her.

Or she could forgive him, take him at his word that he wanted her back, and they could work it out.

Danni frowned. Somehow, his proclamation of love fit her about as well as a pair of size six jeans.

What did Max always tell her? Judge the actions, not the words? It was easy to say he loved her, but was he here with her? Maybe his absence didn't mean anything. But for once, she was taking a deep breath and not making a decision until she was ready. The future would be her choice, not his.

Feeling committed, feeling hopeful that she would not remain pathetic forever, she pulled into Food Lion. She rolled a window down for Punkin and went into the grocery store. She shopped, filling her buggy with healthy foods, a dog collar, and a leash. She knew Punkin already had one, but she wanted to get her something new, something with a bit of bling to cheer her up. In one day, the poor pup had been called ugly and fat—that was a bad day for any girl. Besides, it was Rick's money. What better way to spend it?

Cart loaded, she stood in line, happily envisioning a lighter, healthier version of herself. She felt good—dynamic—until she heard a snicker behind her and a woman's voice say, "I don't think the veggies are working."

Danni's head snapped around. Tori hid her smile behind a hand.

"Oh...Tori."

"You doing all right, Danni?" Tina asked as she joined them in line. Tina handed Tori a twelve-pack of beer. It was Fisher's brand.

God, I hate her.

Danni forced her smile wider. "I'm fine," she said to Tina. Then she turned her attention to Tori. There was no way this bitch was going to take constant jabs at her without Danni returning a single swing. Without consideration for truth or consequences, she said, "Actually Tina, it has been pretty rough, but it's looking brighter. Fisher begged me to stick around a while...and at first, I was against it. But I really owe him, you know? And besides, after seeing so many friendly faces like your own, I can't help but want to stick around. As a matter of fact, Fisher is coming for a late dinner. I was going to grab him a six-pack, but we're hardly kids anymore slugging back beer on the beach. I think a nice bottle of wine would be good. What goes better with chicken legs? Aren't those your specialty, Tori? Red or white? I can never remember."

The color spread across Tori's face, and her hands gripped the cart handle. Danni smiled and started unloading her food onto the conveyor belt.

Her smile remained smug, and her steps light as she left the store and headed out to the car. She loaded her trunk and then drove all the way home, telling Punkin all about her encounter in the grocery store.

Chapter 13

Fisher spotted Tori's car in his driveway from the road. He took a deep breath. The sight of it gave him no feeling of pleasure or comfort. If anything, it made him feel like his shirt collar was shrinking, and it was harder to breathe. He stuffed the bag with the small velvet box in his pants pocket. What the hell had he been thinking? The idea of committing himself to someone for any other reason than love was insane. That had to be the Danni effect.

Tori sat in a rocker on the porch with one leg crossed over the other, leg bouncing like it was made of rubber. Fisher guessed by her body language that today hadn't been a good day. Tori got emotional over any number of things, from a rude cashier to a slow driver. She wasn't exactly a relaxed sort of human being. In his mother's words, Tori was intense.

He was barely on the porch when she let him know exactly what pissed her off today. She flew off the rocker as he approached and met him at the steps. "I ran into Danni. She said you guys were having dinner together. What the hell, Fisher? I thought when we broke up, you said you needed space to think. By space, did you really mean you wanted to screw around?"

"You want to walk it back a bit, Tor? First of all, what I do is my business alone. And two, I'm not sure I know what you're talking about."

Tori shook her head. "Men. You're all a bunch of lying bastards. I ran into Danni at the grocery store. She told me all about you two having dinner together tonight."

Fisher took a deep breath. He'd spent most of his life being attacked and accused of shit he'd never done by a stepdad who screamed and hit first and asked questions later. Logically, he knew it made sense to tell Tori to calm down and explain that he had no clue what she was talking about, but that felt too much like caving into her tantrum. "I'm a big boy, Tor. I can make my own schedule."

Tori's jaw clenched, and she stared at him. He imagined if he could read her mind, she was flipping through all the different ways she could rip his balls off. But he was partial to his balls and had no intention of surrendering them to any woman, so he took a step back.

Tori blinked, let out a long breath, and then smiled. "I'm sorry. I'm jealous. This break has me a little crazy. I love you, ya know?" She took a deep breath in, loud breath out. "Can you forgive me? I'm behaving like a crazy, jealous girlfriend." Tears filled her eyes. "Probably because I'm nothing to you now."

Fisher took a deep breath. He didn't want to hurt her, but he did need that space from her to clear his head and think this all through. He climbed the steps and took Tori by the hand and pulled her to the porch swing. He sat and patted the seat next to him.

"So, are you having dinner with Danni?" she asked.

Fisher rubbed his lower lip. "Danni needs help getting all of Max's affairs sorted out. It's not like it's a date."

Tori pressed perfect hands to her cheeks. "I'm so embarrassed. I thought the worst. I should have asked you what was going on."

"Yeah, you should have."

"Forgive me?" She looked up at him with pouted lips, blue eyes opened wide.

"Don't worry about it." He opened his mouth to ask her why she'd told him to call Danni's husband last night, but he shut it. He wasn't an idiot. Tori had hoped his call would bring Rick riding in like a knight in shining armor. He supposed he couldn't blame her for trying. The blame was on him for being stupid enough to do it.

"Do you want me to go with you? I could help. My grandma died last year, and I helped Momma with the estate details."

He shook his head. "I'd give Danni some space. She's pretty emotional."

Tori nodded. "It hurts that she's acting like I'm the enemy. We used to be such good friends."

"Maybe once she's settled in, she'll be less emotional. For now, I'd steer clear of her."

"Settled in? She's staying?"

"For now."

"Was that your idea?" Tori stiffened against him.

"It was. I told Danni to consider Darby. In the past three years, Darby lost two parent figures to cancer. She doesn't need any more changes. Danni should stay here so Darby can stay in her home."

Tori went silent. Fisher frowned. It was one thing to be jealous; it was another thing to be inconsiderate.

After a few seconds, Tori sighed. "You're right. And what's best for Darby is all that matters. Hopefully, Danni does the right thing, though I can't imagine her staying here for any reason. At least not for the long term." Tori's phone rang. She looked at the number and sighed. "It's work. I have a couple who have looked at nearly every house listing I have, and they want to see more tonight. I swear, I hate lookie-lou's. Buy a damn house or go away."

"Good luck with that."

Tori gave his leg a pat. "Thanks for the support."

"Glad to help."

Slowly she stood and stepped away from the swing, pausing on the top step. "She won't stay, Fisher. Not for the long haul. But I understand that while she's here, you've got to follow your heart. Once she's gone, maybe then we can get back to us."

Chapter 14

After Tori left, Fisher couldn't help but head over to the hotel. He was curious—what had prompted Danni to lie to Tori? The Danni he knew lacked the creativity for game playing.

He knocked, but no one answered. The rental was parked in the lot, so she either walked somewhere or was asleep. He knocked a little louder, still no answer. Suddenly he imagined her passed out and dying from a head injury, so he grabbed the spare key under the planter and let himself in.

A note on the kitchen table from Danni to Darby told him she'd taken the dog to the beach. Fisher thought about walking over and joining her, but not knowing whether she walked to the north or the south ruled that out. Instead, he decided he'd cook dinner. Danni said they were having dinner together, so he may as well go with it.

He found the groceries he'd brought still in the bag in the fridge—as were a few new bags of groceries Danni must have picked up. He went through her bags first—vegetables and whole wheat bread. Fisher frowned and put them back. He pulled out the bag he'd brought her. He got useful food, like burger, buns, and cheese. He ripped open the plastic on the burger and made patties. He tossed them in a skillet and turned on the heat. While they cooked, he found a few boxes of macaroni and cheese in the cupboard.

"Good girl for having taste, Max," Fisher said to the empty room. He put a pot of water on to boil.

He was flipping the burgers when the front door opened, and Danni yelled, "Darby? I'm sorry, kiddo. I didn't expect you back so soon. You don't have to cook." Her words died as she walked into the kitchen. "Fisher? What are you doing here?"

"Tori told me we were having dinner together, so I came over. I didn't realize you inviting me to dinner meant I had to cook."

"Tori told you that?"

Fisher nodded. He toasted the buns, then added a burger to each one. "More like she flogged me with it, but essentially, she informed me I was eating here tonight."

Danni covered her face with her hands and groaned. "I'm sorry. I was just...popping off at the mouth."

He scooped mac and cheese onto each plate then set them on the table. He grabbed them each a beer and motioned for Danni to sit. Red-faced and looking embarrassed as hell, she sat.

"What did Tori say to you to make you tell her that?"

Danni grabbed the beer from him and picked at the label. She offered no explanation, so he prodded her again.

"Seriously, Danni. What happened?"

"She—I'm probably overly sensitive about my weight, and she made a comment about the veggies I had in my shopping cart. It made me mad, so I dragged you into it. I knew it would piss her off, but I never dreamed she'd tell you about it."

"Why are you sensitive about your weight?" She looked fine. Too fine.

"Aren't all women?"

Fisher shook his head. "What's going on with you and Tori? You used to be friends."

"I used to like Barney the Dinosaur too, but we grow out of things. And Barney didn't make fun of my fat ass at my aunt's funeral, so there is that."

"Tori made fun of you at Max's funeral?"

"She didn't know I was listening. I was in a bathroom stall, and she was talking to Tina and telling Tina how Rick divorced me because he said I was fat and he was no longer attracted to me." Danni loosened the edge of the beer label and peeled it off the bottle. "I'm still trying to figure out how she knew about that."

Fisher dropped his burger on his plate. Irritation had ruined his appetite. "That's why he divorced you?"

Danni nodded. "Technically, I divorced him—after he told me we didn't need counseling, I needed fat camp...while we were at the gym...in front of the trainer. The trainer told me to divorce his ass."

"You don't say?"

"It was humiliating. And I guess it's made me sensitive, so when Tori told me the veggies and healthy food in my cart weren't helping, it brought out the evil in me. I wanted to punch her, so I hit her with you. I'm sorry if I got you in trouble."

"I'm not a child. I can't get in trouble."

"Well then, I'm sorry if I made her mad at you."

Fisher no longer cared about what happened between Danni and Tori. He wanted to go back to Rick—maybe snap his neck. "Did you punch the son of a bitch in the face for saying that?"

Danni shook her head. "He was only telling the truth. Sometimes the truth hurts."

"Fuck him. You're beautiful."

Danni's eyes got glassy, but she smiled and patted his hand. "You were always the best friend."

Fisher wanted to kiss her more than he'd ever wanted anything in his life. Maybe it was pity because he definitely felt sorry for her. He knew her better than she knew herself, and he could feel her pain—sharp as a punch in the gut. She didn't deserve to be hurt. He wanted to hold her, wrap her up and shield her from everything.

But he wouldn't.

Giving in to that desire was how he lost her last time. He had to remember that. If he gambled and went for more, he could spook her and send her running from the island.

To say he felt conflicted was like saying the ocean was big. Truth was, he loved her. Always had, always would. But could he flip friendship into something more? He knew Danni loved him—in her way. Even if she didn't realize it.

Danni stood and headed for the fridge. He grabbed her by the hand and pulled her to him. "You're a beautiful woman. Any man would be lucky as hell to have you."

Tears sparkled in her eyes, but she smiled. His imagination took off unchecked. In his mind, it was so easy to kiss her, scoop her off her feet and carry her to another room and —

"Whoa! Maybe you guys should get a room. Impressionable teen in the house."

Danni's reaction to Darby answered his question of whether or not to push things past friendship. The girl caught them holding hands, and Danni about broke a leg getting away. Fisher realized he was a fool to think there could ever be anything more between them. Obviously, Danni didn't want to be connected to him on any intimate levels.

"Darby," Danni said. "I didn't expect you back so soon."

"I see that." Darby grinned and filled a plate with food.

Danni's cheeks turned blood red. "It wasn't anything, I swear. Fisher was just…."

Danni looked at him. He made no offer of explanation. He was curious to know how she'd define the moment. She summed it up as he expected. "…Giving me emotional support."

Emotional support. Fisher rolled his eyes and cleared his throat. "Danni told me her husband told her she needed to go to fat camp. I was telling her she deserved better…so yeah, I was giving her emotional support."

"He said what?" Darby nearly choked on her bite of burger.

"He's not my husband. He's my ex-husband," Danni mumbled, as if the broken connection made his abuse acceptable.

"You mean to tell me that guitar-strumming munchkin had the cheek to call you fat?" Darby said. "Like he's some sort of gift from the gods to the ladies of this universe? If you ask me," Darby said, pressing her napkin to the corner of her mouth, "I think he looks like an ancient-Justin Bieber with a mange-filled beard."

"He's my age," Danni said.

Darby gave her a stare. "You look younger, or at least you would if you didn't look so tired."

Danni grabbed herself another beer. "Thanks, I think."

The teen flashed Danni a smile, then turned her attention to her food and her phone. Her right thumb flew over the phone keypad while the left hand shoveled food in her mouth. Darby's interaction with the people in the room was lost to whatever text required an immediate response.

Fisher sighed. "I suppose I better head home. I have some work I need to do tonight." He gave Darby a pat on the head.

She gave him a knuckle bump. "Later, old man."

The girl's words brought a chuckle out of Fisher. He headed toward the door, saying to Danni over his shoulder, "Thanks for sort-of inviting me over, even if it was out of spite and revenge."

Danni smiled. "And thank you for not calling me out as a total liar and for cooking dinner. You really are the best friend ever."

Fisher nodded. Those were sweet words that always, always cut him to his core.

Chapter 15

Danni's heart suffered a bit of pain as she imagined the *work* Fisher hurried home to finish. It probably had poufy blonde hair and knobby knees. She watched him walk across the path from the kitchen window.

Who he spent time with really shouldn't matter to her. If that she-devil made him happy, who was she to judge? She gripped the counter, her eyes following him until he disappeared, swallowed by the shrunken pines and reed grasses that lined the path.

When Danni was little, she imagined native Hatterasks using the reeds to weave baskets. She'd once asked Fisher's mom if she still knew how to make them. The question inspired a rare laugh from Fisher's usually somber mother. Catherine "Kitty" Cooper Jones was most often found in the kitchen, quietly baking something or another. Rarely was she seen laughing or smiling.

Fisher had his mother's dark skin and height, though Kitty was tall and willowy whereas Fisher was stocky. Kitty said he got his heavy frame from his father. Fisher and Danni had to take her word on it since neither of them ever met Jeremiah Cooper. He died in a car wreck before his son was out of diapers.

Danni shook off the memories and turned to Darby. The girl dipped her burger in a puddle of ketchup and flashed Danni a smile. "Seems I came back a little too soon."

Danni sat across from her. "You are back early. Or at least earlier than I expected."

"Disappointed?" she asked with wiggling eyebrows.

"Not at all. Is everything all right? Did anything happen?"

"Nah," Darby said, quietly. "I just got bored."

"What did you guys do?"

"Smoked some crack. Had some sex."

Danni's eyes popped open.

Darby laughed. "JK'ing, Danni."

"J what'ing?"

"Joking. Don't you text? On your phone?"

"Of course, but I don't JK."

Darby rolled her eyes. "Somehow, that doesn't surprise me. Max always said you checked your sense of humor at the altar."

"She said I did what?"

"I assume she meant checked as in, handed it over—like a coat check?"

"I know what checked means. I'm just.... That's so—"

"Accurate?" Darby laughed for a second but quieted quickly. She twisted a purple-painted fingernail into her smooth black hair. "That doesn't make you mad, does it?"

"No. It's funny. Contrary to your and Max's assessment, I still have a sense of humor."

"You didn't laugh."

"It was at my expense."

"I'm sorry."

Danni sighed and stretched her arm across the table to pat the girl's arm. "No, I just have a lot on my mind."

"Like Fisher?" Darby asked with an exaggerated wink.

Danni shook her head. "No, not Fisher. No chance of that—I messed that up a long time ago."

"Seems he's forgiven you."

"Maybe." He didn't seem angry with her anymore. But still, there was Tori. "Forget it. What guy would ever pick me over Tori? She's gorgeous."

"Oh, bull." Darby shoved her plate to the center of the table. "You're way prettier."

"Ha! Now I'm wondering if you were telling the truth about smoking crack tonight."

Darby stood and walked around the table to Danni. Positioned behind her, she pulled Danni's hair free of the ponytail and fluffed her hair. "You just need a new haircut. And some make-up."

"I'm wearing make-up."

"Well then, the right make-up. I bet you're wearing powder foundation. It creases. Go with the mineral kind. It smooths and covers. And your eyeliner is too heavy—makes you look tired."

"I am tired."

"Well, the goal of make-up is to hide the tired. Let me give you a make-over, and you'll have Fisher eating out of your hand."

Danni blushed and looked away. "I told you—Fisher is just a friend."

"Really?" Darby grinned. "Is that really how you want it to go? You want to be his buddy, maybe his bestie at his wedding, babysit his kids that him and the evil whore have?"

"Darby!" That was just—awful and inaccurate. Evil, conniving bitch was more appropriate. "You shouldn't call other women whores. It breaks the bond of sisterhood."

"That thing ain't my sister."

Danni couldn't hide her smile. It felt great to have a co-conspirator. "You're right; she doesn't deserve to belong to the sisterhood."

"Okay, so seriously, why not go for Fisher? He's hot, even though he's an old guy."

"Would you stop that? We're the same age too." Danni laughed.

"Then, you're perfect."

"We're just friends. He seems happy with Tori."

"Oh my god, no. They are broken up more than they're together. It's just hard to tell when they're split because she NEVER goes away. As his friend, even if you don't want him, you at least have to break that connection for good. Help him find someone who isn't likely to sacrifice babies to get her own way."

Danni laughed. Darby really did know Tori well.

"I suppose looking better wouldn't be a bad thing."

"Now, you're talking." Darby gave Danni's shoulders a shake like she was a prizefighter before going to work on her hair. Darby combed out the tangles with her fingers. "I can't believe how soft your hair is. If I shortened this just a bit. Maybe a chin-length bob, it would be so cute, and it would make it look fuller."

"I can't do it."

"What? Too attached to your ponytail? I could make it a little below —"

"Not the hair. I can't come between Fisher and Tori."

"Can't or won't?"

Darby shrugged. "He obviously likes her."

"Perhaps that's because he's not aware that he has options."

Danni bit her cheek. "No, I'm not taking any chances. I need Fisher as my friend. I didn't realize how much I missed him. One time, a long time ago, I tried to have a...uh...relationship with Fisher." Danni swallowed hard. "It didn't go well."

Darby paused, circled the chair, and looked Danni in the eye. "If all this bumbling is you trying to tell me you and Fisher had sex, you could just say, 'Fisher and I had sex.'"

"Fine." Danni's armpits felt suddenly sweaty. "Fine. Fisher and I," Danni dropped her voice to a whisper, "had...sex."

"So, was it awful?"

Danni shook her head.

"So, what was wrong?"

"I'd rather not talk about it."

"Come on. We are sisters. You can trust me."

"You're a kid. You shouldn't know these things."

Darby laughed. "I could probably teach you a thing or two."

Danni's mouth dropped open.

"Now, don't get me wrong, I'm a virgin. My mother caught an STD that she swore gave her cancer. She made me promise I'd never have sex like she did. And trust me, my mom had a lot of sex. She was using sex for food and shelter before she was my age."

Danni's eyes grew wide. She didn't know how to respond.

"Don't judge her too hard. She wasn't a slut — she just didn't have much choice. Her parents were abusive, so she ran away from home when she was fourteen. The first guy she lived with was in his fifties. Fifty. Mom was just a kid. Then when she turned eighteen and was too old for the pedophile, she was on the streets again. And well, sex was the skill she had to work with."

"Your mom sounds like a survivor."

"She was. And a fighter. She wanted a better life for me and protected me from almost all of it. Sometimes a guy would get rough with her, and she'd come home bruised up."

"Who watched you?"

"People she found trustworthy. When we moved here, it was Ms. Maureen. But then Max offered my mom a room to live in and a job cleaning rooms, and we moved in here."

Danni nodded.

"My mom was far from perfect, but she loved me. I will keep my promise to her."

"You're an amazing kid, Darby."

"I am, truly." Darby laughed. "Now, let's fix your hair. Let me get my make-up kit and scissors. I used to do my mom's hair, so I'm really good. You'll be impressed."

Danni's heart raced a moment. She was trusting a fourteen-year-old girl with scissors near her hair? She felt a moment of panic, but then she caught her gaze in the reflection of the toaster. She looked like hell already. She might as well trust the kid; she had nothing to lose.

Darby returned and went to work. "So," she asked, "if not Fisher, do you want your ex back?"

Danni's shoulders slumped a little. "I don't know. This may sound crazy, but I don't really want him as much as I need him to want me back."

Darby added clips, pushing sections of Danni's brown hair out of the way. "That makes total sense. Getting dumped is a pride killer. Last fall, I was dating this guy, and I barely liked him—like, I liked him so little I was planning to dump him after homecoming—but he dumped me first. I was like, what? Why would he dump me? I was so upset. I came home crying and told Max I didn't realize I loved him until he was gone."

"What did Max say?"

"She told me it was my pride that was broken, not my heart."

Danni nodded. "That sounds like something Max would say."

Darby rested her palms on Danni's shoulders. "I really miss

her, but I swear, I can feel her here. I felt this peace as soon as we got home."

"I feel it too. As a matter of fact, there are times when I think she hasn't left us at all." Danni cleared her throat and decided she'd leave the Max revelations there. No need making Darby think she was insane or that the place was haunted.

"That's why I want so bad to stay here. This place is the only permanent home I've ever had. And for me to stay, I need you to stay, so let's say we make a game plan for catching the big Fish."

"I don't fish."

"You know what, or rather who, I am talking about."

"Whom you're talking about."

"Don't try to distract me with grammar. You need to be with Fisher."

Danni couldn't escape the conversation. She was at Darby's scissor-wielding mercy. The girl's fingers flew, snipping here and there. She definitely didn't suffer from indecision. Danni watched as locks of her hair piled up on the floor.

"Why did you leave here, Danni?"

"To go to college."

"I thought you didn't go to college?"

"I went for a semester and then got married."

"How did you end up in Oregon?"

"Living on the west coast was on Rick's bucket list. That and to be a real estate mogul. Buy low, sell high. Easy money."

"I take it that didn't work?"

"Nope. Total failure. He traveled all over the country, buying high-end real estate in sagging markets. When they didn't sell fast enough, we were left holding the mortgages. Rick burned through cash faster than an old lady in Vegas. I should have known what was coming. When we first got married, before I got my inheritance, Rick got his grandma to mortgage her house to fund his dream. Poor sweet woman didn't have enough income to even make a mortgage payment, but he assured her he'd be flipping this house for double what he was borrowing."

"Did he?"

"Not at all. He invested it in a house that got condemned for black mold. All that money down the drain."

"Did she lose her house?"

Danni shook her head. "Almost. When I got my inheritance, I gave her son the money we owed her and made him promise he'd put the house in his name so Rick couldn't talk the poor woman into putting it in hock again."

"That was nice of you."

"It wasn't nice. It was responsible."

"You sound like Max." Darby paused her work to give Danni a smile. "If I heard it once, I heard it a million times—choices aren't hard; just do the right thing."

Danni nodded. "I should paint that on a wall."

Darby squealed and rolled up on her heels. "We totally should. We should paint this whole place. Give it a total make-over."

"The whole place? Like the entire hotel?"

"Well, I was thinking the apartment, but hey, why not do the hotel?" Darby set her scissors on the counter and plugged in her curling iron. "I mean, if you ever did decide to run it, it would rent better if it didn't look like the Bate's Motel. And if you sold it, it would also be better if it didn't look like the Bate's Motel."

Danni looked around the room—from the flowered vinyl flooring to the cheap wood paneling, this place was a 1970s era nightmare.

"So, are you in? Let's un-Norman this place."

Danni was about to say yes but paused. "I don't have any money. I'm broke. I have $873.29 left to my name." And that was only because Rick put the $500 in her account.

"Do you think Max had money like your mom did?"

Danni shrugged. "I always assumed the money from my mom was life insurance money."

"Didn't she commit suicide?"

Danni nodded slowly. "Yeah, she did. Life insurance doesn't pay on a suicide, does it?"

Darby shook her head. "Doesn't in the movies."

"I have no idea where my mom got the money."

"Maybe your grandparents?"

"I never met them."

Darby looked nervous like she just realized she was poor and might have to give up her cell phone — or whatever it was teenagers cherished these days. "I assumed since your mom had millions that Max did too."

"I have no idea," Danni said. "But don't worry. I'll make an appointment with her attorney on Monday. One way or another, we'll be all right. It's not like I'm incapable of getting a job. I just don't know if we can afford to renovate."

Darby curled and fluffed, then curled some more. She looked at Danni, tilted her head from one angle to another, and then nodded approval. Next, she opened her glittery-gold make-up kit and went to work.

"If we do find some money to fix this place up, Fisher will help us. He's really good," Darby said. "And maybe, just maybe, you can at least stop him from getting with that — woman. God, she's so evil."

"I agree," Danni said. "You know, something has been bugging me since I got here. I overheard Tori tell her friends about my divorce. Do you know how she would know about it?"

Darby shook her head slowly. "No idea. I never knew. I don't think Max knew, because she told me in the hospital that she was going to push you to get rid of him by asking you to divorce him as her deathbed request."

"She mentioned using her deathbed as leverage for something in her letter." Danni smiled.

"You got a letter? Lucky you." Then, as if it dawned on her that Danni only got a letter because Max feared she wouldn't make it back in time to say goodbye, Darby cleared her throat. "I took good care of her, Danni. She wasn't ever alone. She never told me, but I knew. My mom died of cancer. I know what it looks like."

Danni blinked back tears and bit a lip that refused to stop quivering. "I should've come home. I should've been here. You're a kid. You shouldn't have had to shoulder the burden."

Darby gave her a hug, a tight squeeze that forced the breath from her body. "It's okay," Darby said. "You're here now. That's what matters." Darby stepped back and grabbed the dishtowel from the counter. She wiped her eyes and then Danni's. "Now, stop that crying. You'll screw up my good work."

Danni took a deep breath and smiled.

Darby took a step back. "I must say, I did good." She handed Danni a mirror.

Danni's limp hair had a little more lift to it where Darby had cut in wispy bangs and chin-length layers. Her eyes looked bigger, browner, and more awake. Her cheeks were slimmer, her skin tone even. She did look years younger. "You are a friggin' miracle worker."

"You're all ready to be hugging up on Fisher. Bow chick-a-wow-wow," Darby said, adding in a dance that looked part twerk, part seizure.

"Would you stop about that?" Danni tried to sound mad, but she couldn't manage it. "Get out of here. Go text a friend or something. Max left a number for her attorney. I'll give her a call and see if we even get to own this place before we start painting walls."

Chapter 16

Fisher wished he'd have gone to a worksite, or the beach, or the pier—anywhere but home after leaving Danni's. Alone in his living room, the walls were too close, and the house was too quiet. He stood to leave, and the front door swung open. Tori. Fisher sighed.

"Hey, sweets," she said, closing the door behind her. She shoved a peach pie toward him. "I felt bad for causing you hassles with Danni, so I brought you dessert."

"Uh, thanks." Fisher took the pie and set it on the coffee table. He rubbed his chin, trying to think of any excuse for her to leave. Breaking up with Tori never seemed to get rid of her, but it did mean he got more baked goods. His mother said she was like water on a rock and was slowly wearing him down.

Tori kicked off her high heels and followed him to the kitchen. "Sooo. Did you have a nice dinner?"

Fisher cracked his neck, trying to relieve the strain. "It was fine."

"Did you guys talk?"

"Of course." Fisher tried to grin. Tried to keep it light. "It would have been an awkward dinner without any conversation."

She patted his stomach, her hand lingering near his naval. "Was Darby there?"

"Eventually."

Her nostrils flared as she drew a deep breath.

Fisher knew what she wanted to know, but it wasn't any of her business. He didn't ask her what she did on weekends or where she went on her business trips. Broken up meant not keeping track of the other's whereabouts. He left the kitchen without addressing the look of annoyance on her face and sank into his couch. She joined him, sitting so close he could smell her perfume, so strong it stung his nose. He wished she'd go home. He needed space, and fresh air, to think.

Lost in thought, he didn't realize she'd unbuttoned two of the buttons on his shirt. Her hand slipped between fabric and flesh. He closed his eyes, which was a mistake. There, in the darkness, was Danni. It was Danni's hand moving across his flesh in his mind. Her lips trailing across the skin on his neck.

When her hand brushed his waistband, reality hit him. He couldn't have sex with Tori, with his mind preoccupied with Danni. It wasn't right. He grabbed her hand. "Not tonight."

"Are you mad at me?"

"Don't you think broken up should mean broken up?"

She gave him an ornery grin. "It never has before."

"We're getting too old for games, Tor."

She smiled up at him. "Personally, I like our games, but I won't push. I know you have a lot on your mind."

It was an impressive attempt at being light-hearted. If he didn't know better, he'd honestly think his rebuff didn't bother her. But he could read her—that little quiver in her lower lip, the frozen smile that stayed plastered to her face a few seconds longer than was natural.

"Well then, maybe I can interest you in a slice of pie—and a cold beer or a cup of coffee?"

"You don't have to—"

Tori slapped his shoulder playfully. "I know I don't have to. I want to. Put your feet up. Pick out a movie...or a game...and I'll keep you company for a while. Or is that a problem too?"

Fisher shook his head and grabbed the remote. Guilt crept up his spine. Tori was a giver. She worked hard to help people and asked for nothing in return. Why did he always hesitate? He was almost thirty. His only single friends were divorced. They were looking for second wives, and he was still evading a first.

He could blame Max. The old gal's memory made him smile. *It's better to be alone than be with the wrong person.* That was

Max's romantic mantra. She never married and seemed much happier than his own mother, who stayed committed to the man who stole her laughter. After his dad died, it was him and his mom for years. And they were happy years, at least for him—until Bill came along. After Bill, his mother was distracted and temperamental. She was no longer emotionally available to her son. Her entire focus was on keeping Bill happy, so there weren't any fights.

Max was right. It was better to be alone. Unless you found the right one. He thought of Danni and smiled. She was home, and she was single. She was the one for him.

There were only a few problems: how did he flip her out of the comfort of the friend zone, and how did he stop her from lamenting over the asshole who divorced her for being fat?

Fat.

Fisher shook his head. Danni was a beautiful woman. No, she wasn't stick skinny, but she was far from fat. And even if she was fat—what the hell difference would that make to a guy who loved her?

He once told Danni he loved her. She'd come to his house in the middle of the night and pecked on his window. He let her in, and she climbed in bed with him. They should have talked about where they were headed that night, but he never brought it up. He was eighteen, and having a girl like Danni, who willingly stripped herself near-naked before snuggling under the blankets with him, left his brain with little conversation options.

He'd taken her without ever saying a word. Even afterward, all he told her was that he loved her. She held him tight and said she loved him too.

Then he found out about Danni and a guy from school. The rumor was Fisher wasn't the only guy Danni approached that weekend. He didn't believe the rumors until he went to Danni and asked her. She'd looked at him with so much guilt, his stomach knotted. He could still feel that sick feeling almost a decade later. The disappointment gave way to rage—a rage like he'd never felt in his life. He asked her, "Is it true you were with Renzo?"

Danni's body shook. That was the first time he'd seen that

in a human. She knew she was busted. She told him she could explain, but he was too pissed to hear explanations. He told her, "There's no explaining. Just one word is needed, yes or no. Were you with Renzo?"

When she said yes, he'd walked out on her. He couldn't look at her, much less talk to her. He didn't even tell her goodbye when she left for college. It wasn't until she didn't come home for Thanksgiving that reality hit him. He'd been too hard on her. He drove to NC State to talk to her, but she wasn't there.

No one heard from her until Christmas when she came home with Rick, the girly-looking, hipster asshole, in tow. Danni, his Danni, had quit school and gotten married. He still couldn't wrap his brain around it. Was he seriously considering a repeat of that kind of romantic roller coaster? What the hell was wrong with him?

"Beer or coffee?" Tori asked from the doorway.

He could smell the coffee, hear it percolating.

"Coffee would be great."

"I bought some French vanilla creamer. I know you don't like flavored coffee, but I swear, this stuff is such a treat."

"Sounds good."

Tori gave him a look. "Seriously?"

Maybe that was the wrong answer. Fisher rubbed the back of his neck. "You bought it; the least I can do is try it."

Tori smiled. Fisher relaxed. Could he will himself to be in love with Tori? She had never hurt him like Danni had and, she'd been there for him when Danni broke his heart. She didn't play games, and she'd certainly never cheat on him.

He ate the dessert, drank the coffee, and pretended to be interested in the baseball game Tori found for him. But at the end of the evening, when she ran her hand up his thigh, he still sent her home. He needed some time to get himself oriented, and he couldn't do that with Tori so close.

"Are you sure you're not mad at me, Fisher?"

"Of course not." He kissed her on the forehead. "I'm exhausted. Maybe tomorrow we'll go see a movie."

"Tonight, I could give you a massage. Or maybe I could think of some other, more interesting way to help you relax."

She was relentless, but he tried not to be annoyed. "That's not necessary. I don't think falling asleep will be my problem. I'm barely able to keep my eyes open."

"Okay." She kissed his cheek, slipped her feet into her shoes, and opened the door. She didn't look happy about leaving, but after a short pause at the door, she left. "Sleep well, my love," she said. "Hopefully, you'll be feeling more like yourself tomorrow."

"I will. You sleep well too."

Tori paused in the doorway. Perfect nails gripped the door jam. "I don't want to lose you."

"Tori, please—"

"I'm sorry. I know, I know. We need space, and that's pressure. It's just...I'm not an idiot. I know what Danni does to you. Even just as your friend. I'd be worried about you getting hurt again."

"Everything will be fine."

She didn't look convinced, but she left. He closed the door and went straight to the shower and then to bed.

But sleep wouldn't come. He flipped on the lamp by his bed and pulled out the Bible his mom had gotten him for graduation. He flipped to the middle and pulled out the picture of Danni. He'd taken the picture at the top of the dunes during their last spring break. He'd already signed up to join the navy, and she was enrolled in college. They were about to go in different directions, and that worried him.

He talked her into going night fishing with him. His real goal had been to talk her into forgetting North Carolina State and going with him. She could go to college wherever he was stationed. He wanted to tell her he loved her—that he was scared he was going to lose her.

He wiped his thumb over her smile in the picture. He never got the balls to ask. He tucked the picture back in his Bible. He sat up in his bed and pulled on his jeans. He slid his feet into a pair of tennis shoes and headed out of the house.

Down the path, through the fence, he went to Max's window. Danni would be sleeping there.

He tapped on the window, and like he predicted, there she was. She slid the window open and stepped aside for him to slip in.

"You all right?" she asked.

"I'm fine."

"I assume you're not here because your mom and Bill are fighting."

He grinned. Whenever they'd fight, he'd go to Danni's to sleep. "Not this time. At least, not that I know of."

"Then, what—?"

"I wanted to make sure you were okay."

Danni sighed. "To be honest, I haven't been able to sleep a wink."

He kissed the top of her head, sliding his hands into her hair. She looked up at him. The need to kiss her made his body ache. Tilting her head until she looked up at him, he kissed her forehead, allowing his lips to linger a moment, savoring the feel of her skin, the smell of her hair. Lifting her off her feet, he laid her down on the bed. He kicked off his shoes and climbed in next to her. He brushed her hair away from her face. She snuggled into him, tucking her face into his neck.

"Good night, Danni," he whispered.

"Good night, Fisher."

Kiss me, Danni. Like you did that night.

But she didn't. Like so many times in their youth, her body went limp, and her breathing slowed. She was asleep. He kissed her temple and slipped off to sleep.

Right before dawn, when the sun was still a soft glow on the horizon, there was a whisper in his ear. "Rise and shine, big fella. Time to scootch on home."

He woke, expecting to see Max running him out of Danni's room, but the room was empty besides him and Danni, who was still sleeping in his arms. He kissed her as he carefully slipped out of bed. He put his shoes on, climbed out the window, and headed home.

Chapter 17

Danni woke to bright, sunny skies. The memory of Fisher's late-night visit seemed like a dream, but when she hopped out of bed and checked, the window was unlocked. It wasn't a dream.

Danni went to shower with a lighter step. Life wasn't feeling quite so bleak. Fisher might be dating Tori, but he was still her friend. She dried her hair and clipped it on top of her head.

She called Maureen to ask her about planning Max's wake. If Max was going to haunt her, she wanted it to be for a good reason and not as punishment.

"Of course, I will. I think she'd want her ashes scattered in the cove there by the hotel. We could have a fire, some music, and of course, beer. Plenty of beer and a whiskey toast to send her off with."

"Whatever you think's best. Just tell me what you need me to do."

"Absolutely nothing. I'll take care of everything."

Danni thanked her and hung up. If she planned to host a party at the hotel, she needed to whip this place into shape. The carpets needed a good scrub, as did the walls. She wasn't sure they could afford renovations, but she could afford soap and water. She'd also need to clear out the cove, so they could stand around a fire without getting cut up by bramble bushes.

What she needed was a to-do list. But before that, she needed coffee.

Danni went to the kitchen and made a pot and some toast, then settled in at the table with a notebook. She turned to a fresh page and started at the top. First, she had to clear the cove of brush. There were most likely snakes, so she'd need boots and leather gloves. She paused, wondering if Max's chainsaw still worked. Some of the brush had undoubtedly grown too thick to pull or cut with clippers. It was going to be a lot of work, but it felt good to be doing the things that would make Max proud and getting this place looking as good as she could would honor her.

The click of dog claws on the vinyl flooring drew her attention from her list. Punkin looked up at her, head cocked, tail wagging. Danni shoved away from the table and walked to the door that led to the fenced yard. She pushed the door open and walked Punkin out.

Standing on the back porch, she was hit with a punch-in-the-gut longing — not just for Max, but for life the way it used to be. So much of her life was spent in this spot. Her real life. Those quiet, unscripted moments she didn't even realize meant so much until they were nothing more than sentimental longing.

The hotel was a public place. From the wide wooden porch with the cane back rockers to the pool and deck at the rear of the hotel — those areas were always alive with strangers. But this area, this little square of the yard, was theirs alone.

Danni leaned against the spindle post as she watched the dog nose around the yard. She'd forgotten what this place meant to her. How many conversations did she have with her aunt on this porch? Visits with friends? Punkin inspected every bush and the perimeter of the wooden fence. She was obviously in no hurry to go inside.

Danni sat on the porch swing. The rusting chain creaked and groaned as she pushed back and forth and remembered. Bittersweet thoughts of what had been a good life, an unappreciated life. If only she could go back in time for one day, she'd pay any price. Even her worst day then was better than her best day now.

Her phone rang, and she pulled it out of her pocket. It was Rick. She shoved it back in her pocket. He was feeling more and more like nothing but the detour of regret. It rang again and again.

"You going to answer that?"

Danni's head turned with the sound. Fisher. She wiped at unshed tears as a smile crept across her lips. Danni patted the seat beside her and scooted over. Fisher opened the back gate and sauntered up the crushed shell path. Seated beside her, his long legs took over, moving the swing back and forth.

"You didn't answer your phone. Telemarketer?"

"Something like that." It rang again. She could feel it vibrate against her hip. Rick was evidently feeling eager to talk today.

Fisher looked down at her leg. "You're vibrating."

Danni pulled her phone back out of her pocket and shut it off. "It's Rick."

"The love of your life? You don't want to talk to him?"

"Don't be a smart ass."

"I'm not—at least not completely. I thought you wanted to save your marriage."

"I never said that."

The sun sparkled off the water along the horizon. Another few weeks and it would be hot enough to swim. The sweet smell of wild rose and gardenia saturated the still cool, moist air. This was a good moment. She didn't want it interrupted by Rick.

She said to Fisher, "Darby suggested we renovate this place, and I think it's just what I need."

"That will take some time."

"I promised Darby I'd stay at least until she graduates."

"High school?" Fisher sounded shocked.

Danni nodded. "She loves it here, and she told me a bit of her history. The kid deserves a break."

Fisher smiled. "Then, I think renovation is a great idea."

"Will you help?"

He turned to her, giving her a look that sent instant warmth through her veins to her heart. "You know I'd do anything for you."

Danni bit her lip. Her eyes stung, but she smiled. Like a surge from a rogue wave, a feeling of buoyancy washed over her. Was this happiness? She looked up at Fisher. For a moment, she thought he might kiss her. As if it had a mind of its own, her tongue flicked across her lips. Fisher smiled down at her, causing a blush to spread across Danni's cheeks.

"What did you have planned?"

Kissing you? Was her only thought.

"With the renovations," he said, his voice low and husky.

"I was thinking art deco, but beachy. Maybe some pink flamingos and palm trees."

"That sounds like Key West."

Danni chewed on her lip and thought a minute. The Outer Banks wasn't a flashy sort of place. It was more low-key. More humble in its beauty than the colorful Caribbean flair of the beaches farther south. "You're right. Bad idea."

"Maybe go for a laid-back art deco style. I have a picture of my grandma and grandpa in one of those wood-sided Jeeps they'd drive on the beach."

"The Woodie? I remember that. Remember how we'd pretend to drive it? Take it on adventures?"

"I do. As I recall, a picnic in the mountains was your favorite place to pretend to go."

"Because it would be cool there, and sand wouldn't blow into my sandwich."

"That thing sat in the backyard until…well, until Tori moved in. She had me junk it. She worried it would attract snakes."

"Tori lives there? You live with her?" Danni's heart fell to the bottom of her stomach for an acid bath. Fisher, her best friend, was consorting far deeper with the enemy than she ever imagined.

"Years ago. We broke up, and she moved out."

"But you're getting back together?"

Fisher shrugged. "Who knows what will happen? It seems we're always trying to work things out, but never can."

"So, all this time, you're harassing me to get rid of my asshole ex, you're dating yours?"

"Tori never cheated on me. Or stole my money. Or left me in a hospital alone. Or — "

"I don't need a recap. I know what kind of jerk he can be."

"Come on, Danni. I'm not trying to pick a fight. I only want what's best for you."

"I don't need a keeper." She crossed one leg over the other, her top leg swinging up and down. She had to take deep breaths. Why did he have to keep coming over? It was torture. "You're a shitty boyfriend, you know. Being here now...last night."

"I'm not her boyfriend."

"So, what are you?"

He shrugged. "A friend?"

"Is that why she's always around? She acts like she owns you."

"No, she doesn't. She checks in on me; she's a caring person."

Danni laughed. "Oh my, she has you fooled."

"She treats me better than you do."

"Well, if you like her so much, why don't you marry her?"

"Childish taunts? That's your comeback?"

Danni shrugged.

"I don't want to fight with you. I came over to check on you, not piss you off."

"I'm just saying us as friends won't work with Tori in the mix."

"What are you saying? That you can't be my friend unless I end my friendship with Tori?"

Her breath caught in her throat. That wasn't what she meant at all. Honestly, she didn't know what the hell she meant by any of it. When it came to Tori, it was like her brain turned into a bull raging at the color red. "I'm done with Tori. I'm not telling you what to do, but I don't want to be around her, and I don't want to talk about her."

"If it's the comments about your weight, she admits she was jealous—"

Danni held up her hand to stop him from talking. "I'm done talking about Tori. I have work to do today."

Fisher stood slowly. "I'd help, but I have to be somewhere by noon."

"A date with Tori?"

"It's not a date. It's a real estate opportunity. Am I allowed to have a professional life?"

"Of course. Don't tell her I said hi. I don't need her turning anymore of her vindictiveness on me."

"I already told her to leave you alone."

"Men are so stupid," she mumbled, arms crossed tight over her chest.

"Are you talking about me or the fat-shaming ex your trainer pressured you into divorcing?"

Danni glared at him. Her jaw clenched so tight it hurt.

Fisher rubbed his face with his hands and groaned. "Come on, Danni. Why the hell are we even fighting?"

"I'm not fighting. Are you fighting?"

"You're impossible."

"So leave."

"Fine, I will."

"Fine, go."

Fisher stood and walked to the steps. Without turning to her, he said, "I'll be back, and we'll get started."

"On what?" Danni asked.

"Renovations."

"Oh, that. Forget it. I can do it myself."

"Don't be so damned stubborn."

She wanted to tell him to go to hell. She wasn't stubborn, but suddenly she got a mental picture of herself—slumped in the swing, arms crossed tight over her chest, and lower lip stuck out so far a bird could land on it. Danni tried not to be so obviously bitchy, but her words came out terse, irritated. "I'll order pizza if you make it back alive."

"Is there some other reason Tori upsets you? Should we talk about this?"

Danni snorted. "She stabbed me in the back. It's that simple."

"Is this about Renzo?"

Danni shot out of the swing so fast it upset the balance and sent it sideways, banging off the porch railing. "Just go."

She turned and headed for the door. Punkin was right on her heels, so she scooped the dog up, buried her face in her fur, and hurried inside.

Chapter 18

Fisher took a deep breath. Was this how his mother felt? An inexplicable draw to someone who hurt her? He evidently hit a nerve bringing up Renzo. Mystery over the hate for Tori solved. It was Tori who had told him about the party at her house where Danni was with Renzo. He supposed that was a pretty deep stab in the back.

But Tori cared about him. She'd told him because she didn't want him to look like a fool. And she was concerned for Danni. It wasn't like her to have sex with a guy she barely knew. Or was it? She married Rick three months after meeting him.

A thought occurred to him, ever so slowly, as if his mind was resisting it. Danni never cared about him, not in a romantic way. He cared about her. He pursued her. Even now, he was the one pushing himself on her.

It was time to walk away. No more games, no more acting like a lovesick fool. Danni made her choice when she chose Renzo over him. He stepped off the porch that he'd stepped off a thousand times before. Only this time, he felt like he had the weight of a changed world on his shoulders.

As he approached his house, he saw Tori's car. He took a deep breath. It was time to do the right thing. The adult thing. No more games.

"Hey, Tor."

"Let me guess, Danni had another emergency?"

Fisher sighed. Danni was right. It was insane to think he could be friends with both women. If he committed to Tori, he would forever lose any connection with Danni.

"I suppose I'm a fool to think I can be friends with the both of you."

Tori's eyes widened. "I'll behave."

"You don't have to behave. Hell, you haven't done anything wrong. Danni's damn near impossible to even talk to. At least you've been a good sport about it all."

"No, I haven't been a good sport. Not really. I'm insanely jealous of Danni. I know she has a spell over you. I'd call it love, but that hurts too much." Tori offered him a weak smile. "She says jump, and you say how high."

Fisher scratched his head. He'd spent a lifetime thinking his mother was a damned fool—was it genetic?

"I guess I just keep hoping that one day, you'll be that insane for me." A tear slid down Tori's cheek. She wiped it away.

Fisher pulled her in for a hug.

"And it hurts me that Danni hates me." Tori played with the collar of his shirt as she talked. "She was my best friend growing up but treats me like I'm the enemy. And I'm not. I just don't like to see her toy with you."

"She's not toying with me. She's a friend, that's all."

"Sure. And I'm the queen of England. Why else is she hanging around here, if not to trap you in her web again?"

Fisher pushed away from her, dropping himself into one of the chairs on his porch. "She's not staying for me. She's staying for Darby. Her being here has nothing to do with me."

"Right. You mean to tell me that after one day with that girl, she's ready to change her whole life?"

"Seems so."

"I'm not buying it. She has another agenda."

Fisher looked up at her. Her eyes were narrowed in thought, toe tapping on the floorboards. "So, what do you think Danni is staying for?"

She looked down at him and swallowed hard. "Maybe it is Darby she wants. I did hear through the grapevine that her and Rick couldn't have kids. Maybe she sees Darby as her chance to be a mom?"

Her words hit him like a punch in the gut. If that was true, his heart ached for Danni. Slowly, a thought occurred to him, and he had to ask, "How the hell do you know so much about Danni's marriage?"

Tori's mouth dropped open. "I...I don't. I told you that was a rumor I'd heard. I don't even know if it's true. I'm just saying...."

Irritation was giving him a headache. He needed a beer and a break from the women in his life.

As if the universe knew he was fed up with the female species, a text came in from Darby. *Will u still help,* (happy face)? *D's just* (crazy face). *Mostly cus of u* (double hearts).

Fisher wasn't the best at deciphering teen texts, but he assumed even Darby realized he was driving Danni crazy. Maybe he was. Tori was wrong. Danni wasn't manipulating him. He was the one telling her what to do. She was here to bury her aunt and take care of the estate and Darby. He was the one who hoped she'd never leave here. Never leave him. Damn, he was pathetic.

Chapter 19

Danni stared into her cup of coffee. All of her earlier energy and hopefulness was gone. Why did she pick a fight with Fisher? She wasn't even sure what started it, or what all she'd said. Did she give him an ultimatum?

Someone patted the top of her head. "I see you didn't bother doing your hair this morning. Bad, Danni."

Danni turned. Darby looked even cuter in the morning, with puffy eyes and skin so smooth and perfect the girl could have been molded out of porcelain.

"Hey, Darby," Danni said as she rose and looked through the fridge for something for breakfast—or rather brunch since it was almost noon. "I didn't have time for preening."

Darby shook her head, her mouth twisted in a smirk. "You're going to be a problem, aren't you?"

Even as miserable as Danni felt this morning, Darby could still make her smile. "Probably. I seem to have woken up on the bitch side of the bed this morning."

"I heard you and Fisher arguing. What was that all about?"

"You want some eggs?"

"Sure, but I also want you to tell me what you guys were arguing about."

"Tori. Fisher was telling me how great she is, and I just had to open my big mouth and try to set him straight." Danni cracked the first egg on the edge of the pan with so much force, she smashed it. "Damn it," she muttered and threw the mess in the trash before washing her hands. The next egg didn't fare much better. In frustration, she threw an egg against a wall. The exploding egg did little to calm her down, but the embarrassment of throwing a temper tantrum in front of Darby did make her take a breath.

Darby grabbed her by the arm and shut off the stove. "Whoa there, Babe Ruth. You need to calm down." She grabbed Danni by the arm and pulled her toward the back porch. "Come with me. You need to relax and get centered."

"If you think I am going over to talk to Fisher —"

"We're doing yoga. You need to unwind and relax."

"I'll have a beer."

Darby gave her arm a jerk. "Nope. Not healthy. Trust me, I've had my fair share of anger management training; I could be certified a therapist." Darby opened the door and pushed Danni through it. "Besides, what kind of a role model would you be? Going for alcohol to reduce your stress rather than natural, healthy exercise?"

"Fine. I guess if you put it that way."

"Not only will this help your frame of mind, but it will give you a perky little yoga butt."

"A yoga butt, huh? I could use one of those."

"So, come on."

"In the yard?"

"Yes. You can look out over the trees to the water — it's calming. That way, you can keep your temper and NOT be direct when fighting Tori. You have to be subtle. Cut her out of his life with scissors, not a sledgehammer."

"I'm not very good at subtle."

"I heard. Now, yoga is your punishment."

"You're kinda mean for a sweet-looking kid."

Darby kicked off her slippers and sat in the grass. "Get down here. Then you can shower and do your hair before Fisher comes back."

"I seriously doubt he'll come over again."

"Then you'll go to him and apologize."

"The hell I will."

"You can consider that while you find your body's center." Darby sat cross-legged, hands held like in prayer, and closed her eyes.

Danni sat and followed suit.

"Mountain pose." Darby hopped to her feet. Danni followed. Her transition from seated to standing wasn't as smooth as Darby's, but she didn't fall on her face either.

"Stand tall and breathe," Darby said.

Danni felt confident. This wasn't so hard. She could do this. "No wonder yoga is so popular," she said to Darby.

"Sun salutation, Danni. Get with the program, you're falling behind." Darby inhaled and circled her arms to the sky.

Danni mirrored the girl's movements. "I can't believe this even qualifies as exercise."

Darby shrugged as she folded her body forward and stepped back.

Darby's movements were so fluid, so fast, Danni was quickly tripping over her feet, trying to keep up. She almost did a face plant in the grass, transitioning from sun greeter to downward dog.

"Return to mountain pose."

"Thank God." Danni let out a puff of air. "I like the mountain. Screw the sun and the dog."

Darby laughed. "It's easy. Don't wimp out on me now."

"Screw you too, Darby." Sweat rolled down her forehead.

"Deep forward fold."

"Listen, little yoga master, my gut is in the way of my forward fold."

Darby laughed. "Suck it in."

"Easy for you to say, string bean. If I could suck it in, where the hell do you think it could go?"

"That's why you're doing this. To tighten your ab muscles."

"I've got to develop some first. Dear God...." Danni muttered as Darby walked her through all kinds of poses that Danni did her best not to completely butcher.

Finally, Darby suggested a child's pose. Danni felt a surge of relief. If it's for a child, it had to be easy...but it wasn't. Danni squealed as she pressed her weight against her heels. "This could cripple my knees. How the hell could this be healthy?"

"It's good for your back. Lean forward, rest your forehead to the ground, and enjoy the relaxation."

"Enjoy?! My ass!" Danni squealed.

"I'm enjoying," a man's voice said from the porch.

Danni wrenched a muscle in her lower back, flipping around to see who was there. "Fisher. You're back."

"You said you needed help." Fisher grinned, which Danni had to admit was a beautiful sight. His eyes crinkled, and tiny dimples appeared at the corners of his mouth. "I came to work; I didn't realize I'd get a show too."

Darby laughed. "Hey, Fish."

Of course, Darby thought it was funny. She was skinny and didn't look like a hundred-year-old dog with a crippled leg stumbling through dumb poses with idiotic names.

"So, what's the plan, Danni? You still wanting to renovate this place as a hotel, or are you leaning toward opening a spa?"

Danni rolled her eyes and wiped at the sweat on her brow. "You're the funniest man."

Danni made them all a quick sandwich before changing into work clothes and heading to the cove. Darby sent out a text, and in no time, there were eleven teenage kids ready to help. Darby informed her they'd work for pizza and access to the pool once it was open. Danni agreed.

They worked the better part of the day and had the area cleared and a bonfire ready before sunset. Danni pulled off her work gloves and turned to Darby. "Go ahead and order the pizza. My wallet is in my purse in the office."

Darby and her friends left.

When she turned back to Fisher, he was staring at her. As if by instinct, she wiped at her face, assuming she had something on it. After a few more seconds of silent observation, Danni had to ask, "What?"

He looked solemn as his head dipped close to hers. "You're good for Darby. It's good to see her happy."

"I like having her around. She's a good kid. Way smarter than me in most everything. Hell, she might be more the adult in this relationship. I don't help her half as much as she helps me."

"I can see how you're helping her. Her attitude is more

relaxed. The old Darby could be...quite intense. You're softening her. You're a natural momma, Loonie."

His comment made her physically wince. Danni shook her head and slapped her gloves against her hand.

"I'm sorry; I wasn't—"

Danni dropped and sat in the sand. The sky was starting to turn from blue to pink as the sun set on the horizon.

Fisher sat beside her.

Tears burned her eyes and made her nose itch. She rubbed it with the back of her hand. "I'll never be—" Danni stopped and took a deep breath. Part of her wanted to just toss it out there—I'll never be a mom, period. But she couldn't. The words felt stuck in her throat. "I'm not trying to be Darby's mom. She had a mom."

"That's what I was meaning when I said that. Your instincts for what's best for the girl are right on target."

His words were quiet, and he was so close. Too close. She could feel the heat from his body, smell the soap he'd showered with. Her heart hammered so wildly it made her feel hollow and dizzy. "Please don't."

"Don't what?" Fisher licked his lips.

"Kiss me."

Fisher grinned. "That's pretty damned arrogant of you. Who said I was considering kissing you? I was just talking to you."

"You don't need to be so close for that," Danni's voice was a whisper.

Fisher frowned and leaned away.

Danni instantly regretted opening her mouth. "I'm sorry. That was a stupid thing to say. And I'm sorry about what I said about Tori earlier. I'll do my best to get along with her. I'm being a brat. I don't want to do anything that will lose you as my friend. I...I don't really have much left in my world if I lost you."

"You'll never lose me."

"I hope not. But I promise I'll be nice about Tori. If you like her...well, I can get over my issues, for you."

Chapter 20

Fisher looked out over the water of the Currituck Sound. He had wanted to kiss her. Hell, he still wanted to. It was embarrassing to know he was so easy to read, and even more embarrassing to know she'd shot him down—fast.

Sharing a sunset at the cove suddenly felt like a bad idea, especially when she confirmed Tori's rumor with her reaction to his mom comment with pure heartache on her face. He wanted to ask her, tell her he loved her no matter what. But he wouldn't. She wanted to be friends; they'd be friends.

He stood and offered Danni his hand, helping her to her feet.

On the walk to the apartment, Danni said, "I'm also sorry about the kiss comment. I swear, sometimes things just float out of my mouth without my brain considering them."

"You're full of sorries today." He opened the door to the kitchen and held it for her, but didn't follow her inside. He took a step toward the porch steps. "I should head on home."

"Absolutely not. You'll stay and eat pizza with me." She pointed to the boxes of pizza on the counter.

Fisher nodded. He grabbed a box of pizza and sat at the table.

Danni pulled a carton of beer out of the fridge and joined him. "Fisher, I want to keep things right between us."

Fisher shoved the box of pizza toward her, and she took a small slice and picked at it. He took a deep breath and shook his head. He wished he could wrap his hands around Rick Cee's neck and give it a good squeeze. It killed him to see her so insecure and broken.

Danni never had a bold personality. She was always on

the shy side, but she never cringed from people. Ever since she married Rick, it was like she avoided contact. Even at the funeral, he could tell she acted physically pained to be there—and it wasn't the grief over losing Max that was causing her pain.

"So, I won't take advantage of you, I swear. One way or another, I'll pay you," Danni said.

Fisher stopped chewing and stared at her.

"For the help," she explained.

"I don't want your money."

"I don't want to take advantage of you. Or feel like I'm a charity case. I feel like when you look at me, you always look disappointed."

"What is it, Danni? Am I trying to kiss you or judging you?"

Her cheeks turned red instantly. She picked up her beer and took a swig, then studied the label like it was the most interesting thing in the world.

"Listen to me," he said. She didn't look up at him. He scooted his chair closer to hers and took her by the hand. "I'm not disappointed in you. I'm worried about you. I want you to stop beating yourself up. And I definitely want you to stop letting people treat you like shit. You shouldn't have to be doing yoga and feeling guilty about a slice of pizza."

"Darby made me do the yoga. She said I wasn't centered."

"No, you're trying to lose weight to get that asshole back."

The comment made her pull her hand away and hide it under the table. "No. I'm not." Danni shook her head. "Max was right. It's better to be alone than with someone I don't love."

Fisher took a deep breath. His pulse went nuts.

"Max used to tell me that all the time," she said. "It was like she psychically knew I'd make dumb choices in love."

It was his turn to study his beer bottle. He brushed the sweat from the glass. He couldn't look at her, not yet. She'd see his truth and hate him for it.

"I used to think Max was nuts for never dating after her fiancé died. But I think I understand—if you've had the perfect person for you, you can never settle, at least not happily, for less."

He took a long swallow, trying to think of who it was Danni

loved. Renzo?

"You all right?" Danni touched his arm.

"I'm fine." He grabbed another beer from the carton.

Danni nodded. "I wonder what Max's guy was like. I suppose she loved him, though she never talked much about him."

"You could ask my mom. Or Maureen. They were all friends."

"Or do you think it was me? Maybe I put the wet blanket on dating. She was left with an infant to care for. Isn't that like kryptonite for single men?"

Fisher wasn't answering that question. If he said yes, he sounded like an ass. If he said no, it sounded like he wanted kids, and that would be pressure on a lady who probably couldn't have them.

"Well?" she asked again.

Fisher held out his hands, palms up. "Shit, Danni, I was the kid without a dad. If I loved someone and she had kids, the kid would not be a problem."

"You're one of the good ones, Fish."

He nodded and stuffed the last of the pizza in his mouth, chewed, and swallowed. He stood. "I better head out."

Danni hopped up, circled the table, and grabbed his arm. "Don't leave. Maybe we could search through the closets. Maybe Max had love letters or hidden journals about her mystery man."

Danni loved a good mystery and turned every story into a star-crossed-lover story. He'd love nothing more than any excuse to stick around if even to dig through Max's closets, but he couldn't. He'd done a shitty job hanging loose in the friend zone. "That's not a good idea."

"Why not? Max evidently wanted me to be the one to deal with her life. She'd know whatever I found, I'd tell you."

"It's not that."

"Is it Tori?" Danni bit her lip. "That's fine."

"No, it's not Tori." He ran a hand through his hair. "Shit." He shook his head. "The problem is you were right earlier."

"I was? About what?"

"Nothing," he said as he stood and headed for the door.

She grabbed his arm. "Nothing, my butt. Fisher, what's going on?"

"You were right earlier. And I'm doing my damndest to stop pressuring you, but I—"

"I was right? What in the world are you talking about?"

"You were right down at the cove."

She stared at him, face blank of understanding, but full of worry.

"You were right about me wanting to kiss you. I did. Hell, I do. That's why I need to go."

Chapter 21

Fisher dropped the confession like a bomb then headed for the door. Danni ran in front of him, blocking his exit with her body. "You can't say something like that and just leave."

"Say something like what?"

"That you want to kiss me."

"Why can't I?"

"Well, because...we need to talk about it. It just seems like something that can't be said and then ignored."

"Yes, it can. It's a foolish idea."

Danni's heart sank. "Of course, it's foolish. But still, you can't just say that and walk away."

"Fine." He took a step toward her. "You want to hash it out, let me explain. You and I were great as friends. Honestly, the best friends ever. As friends, I could always count on you. Any time, for anything. But then we messed that up, and you were gone."

"I—"

"You don't need to explain. I just want you to know I'm trying not to cross the line and do shit without thinking—it screws everything up. I won't make that mistake again. As great as we were—together—it wasn't worth it."

Tears burned her eyes. She tried to force her thoughts to logic and reason. Wasn't he saying exactly what she'd been thinking? Did she seriously think he was going to fall in love with her? Ditch the Barbie-doll perfection for her?

Damn it, don't cry.

If she blinked any faster, he'd surely think she had something in her eye. She swallowed her pride and her tears. "I'm glad you're thinking it through. We wouldn't want to make another epic mistake."

He took a step toward her, and she stepped back. "That isn't—"

Her phone rang. Danni pulled it out of her pocket and hit answer. She'd gladly talk to the devil himself or a telemarketer in order to end this conversation.

"Rick," she said. "What's up?" Danni turned her back on Fisher.

"Hey babe, I've been thinking. I should come there."

"You should what?" Her tears forgotten, she almost swallowed her heart in exchange for the distraction.

"I said, I should come there."

"Why would you want to do that?"

"I miss you."

"Seriously, why? What do you want?"

"Can't I miss my wife?"

"Ex-wife, and no." Danni forgot Fisher was behind her. The idea of Rick here almost gave her a panic attack. She couldn't take his constant criticism right now, or trust him not to hit on Darby. "It's been more than a year, and you never missed me. I don't want you here."

"Jesus, Danni. You don't have to be a bitch about it. I was trying to be nice."

"I'm sorry. I wasn't trying to be mean; I need time alone."

"Time alone, my ass. I know what you're doing. Doesn't he have a girlfriend? Or does that not matter to you guys?"

"It has nothing to do with Fisher. He's a pain in my ass too." Danni hung up the phone and shoved it in her pocket. She was so pissed, her face burned like it was on fire.

"What was that about?" Fisher asked.

She pressed cool hands to her now burning cheeks. Was there any chance he missed the part where I called him a pain in the ass? "Nothing."

"I take it that was Rick?"

Danni nodded.

"I may be a pain in your ass, Danni, but I'm nothing like

him."

"Really? Could've fooled me." Danni knew that was a lie, but what else could she say? *You're breaking my heart by accident; shame on you?*

Fisher grabbed her by the arms and pulled her close. "I don't want to change you. I love you just the way you are."

"Stop. I don't want to hear that. Please, just leave."

He didn't let go. Instead, he pulled her closer, hugging her against him. "Fine. Enough personal talk, let's discuss the renovation."

"What?" Danni pushed against him. Was he seriously this clueless or stupid? Did he really think he could shove her into the friend zone after saying he wanted to kiss her, but regretted sex with her...holy shit, one more mixed message and her head might explode.

He let go of her and walked from the door toward the kitchen. "What kind of changes do you want to make?"

Danni shook her head. "The change I want is for the men in my life to leave me alone. I don't need your pity, and I certainly don't need Rick's bullshit. Do you guys think I'm stupid? I know you want to keep me as a pet, and Rick probably thinks I have more money for him to steal. But what I really want is some peace in my life, so go."

He grabbed her by the arm and pulled her close. "I don't pity you." He almost looked like he was in pain. "Jesus, Danni, don't you get it? I love you. I've always loved you."

Tears sprang to her eyes. She opened her mouth but closed it. She couldn't trust herself to speak.

He took a step toward her, brushing his thumb across her lips. "I wish I knew if kissing you would be the solution to the problem or the beginning of bigger ones."

"Seems you've got a lot to think about too."

"Not really. One day, I'm just going to say fuck it."

"And then what?"

"I'm going to kiss you and let fate decide."

"That's a big risk. Fate hasn't always been good to me."

Chapter 22

Danni woke bright and early the next morning to the sound of Darby showering. She grabbed her phone to confirm it was Sunday. It was. She groaned—hadn't the kid heard that Sunday was for sleeping in? She was about to nod off, but the guilt of Darby being up and cooking for herself made Danni roll out of bed.

She pulled on a pair of jeans and a T-shirt. She needed to make a Goodwill run and pick up some old clothes. Or fly out to Oregon for a few days and clear out her apartment and bring some of her stuff back with her. She'd only come out with two small bags, and her puffy coat had taken up most of the space.

She made her way to the kitchen and started a pot of coffee. The sun pouring in the window promised a pretty day. It was already shining bright, scattering a shimmering pattern off the inky water of the Currituck.

Danni poured pancake mix into a bowl, added water, and mixed it up. She set it aside and pulled out the skillet and set it on the stove to heat. She grabbed a stick of butter out of the fridge and cut off a chunk and tossed it in the frying pan. It sizzled and melted. She used the spatula to spread it out before pouring in the batter.

"Real food?" Darby grabbed a glass from the cabinet above Danni's head. "Are you feeling okay?"

Danni nodded. "I'm going to start fixing the place up today."

"All right, where do we start?"

"I thought I heard you say you were going to Ocracoke for a festival or something."

"That was before I knew we were working today."

"Well, you go to your festival. I'll save the heavy work for you. I'm going to make a list of all the things I want to change. And maybe I'll start with the easy stuff, like cleaning and decluttering."

"Are you sure you don't need my help?"

"Positive."

Darby hopped on the counter, sitting next to the stove. "So, what were you and Fisher fighting about?"

"We weren't fighting."

"It sounded like you were fighting. You were screaming at him."

"I was not. I was just...stressing my point."

"What happened between you guys?"

Danni shook her head. "Honest to God, I don't know. On one hand, he says stuff like he loves me but doesn't want to be anything more than friends. Then he says he'd like to kiss me but is certain that will ruin our friendship. Which it probably would." Danni tried flipping a pancake before it was ready, and it fell apart in a goopy mess. "Damn it," she said, throwing the offending thing in the trash can.

"Do we need to pause to get centered?" Darby asked.

"No. No more damn yoga. Let me scream and yell like a normal freaking human being."

Darby laughed.

Danni poured another pancake in the pan. She went to flip it, but Darby said, "Not yet. Wait for the bubbles to pop."

Danni took a deep breath. "Stop being so damned smart."

Darby smiled. Making a half turn on the countertop, she poured herself a cup of coffee. "Obviously, he loves you."

"No, not obviously." Danni closed her eyes and took a deep breath. "I'm tragic. Fisher can't pass wreckage without cleaning it up. He's the kind of guy who changes flat tires for old ladies and gets all twitchy if something is broken and you don't let him fix it. And right now, I am the pitiful project."

"Is that so bad?"

"It's horrible. That's not love. That's Fisher taking that

feeling of friendship and comradery that we shared as kids and transferring it to something emotional. It's a lie."

"I take back what I said yesterday. I'm no therapist—you're talking some crazy shit that makes no sense to me."

"Trust me, I know Fisher."

"Why don't you just talk to him? Tell him you love him."

"I've thought about it, but I don't know how. I mean, I know how, but it's like I've got this wall in my brain that screams at me to keep my friggin' mouth shut. That if I say it, I'll ruin what we have."

"Which is...?"

"We're friends."

"Friends who scream and yell and look like they're being tortured by Cupid? I can see why you'd never want to risk losing that."

Danni dropped a perfect pancake on the plate. Darby was right about those. They were easier to flip fully cooked.

"You're learning." Darby dug her fork into the pancake and slapped it on a plate. She slid off the counter and grabbed more butter from the fridge.

Danni poured herself a cup of coffee and sat at the table with Darby. "I'm tired of always trying to second guess everything. And I'm tired of feeling like I'm to blame for everything. With Rick, he expected physical perfection, and I couldn't deliver on that. And with Fisher, he expects me to never be human, and I can't live up to that standard either. I need a break from it all. When is your spring break? Maybe we could go to Oregon. Would you want to?"

Darby's face fell, and her eyes were suddenly glassy. "You said—I don't want to leave here—"

Danni grabbed her hand and gave it a squeeze. "A vacation, of sorts. Not a permanent thing. It would only be for a few days. My lease on my apartment is monthly, and I could clear it out and not be paying rent on the place. And I need to get my stuff. I have nothing here."

"So...you'd essentially be moving here?"

Danni nodded. "My life might be a screwed-up mess, but I

swear, I'll do my best not to let the insanity rub off on you. You're happy here, here is where we stay."

Darby's smile was huge. She kissed Danni on the cheek, which made Danni smile. It felt good to be a solution to a problem, for once.

"Oh my God. Oh my God. I was afraid if you guys split up, you'd go back for good. But you're staying! This is awesome. Of course, I'll go with you. When can we go?"

"I'll look at costs—see if it's better to drive, fly, or take a train."

"I have some money. Not a bunch, but—"

"You keep your money. I can put it on a credit card for now. Then, I'll meet with the attorney tomorrow and find out what I need to do to start renting rooms so we have an income. We'll go when you're on spring break."

"Awesome. This is going to be sweet."

"Our first road trip."

Danni took the last swig of coffee and set her cup in the sink.

Darby's phone pinged. She read the text. "Candy and her mom are here."

"Go. Have fun."

"You're sure you don't need me?"

"Nope. Trust me. I'm fine on my own."

Chapter 23

Fisher threw a stepladder and a toolbox into the back of his truck. He had been up half the night trying to think of how to deal with Danni. He told her he loved her, and her response was to fight him. It should be no surprise that baring his soul would start an argument, but it did. He could not win with Rodanthe Luna. He said he'd help her flip the place, and that's exactly what he'd do, but that was it—starting today, no more love bullshit.

Maybe working on the hotel would make her feel the connection to this place. Accomplishing something would give her some pride and make it her own. Whenever he flipped a place, it became his baby. He'd pass the houses he'd worked on and feel like he was visiting children he'd raised.

Danni could use that feeling. She needed a home. She was like a ship without an anchor, and when storms hit, she blew from place to place. One day she'd either have to drop anchor or drift forever.

He took a deep breath. He loved her too much to let that happen. At least not without a fight.

There I go with the love shit again. He slammed the door of the truck, texted her he was on his way and headed to the hotel.

There she was, hard at work, positioning a folding chair against the hotel wall. Fisher frowned and shook his head.

He called to her as she climbed up, but she didn't hear him. She stuck both feet toward the back of the chair. The seat collapsed, sending her face first toward the hotel. Fisher reached out and grabbed her around the waist. She let out a gasp and wrapped her arms around his neck.

"What the hell are you doing?"

Her body leaned against his. She tried to pull away, but he held her.

"I was getting started. I figured I could take down the shutters and paint them, grumpy."

"I'm not grumpy."

"Really?" Danni shoved away again, but he wasn't letting go. "If you're mad that you have to help me, you don't have to. I can hire a handyman. There's more than one on the island, ya know?"

Part of him wanted to give her hell for being stupid enough to put her feet on the back of a folding chair, but he bit his tongue. She was eager to start. That was a good thing. "I'm not grumpy, I just didn't want to see you go headfirst through the window." He lifted her off the chair and set her on the ground.

"Trust me, I didn't want to go crashing through the window either, and that's exactly where I thought I was headed. I should have gotten a kitchen chair."

"You need a ladder."

"Thank you, Captain Obvious. I looked for one this morning but couldn't find anything."

"I texted you that I'd bring you tools."

"I missed that." She dug in her pocket. "Oops, I forgot to turn my ringer back on. Rick wasn't taking go to hell for an answer." She turned it on and shoved it back in her pocket.

Fisher headed to the truck for the tools. Was he being a pain in the ass like Rick? Refusing to read the writing on the wall and leave her alone? Lost in that thought, he didn't realize Danni was walking beside him.

"Thanks for the tools. I couldn't even find a screwdriver."

"I'm not surprised. Max would call me to change her light bulbs — she sure as hell wasn't fixing anything that took a tool. I doubt she even had a hammer."

"Life was too short to waste a minute on the boring stuff," Danni repeated her aunt's words. "Maybe that's why I'm such a vagabond. I'm trying to get away from the boring stuff."

Fisher nodded and quickened his steps. Her words felt like

jagged needles to his nerves. Obviously, he hadn't been exciting enough to commit to all those years ago.

He pulled out the ladder and the toolbox. Flipping open the lid, he grabbed an electric screwdriver. "This is —"

"I know what it is. And you'll be shocked to know I know how to use it. I'm actually pretty handy."

"Well then, you don't need the tutorial." He handed her the tool. "The charger is in the toolbox. It should last for a while. I charged it last night."

Danni tossed a butter knife in the toolbox. "Your tool kit tops mine."

"That's all you had?"

"I have a brick for a hammer."

"You could've called me."

"Sure, but where is the creativity in that?" Danni's smile looked genuine.

It bothered him that she was happy as hell trying not to need him. Damn her for ruining a beautiful morning.

"You want to come in for some breakfast? I made pancakes. Like for real made them, in a pan."

"I am impressed." He tried to sound like he truly was impressed, but he had too much of the conversation digging at his mood.

"Coffee?"

"No, thank you."

"Are you sure?"

"Yes, I'm sure." His words came out like a bark — much harsher than he'd planned.

"I'm sorry for being a bitch last night. It's just...I'm tired of my happiness being at the mercy of other people. But I suppose it sounded more like a screechy rant than me trying to figure out what the hell to do with my life." She shook her head. "It's just — I think I need to focus on something simple for a while, like painting. That's why I grabbed my butter knife and my lawn chair and went to work. I hope I didn't make you mad."

He rubbed away an itch on his chin. "No, I'm not mad."

"You seem antsy."

You're killing me. "I'm late for work."

"It's Sunday."

"I just need to check on a few work sites, then I'll be back with primer and paintbrushes, so you're not trying to redo the shutters with bird feathers and toothpaste."

"Give me some credit. I have a few bottles of nail polish."

Danni's laugh made him smile. He'd promised himself he'd give her space — ten minutes later, and he was promising to come back.

He dragged himself away and drove to the worksite, but didn't get out of his truck. Crossing his arms over the steering wheel, he dropped his head on his forearms. What was he to do about the impossible dream that was Danni?

Chapter 24

Danni watched Fisher leave. Something needed to be said, but she didn't know how. Her attempts to keep him were causing more harm than good. He was perpetually irritated with her. When he told her he loved her, what if she had simply said she loved him too? It couldn't be any worse than things were now. If he had come over last night and pecked on her window, she'd have told him how she felt. But he didn't come over. He'd threatened to kiss her, told her he loved her and then left, only to return today with a business-only attitude.

He waved as he backed out and headed south. Danni rubbed the back of her neck. "Where are you, Max? I could use some advice about now."

Silence. Or at least no Max. Cars swooshed by periodically. The wind rustled leaves and branches. Danni suddenly felt lonely. All of this morning's determination to make her life better one job at a time fizzled with her worries about Fisher. She was trying so hard to do everything right. To play it safe. Play it smart. All that accomplished was pushing him further and further away. Her fear of losing him was making her lose him.

"I love you, Fisher," she said in the empty parking lot. That was easy enough. Why did she choke on those words whenever he was around?

Punkin barked.

Poor dog had been alone all morning. Danni hurried across the gravel drive to the office door. She could see Punkin in the large office window. Perched on the office chair, paws scratching the glass, Punkin made it known she needed out post haste.

Danni opened the door, and the dog hopped off the chair and headed off the porch quicker than Danni could yell stop.

Danni expected her to stop at the grassy area to do her business, but the dog was off the porch, down the steps, and headed for the beach. The problem was, to get to the beach, she had to cross the highway. Danni screamed her name and chased after her. An RV barreled down the asphalt, probably driven by some old fella with poor vision. She imagined the hypothetical driver would never see a little dog with fur the color of tar. She ran faster, yelling for the dog to stop.

At the edge of the road, Danni's foot landed in a pothole, and she shot forward. Her knees hit the gravel first, then her elbows. Laying herself out and reaching as far as her arms could go, she snatched a hind leg and jerked. Punkin yelped but stopped. She turned her furry face to Danni.

"Don't look all innocent, young lady. That was a stupid thing to do." Danni crawled to the dog and scooped her up, settling her in her lap.

The RV passed by. The driver tooted his horn and waved. Danni, shaken, held the dog tight. Punkin licked Danni's cheek. "You should suck up," Danni said. "If you'd have been smashed —"

She couldn't finish her comment. Her eyes burned, and her nose tingled. She sat at the edge of the road, gripping the dog. She might have sat there all day, but Fisher's truck pulled in the drive. Her first feeling on seeing the beat-up brown pick up was relief, followed quickly by mortification.

Holding onto the dog, she stood and wobbled toward the hotel. Her knees hurt like a son of a bitch, and her hands and elbows felt tight in the places where they didn't burn like they were on fire.

"What the hell happened? Are you okay?"

Danni blinked away instant tears and did her best to look composed.

"Punkin...she got away. I thought." Danni choked on the words. She took a deep breath. "I thought she was going to get hit by a car."

"You all right?"

"I'm fine."

"You're bleeding."

Danni looked down at her torn jeans and exposed bloody knees.

Fisher grabbed her arm and gently pulled her toward the apartment, escorting her to the bathroom. "Lose the pants."

"What, no wine or roses?"

He turned red. Danni enjoyed the look that crossed his face. It was part dumbfounded, and part flustered. When she unbuttoned her pants and dropped them to the floor, he watched as if mesmerized. Danni thought instantly of the cellulite on the back of her ass. He'd notice it in the harsh light of the bathroom. She grabbed a towel from the rack and wrapped it around her waist.

Fisher turned away. He dropped the toilet lid and made her sit, then ran hot water into the sink as he went through the cabinets, pulling out supplies.

"I'm fine, you know," she said.

"You look like hell."

"Thanks." Danni's eyes felt grainy from her desire to cry like a baby.

"You're lucky you didn't get hit by a car."

"Am I?" Danni meant it to sound like a joke, but it came out sounding whiny and full of self-pity.

Fisher shut off the water with way more force than was necessary. Danni thought he might have ripped the handle off.

"Don't say shit like that."

Logic told her she should apologize. It was a dumb thing to say, but contrariness made her shrug and remain silent.

Fisher put a folded towel behind her knee and poured peroxide over her cuts. It was cold, and she couldn't help but jerk her leg back, but he wrapped a hand around her calf and held her still. "It needs cleaned."

"I can do this myself."

"Kill yourself for a stupid dog."

"My dog isn't stupid."

"She's not your dog. She's my dog."

Danni rolled her eyes. "You're full of it."

Fisher moved from one leg to the other. "Max told me in the hospital—if you leave, I get the dog."

"Why would Max do that?"

Fisher shrugged as he wet the washcloth in the hot water and cleaned the gravel from her knees.

"I guess if you think she's stupid, you'll give her to me?"

"Nope. You leave, you leave alone."

"That's mean. You're just being mean."

"Why should I give you my inheritance?"

Danni's voice was shrill. "She's just a stupid dog."

Fisher grinned and gave her a wink. "Seems you don't appreciate her either."

She shoved him out of her way and stood. "You're being a jerk."

"Bullshit."

"Don't curse at me."

"It wasn't a curse. It was profanity."

"Semantics? You're going to argue semantics?"

"Are you calling me stupid? Saying I can't argue semantics?"

He was impossible. There was no talking to him. Danni growled and stormed out of the bathroom to her bedroom and slammed the door. She tossed the towel to the floor. Her shirt had black streaks from the asphalt. She pulled it over her head, bitching under her breath as she threw it on the floor. "If he thinks for one second I'll use his stupid ladder, he's got another think coming. I will go to Ace myself and buy my own. I don't need him."

The door swung open and there was Fisher. She was stuck in the middle of the room—too far from the T-shirt on the floor to grab it, and not close enough to her suitcase to grab another. So, she squealed and covered herself with her arms.

Fisher turned red faster than he could stammer, "I'm sorry. I'll just go."

Chapter 25

Fisher closed the door and headed for his truck. Images of a half-naked Danni slowed his steps. If he left now, things between them would only get more strained, more awkward. If he was to have any chance at repairing what was between them, this was it. It was time to put pride aside and take a chance. What was the worst that could happen?

She could reject him? He'd survived that a few times already.

She could go back to her husband? Leave the island....

His feet slowed to a stop. He was stuck. Damned if he did. Damned if he didn't.

Good manners told him the least he could do was apologize for storming in on her while she was changing clothes. He took a deep breath. It wasn't always easy to do the right thing. He walked back into the hotel, past the office to her room. He took a deep breath and lifted his hand to knock. Before he could exhale, the door swung open and she was standing in front of him.

"I thought you left."

Long breath out. Short breath in. "I'm sorry. I shouldn't have barged in like that. I was...."

Danni sure as hell didn't let him off the hook. She crossed her arms over her chest and stared at him, as if daring him to mess up his apology.

"I shouldn't have walked in on you."

Danni stared at him as if studying him. Her shoulders dropped, and she rubbed her temples. "You don't need to be sorry. I'm sorry. I don't know why I'm being such a bitch."

"You're not being—"

"Yes, I am. Maybe I've just grown to expect things to turn on me. Everything I do turns to crap...it's just a matter of time. And I don't want us to be one of those things that I ruin."

"It doesn't have to turn on you."

"You have a solution to my jinxed life?"

Fall in love with me and live happily ever after? He said nothing.

Danni took a deep breath. "I swear, sometimes I think I can smell Max's perfume. Kind of like a warm brown sugary smell." She cocked her head and looked at Fisher. "Do you smell that?"

He shook his head. The place smelled like Murphy's Oil Soap and clean laundry.

"It's weird. I smell it now and then. But it's faint. Maybe I'm honestly going crazy."

"Don't say that."

"I'm joking, sort of." Danni pulled her brown hair back and secured it in a ponytail. "I'm not unstable, I swear. And I truly am sorry I keep fighting with you. Maybe it's the stress. Maybe I have too much bad energy." She squared her shoulders and said, "Energy I could burn working. Now that I have the proper tools and Punkin is secure in the backyard, I can make progress."

"Come on, I'll help you."

Danni nodded and headed outside, Fisher following her. He grabbed the ladder and screwdriver and went to the first window.

"I thought you had work to do."

"I just had to make sure the work crews were on schedule."

"So, you're the boss?"

"I suppose." He unscrewed the first shutter and handed it to her.

"That's a very appropriate job for you."

"Construction?"

"No, being bossy." Danni chuckled as she carried the shutter to the porch.

As he undid the next one, he said, "Is that any way to talk to your free labor?"

She returned to the ladder and looked up at him and smiled. "I'm sorry. I'll be nice."

He pulled the next one down and handed it to her.

"Just out of curiosity," she asked, "what would it take to get you to give me Punkin?"

He looked her over. From the fresh holes in the knees of her pants to the simple baby blue tee that hugged her breasts he now knew were the color of porcelain and just as smooth. And he knew from the memories that haunted him they were subtly larger than when she was eighteen, but were probably still as soft. "Are you offering silent bids, or would I have to ask and risk getting busted for sexual harassment?"

Danni gave him a look, like she was slowly piecing together what he'd said. Once it made sense, her mouth dropped and she shook her head. "Oh my gosh, you are the world's worst boyfriend."

Fisher laughed. "How many times do I have to tell you I don't have a girlfriend?"

"She's at your place every night."

"You jealous?"

"Uh, no. Not really." She looked flustered. Her eyelashes fluttered, her lips moved but made no words until she said, "I wouldn't call it jealousy. Concern, maybe."

"Funny. She says the same thing about you."

Danni looked at him with eyes as round as full moons. "Me? How can I be bad for you?"

He looked at her. She really didn't have a clue. No human being on this earth had ever hurt him like she had. If she didn't understand that he wasn't going to explain it. He shrugged.

Danni put her hands on her hips. "I'll tell you why she doesn't want you around me. It's because she's a conniving little bitch. She knows I know it's her fault you hated me."

"How did she do that?"

"I know she was the one who told you about...." Danni shook her head. "It's just her fault."

"Have you ever thought it wasn't her telling me about what happened that was the problem, but that it happened?"

Danni's arms dropped to her sides.

"Forget it," he said. "We were kids. It's not a big deal anymore." He grabbed the ladder and moved it to the next window.

"You know," Danni followed him to the next window, "I felt really bad for a long time about that. But the truth is, I didn't do anything you hadn't done a hundred times. I don't understand why I was the villain."

Irritation moved up his spine, but he took a deep breath. She was right. She never made a commitment to him. He'd assumed sex was an implied form commitment. But hell, it wasn't the 1950s anymore. Sex was sometimes just sex.

"I was jealous, Danni. Call me irrational, but I only wanted you to be with me."

Her face puckered and she pressed a finger against her lip. He knew she was trying not to cry.

Stepping off the ladder, he pulled her closer and kissed the top of her head. "Let's forget about the past. We're going to make this place look better than it's ever looked."

She nodded her head, brushing her cheek against his T-shirt. He held her a minute, appreciating the feel of her tucked into him. "You ready to get to work?"

She nodded and sniffed. He kissed her temple and pulled away. The smile she offered him looked shaky, but he considered it a valiant effort.

"Then let's get this done."

They finished the rest of the shutters without speaking of anything more exciting than current events and weather changes. He unscrewed shutters. She carried them to the porch. Eventually, all the shutters were off the hotel and stacked on the porch.

Fisher pulled a large tarp out of the back of his truck and laid it out on the gravel drive. He started carrying the shutters over to the tarp and laid them out in rows. He motioned for her to follow him to the truck. He pulled a ten-gallon bucket off the truck and twisted off the lid.

"Shit," he said.

Danni looked at him with big eyes.

"I asked for white paint," he said.

"What color is it? It looks white."

"It's light blue."

Danni pinched her lower lip and looked into the bucket of paint. "I think I like the idea of blue shutters. Max always said blue warded off evil. That could be useful. Maybe they'll keep Tori away."

He gave her a look, but she said no more.

"So paint them blue?" he asked.

"Yep. If I hate it, I'll repaint them white."

"Nothing in life is permanent."

Danni nodded. "Damn straight."

"Come on," he said. "Let's do this."

Together they marched back to the tarp and set about painting all fifty-two shutters. It was well after dinnertime when they finished.

Danni stood and rubbed the small of her back. "I don't think I've ever bent over for that long before."

"I'd offer you a back rub, but I've crossed the line enough lately. I don't want to end up gelded."

"Coward," Danni laughed. Her eyes sparkled with humor. There was the girl he used to know.

"I worry—is there is a limit to how many times I can openly hit on you before you think I'm as big of a jerk as your ex?"

"You've been hitting on me?"

Fisher shook his head. He didn't know what to say—wasn't he being obvious? Like a man floundering in water, he slapped at a life raft. "I'm joking. But seriously, I don't want to be a pain in the ass like your ex."

Danni laughed. "Oh, sweetheart, you're not even on his level. My dear ex-husband bought one of his girlfriends a car. I got the bill from a Chevy dealership in Florida. When I asked him about it, he said he'd bought it to lure in a big investor."

"And you divorced a generous guy like that?"

"Oh, he was generous, all right. He also spent $135,000 on plastic surgery."

"One hundred and thirty-five thousand?"

"He claims it was a bargain."

"What did he get done?"

Danni shrugged. "I know he got calf implants. I'm not sure

what else he had done."

"Calf implants?"

"Yeah." Danni slapped her calf. "So, he didn't have chicken legs."

Fisher was stunned. No wonder she was broke. "Okay, I'd never be that big of an asshole."

"It's finally starting to be funny. But when we were going through the divorce, and the accountant kept finding one insane expense after another, I thought I had to be the stupidest human being alive."

He wrapped a hand around the back of her neck and pulled her to him. "Ah, Loonie. Don't beat yourself up. We've all loved someone who's made us look like a fool."

The look she gave him was full of hurt. He wasn't sure why he said it—to punish her a little for leaving him? For choosing a dipshit over him? Or was it for coming back and making him love her all over again?

Chapter 26

Danni tried to ignore his comment, but she couldn't. The idea of Tori having the power to hurt him was a tough pill to swallow. In her heart, she wanted Fisher to be the one who got tired of Tori and sent her packing. Not for him to be the one with the broken heart.

She reminded herself that Rick was the one who'd dumped her. That didn't mean she still loved him, even if she did want him to regret what he did.

Oh my God, I'm a lunatic. Danni stared blindly over the shutter filled tarp.

"Do you think they're okay? They look almost white."

Shaken from her thoughts, Danni jumped. "Yes. They're perfect. They're the color of a clear, sunny sky."

"Good. You were looking at them like you wanted to vomit."

Danni swallowed and shrugged. "I think I'm hungry. You want a beer and a sandwich?"

"You know, I do." He followed her into the hotel.

She kicked off her shoes; he kicked off his work boots. When she went to the kitchen and let Punkin out the back door, he hovered close behind.

"Roast beef all right?" she asked as she turned, almost bumping into him.

"Sounds great."

She paused at the kitchen sink to wash her hands. He stood next to her, waiting for his turn to wash up. She soaped up a dishcloth and scrubbed her face, down her neck to her arms. He leaned his hip against the counter and watched her. Tendrils of hair escaped her ponytail, curling in damp wisps around her ears and her throat. He brushed them back, his fingers cool against her skin.

"You missed a streak." He rubbed her cheek with his thumb, allowing his hand to trail down her neck. Her pulse jumped, quick and strong against his fingertips. She swallowed hard. His touch felt intimate, but she suddenly feared it was wishful thinking. She took a step toward him, closing the gap between them. He smiled and wrapped his hand in her hair. He paused only a moment before he pulled her closer and kissed her, slowly at first. Her body felt warm and fluid. She leaned her body into his, and he deepened the kiss.

When she wrapped an arm around his neck, he grabbed her by the hips and pressed her against the cabinet. His lips moved slowly from hers, down the smooth, silky white skin of her neck to the hollow of her throat. A moan escaped her lips.

She wanted this more than anything in the world, but it couldn't be real unless he knew everything. She owed him the truth. When his hands slipped under her shirt, she took a deep breath. "Stop, Fisher. We need to talk."

His lips lingered against her throat. "I don't want to talk."

She pushed away from him. "There are—is something we need to talk about."

"Don't do this, Danni. Can't we just let go of the past and all the bullshit?"

"It's not that. I want you to promise me that when this is done—"

"Save it, Danni. Damn it. Why does it have to end? Why in the hell does everything have to be so difficult with you?"

"I'm not trying to be difficult. There are things we need to talk about. We can't make a mistake."

"Now I'm a mistake. Nice, Danni. Real nice."

"I didn't say that."

"Sure is how it sounded."

"All I'm asking is we make this choice with clear heads."

The front door opened and closed. Footsteps moved through the apartment.

"Danni!" Darby yelled. The girl appeared in the doorway, holding up her phone. "Travel Hopper has tickets to Oregon for $385 each. Now, can we book?"

"You know what, Danni? Forget it. I'm done trying."

Chapter 27

"No, no, no." Danni chased Fisher through the apartment and out the front door. "It's not what you think, Fisher. We're flying out to close my apartment and get my stuff." He kept walking. "Fisher! Are you listening?"

He never answered. He got in his truck and left without looking back. Danni ran to the kitchen and grabbed the keys to the rental. She had to explain.

Darby looked worried. "Oh my God, I messed things up, didn't I? He thinks...oh shit."

"We were already fighting. It wasn't you."

"Why were you fighting?"

Danni let out a sigh and gripped her purse. "Because Fisher always lets his temper fly. I try to be reasonable and look at all the things that need to be considered, and he gets mad at me."

"Like what kind of things need to be considered?"

"It's kind of a long story. Can I—?"

Darby waved her from the room. "Go."

Danni took off. She drove all over the island but couldn't find him anywhere. She called Darby, who was asking around, but none of her friends had seen him either. Danni imagined him going to Tori's, venting all his frustrations with her.

Defeated, Danni went back home. Darby was waiting in the living room. "No luck?"

"None." Danni flopped down on the couch and tossed her car keys on the table.

"Okay, so I've been waiting to hear what things need to be considered."

"I drove all over," Danni said. "The longer I drove, the more I started to wonder why it's always me in trouble. He's being a bitch about this, storming off without listening to any explanations. I don't know why I bother."

"Because you love him?"

Danni groaned. "This is why I didn't want to do this. This feeling…this fear of losing him seriously sucks. I hate it, Darby. I seriously hate it."

"I don't get why this is so hard for you two."

Danni took a deep breath and let it out loud and long. "I have a tendency to screw things up, and Fisher has a tendency to be a prick about it. Ever since…ever since I screwed things up."

Darby laughed. "I think I deserve more information than that."

"It's ancient, humiliating history."

Darby leaned closer. "You know, I would never tell. And imagine — it could be a teachable moment for me."

"I know you're trustworthy, kiddo. And you're right, maybe there is a life lesson in it, although I think you have more maturity in your little finger than I ever had or ever will have in my whole body, so you probably won't need the lesson."

"You're pretty okay for an old chick. A little hard on yourself, but definitely okay."

"This old chick thanks you."

"Now, what happened?"

Danni pulled her hair out of the ponytail and rubbed her scalp. "It was the summer after we graduated. Much to my embarrassment, I was still a…," Danni lowered her voice and whispered, "Virgin."

Darby laughed. "So?"

"Well, my friends, AKA Tori and Tina, told everyone. Not that it was much of a surprise to anyone. I was like the biggest dork. I mean, when I say I was a virgin, I mean virgin. I hadn't even been on a date, at least not a proper one, unless you count movies with Fisher, which I didn't. I hadn't even kissed a guy — well, besides Fisher, and that was when we were six and playing house."

"There is definitely a Fisher pattern to every story. So, the not dating—were you the problem or was he? Or was Max totally psycho overprotective back then?"

"No. Max always tried to get me to date, but no one ever asked me out."

"Probably because you were with Fisher all the friggin' time."

"That never stopped girls from asking him out. He always had a prospect."

"Fisher can be a pretty scary guy. If guys thought you two were a thing, they'd be crazy to ask you out."

"Well, whatever the reason was, I'd never been asked out on a date until that summer. This guy moved in with Tori's family. He was from Italy, and he was hot. He had oodles of charm and the accent. All the girls fell for him."

"Sounds like a player."

Danni nodded. "Anyhow, Tori told me Renzo liked me. Like more than a passing fancy liked me."

"Passing fancy?" Darby laughed. "Gotcha, Grandma."

"Shut up, or I won't tell you the rest."

"Come on. I let prospect slide. I can't just let you say weird crap like that too often without saying something. I might break out in hives."

"Anyhow, Renzo and I hung out a few times, and I liked him. He was cute and funny—and he acknowledged I existed." Danni laughed.

"Good to hear you maintained some high standards for yourself."

"I definitely had none of those. I was too desperate not to be a freak. Besides, all the girls liked him—like fan-girl crazy. And he was interested in little old me."

"You realize he was probably just trying to nail you?"

"Oh, Definitely."

"I'm beginning to imagine how this turned into an epic fail."

"At the time, it seemed like a good idea."

"So did bell bottoms, big hair, and the treaty of Versailles."

"Do you want to hear what happened, or lecture me on what I've already messed up and can do nothing to change?"

"Can I just guess? If I get it right, you give me twenty dollars?"

"I'm not paying you, turd."

"Fine, I'll guess for nothing." Darby leaned forward. "You had sex with this guy, and that pissed Fisher off."

Danni shook her head. "Tori threw a party at her house while her parents were out of town. Renzo asked me to stay over. I told Max I was staying with Tori to keep her company while they were gone, but really I was staying with Renzo."

"How sad. You waited all that time, just to do it with a cherry collector?"

"A what?"

"It's a guy who preys on virgins for sport."

"Sounds about right. At the time, I didn't really think about it much. I was just excited to finally have a guy, any guy, interested in me."

"That's sad, Danni. I told you...no confidence. Why didn't your friends stop you?"

"My best friend was Tori. It was her idea."

Darby groaned.

Danni nodded. "Looking back on it, she was pushing me hard. She convinced me that the life of a crazy cat lady was waiting for me. So, I went with Renzo. We had fun at the party, but by the end of the evening, we kind of made our way to Tori's room."

"So I'm right, you had sex with him, and Fisher got pissed."

"Not completely."

Darby gave her a look—eyebrows squished together, lip curled.

"I never had sex with him. I was going to, but at the last minute, I panicked."

"Did he...?"

"No. He was cool about it, but everyone made their assumptions, which Renzo did nothing to correct. And you know how kids are...there were catcalls and rumors, and suddenly, guys were noticing I was alive, and girls were giving me the evil eye. It was humiliating. I hated it."

"Guys can be such dicks."

"Some of the girls weren't much better. I went from just being Danni to — it was like they hated me in an instant."

"You were a threat. Guys assume if one guy can get you on your back, they all can. Sluts hate the new competition. And goody-two-shoes hate it when you leave their ranks and put extra pressure on them."

"Well, I hated it. I felt dirty and cheap like everyone was talking about me behind my back."

"Oh, they were."

"You're real helpful, ya know?"

"Just keeping it real." Darby gave her a playful poke on the leg with her toe. "So, then what happened?"

"I wanted out of there, so I went to Tina and asked her to take me home. On the way there, I decided I wanted to see Fisher, so Tina dropped me off at his house."

"Did you tell him what happened?"

Danni shook her head. "But I realized the guy I was looking for was right there all along. I kissed him, and it felt so natural... the rest just happened."

"So how did you two break up?"

"We were never a couple. He found out about Renzo by the end of the weekend, and he flipped out. He was so mad at me for it that he refused to talk to me." Danni's eyes burned with tears. "I called him over and over, but he wouldn't talk to me. He hated me for it, so I hated myself a little more than I already did."

"And that's why you left?"

Danni shook her head. "I left to go to college. But he is the reason I never wanted to come back."

"Dang, that's harsh. So, just because you made out with another guy, he dropped you like a bad habit?"

"He was furious with me. I don't think I've ever seen him so mad. You're right; he can be scary as hell when he's provoked. Just thinking about it makes me shake." Danni held out a trembling hand.

"That's pretty messed up. I thought Fisher was a better guy than that. You weren't doing anything he wasn't doing."

"After about the second month of him ignoring me, I did get

mad. I felt like he hated me for being human. I couldn't be with a guy who expected me to be perfect. I'm too screwed up to be perfect."

"We're all human, Danni."

"I know, but still, I blamed myself for messing things up. I'd try to stay mad at Fisher, but it would always circle back in my head that I was the fool. Then I met Rick, and he acted like I was the best thing since sliced bread, and honestly, it felt good to have someone think I was...I don't know—not an idiot? Does that make sense?"

"Yeah. And he is cute, though I will deny I ever said that."

"It wasn't so much that he was cute. It was more like he was the polar opposite of Fisher. Rick didn't have a serious bone in his body, and he didn't make me feel like I was the biggest tramp to walk the earth. And he was fun. For Rick, life is one big party. One day he told me we should spend spring break in the Bahamas. Got to the Bahamas, and he suggested we get married. It seemed, at the time, very romantic."

"When did he turn into the douche?"

"After about a year of marriage. I was given my inheritance on my twenty-first birthday. Once he had that, I was nothing but baggage."

"Did he know you were getting money?"

Danni shook her head. "It came as a surprise, but it gave him enough to bankroll his dreams—which all failed. That's when the real stress started."

"What were you and Fisher arguing about when I got here?"

"I told him I didn't want to rush things. I mean, if we rush things and it blows up again, or he gets mad at me, I'm stuck here with a furious Fisher. Like now. This is what I wanted to avoid."

"I didn't realize Fisher could be such a moody little bitch. He's usually pretty cool about things."

"Not where I'm concerned."

"And why would that be?"

Danni grabbed her shoes.

"Where ya going?"

"To find Fisher. I'll decide if I want to hug him or slug him after I find him."

Chapter 28

Fisher wasn't home five minutes before Tori showed up. He looked her over objectively. She was a beautiful woman, with long blonde hair and a body that made men stop and stare. She was hard-working and focused. Maybe too focused. Tori could become annoying when she was on a quest. She wasn't the type to relax. A Sunday spent fishing wasn't ever on her agenda — that was nothing but time wasted when she could be working.

Fisher was too complacent for that. He didn't want to own the world. He had his little piece of the planet, and that was enough for him. After they broke up, Tori said she understood, but he was never sure if she really did, because, unfortunately, Tori was also more than happy to be whatever he wanted her to be to make him commit.

She loved to please him.

Was that so bad?

Dressed to perfection in gray slacks and a white sweater, she looked stunning.

"Hey, handsome," she said as she got out of her car. She gave him a smile so broad and happy, he hated himself for not being able to fall in love with her. Wasn't that the sane choice, love the woman who already loves you? Or keep banging his head against the wall with Danni....

"Hey, Tori." He stuffed his hands in his pockets as he watched her walk toward him.

She kissed his cheek. "I have food. I was thinking today that you take care of everyone, but who takes care of you? So, I made steak and potatoes. I promise I won't even nag about how much butter or sour cream you drown them in."

"That was nice of you."

"You look half sick. Is something wrong?"

He took a deep breath. "I'm fine. I just...I feel guilty that you're doing so much for me."

"I enjoy it."

"I don't want to take advantage of you, Tor. Or give you false hope."

Tori shifted her weight from one foot to the other. "I thought we were friends."

"We are. But if I keep having you take care of everything—"

"Like you do for Danni? Is that why you're suddenly suspicious of my motives? You know you're bending over backward for her, hoping she'll be so grateful she falls in love with you?"

Irritation crept in...at her for being right and at himself for being stupid enough to think anything could ever work with Danni. "This isn't about Danni. It's about me not wanting to lead you on."

Tori laughed. "Dearest Fisher, I have no delusions that you're anything but my friend. Would I like for you to be more?" She shrugged. "I won't lie; of course I would. But I know it isn't going to happen. But if we can't even be friends, then I guess I'll go."

She turned to leave, but he grabbed her by the arm. "You don't have to go. Come on in. It was nice of you to bring dinner."

"I thought it was." She flashed him a fake pout before breaking into a big smile. "Just to make sure you know it's a friendly dinner, I won't give you roses or light candles."

Fisher smiled. Tori always was a good friend, and it felt good to have some support right now.

In the kitchen, Tori unloaded the food from her canvas tote. There was steak, potatoes, and a salad, each done to perfection. The steak was tender and juicy, with just the right amount of seasoning. The potatoes were buttery with crispy edges and a hint of garlic and sour cream. Fisher skipped the salad for an extra helping of potatoes. The woman was a wonder in the kitchen. She approached cooking like she did everything else in her life. If she was going to do it, she'd do it best.

Plates emptied and cleared, she poured them each a glass of wine. They sat and talked, slowly draining the bottle of top-notch Chianti. Tori went to the counter and pulled another bottle out of the bag. Like a pro, she removed the cork and carried the bottle back to the table. Leaning over his shoulder, she filled his glass. Her breast brushed against his shoulder. He looked up at her, and she ran a hand through his hair.

He closed his eyes and shook his head. "I love her, Tor. I don't want to, but I do."

She rubbed his shoulders. "I know, sweetheart. I hope she either comes to her senses and sees what she could have with you or goes away and leaves you alone. The thing is, she won't mean to hurt you, but she will. Hurting people is just what Danni does. I don't think she means to be selfish, but she's so caught up in her own problems that she can't see what she's doing to the people around her." Tori stepped away from him. "The Lowrys were always an odd group of gals. They don't do personal connections very well. None of the Lowry sisters ever married. Not Danni's mom, or Max. I don't think the youngest one ever married either, though I honestly don't know much about her."

"There was a third sister?" Fisher had never heard that.

"Yeah, there was a third daughter before they moved to the mainland. I think her name was something common, like Lynn or Leigh."

"Are you sure? Max never said anything about another sister."

Tori gave him a look. "My grandmother was best friends with Max's mom. She told me all about them. There are stories I could tell you that would make you sick to your stomach."

"If the stories are true, of course."

"Nana Moore would never lie, Fisher."

"I'm not saying she would. I'm just saying I knew Max a long time, and she never mentioned —"

"She never mentioned anything, because she never told anyone anything personal. Think about it — did you ever hear Max talk about Vi? The only things we honestly know about

Danni's mom is that she had a baby before she was seventeen and jumped off the Bonner Bridge when she was nineteen. Oh, and she somehow managed to leave her daughter an estate worth several million dollars, yet she came from a poor fishing family."

Fisher thought a minute. Tori was right. He'd known Max his whole life, yet not once did she mention her personal life. He would never have known she dated a guy if his mother hadn't told him. And she never did talk about Vi. What he knew about her, he got from town gossip. "I guess you're right."

"I know I'm right. I'm telling you—emotionally disengaged, all of them. That's what's wrong with Danni. She's broken. That's why I never really get mad at her for being so mean to me. It's just her way."

"You're a good woman, Tori. You're beautiful and generous. Hell, you're smart and motivated—a woman like you should never settle for anything less than perfection."

Tori sighed. "That's nice of you to say, but I'm far from perfect." Her hand stroked the back of his head as if he was a child or a pup. "I've been on pins and needles since Danni came back, and I've said things to her that I regret. I wasn't being nice. I was being petty and childish. Hopefully, she can forgive me."

"You're one of the nicest, most generous people."

"Yet, your heart pines for the fair, Danni."

"Seems it does."

His confession made Tori's face drop. It took her a minute to recover, but she did. Offering him a big, wide smile, she grabbed her jacket and her tote. "On that note, I think I will leave you to wallow in your Danni grief. I'm going home for a long, hot bubble bath."

"I'm sorry, Tor. I—"

"No need to apologize. I appreciate that we can be friends and can be honest with each other."

He nodded and followed her out on the porch.

At the edge of the steps, she stopped and turned to him. Pressing the collar of his shirt with her hands, smoothing out the creases, she said, "I'll tell you what, Fisher Todd Cooper. I hope all of this works out for you. If Danni is what will make you smile, I hope you get her. But if it all goes to hell, remember, I'm always here for you." She gave his chest a pat. "She is quite the tragic figure, and you are a rescuer. Please, promise me you won't drown trying to save her."

He looked down at her, and she looked up at him. "Thanks for worrying about me, but I'll be fine."

Tori leaned closer and kissed his cheek. "Follow your heart. I know this is something you need to do. If she's playing games or loses interest, you know where to find me." Her voice quivered a bit, and her hands were shaky as she wiped lipstick off his cheek. "I'm not saying that to sound desperate or pathetic, but because you're my friend and you're very special to me."

He took her hand and pulled her in for a hug. "Thank you, Tori. You really are a good friend."

"The best you'll ever have," she said before she left.

Chapter 29

Danni ducked into the shadows cast by the porch. Her excitement in seeing his house lights on was dampened by the sight of Tori's car. Her first response was to turn and leave, but then her spine stiffened, and she decided if she lost Fisher again, it wouldn't be by tucking her tail and running away. She'd walk right up to his front door and demand he listens to everything she had to say.

Fortified with a righteous plan, she made it to the front steps. When she heard the door open, she ran and hid. After Tori left, she debated popping up from her hiding spot, but wondered how in God's name she would explain spying on him. Would he buy that it was by accident?

"Danni?"

Danni almost fell over. "Fisher."

"Are you hiding down there?"

"I...." She stood and brushed the sand off her butt. "Just hanging out...feeding the mosquitoes."

"Good night for it." He leaned against the porch column.

"Actually...." She gripped the railing as she climbed the steps. "I was coming to talk to you, but you had company."

"If it's about the trip to Oregon, I got about a thousand texts from Darby explaining."

Danni nodded. "She felt awful."

"She doesn't need to."

"You seemed pretty mad when you left."

"I overreacted."

"Maybe a little." She held her fingers an inch apart. "But I should have told you sooner—I need more clothes, and I need to quit my job and get rid of my apartment."

Fisher crossed his arms over his chest. "You're seriously staying?"

She nodded. "For the rest of the near future."

"I'm glad to hear that."

"Are you?" Danni bit her lip.

"Of course."

"Even though I seem to be the worst thing to happen to you since—well, ever?"

"You know better than that."

"Do I?"

He grabbed her by the elbow and pulled her toward his house. "We need to talk."

Inside the house, Danni stood in the doorway, arms locked over her chest.

"Can I get you a drink or anything?" Fisher asked.

Danni shook her head. The smell of steak hung in the air. A bottle of wine sat on the kitchen counter. How very cozy...Danni wished she was still hiding in the shrubs being feasted on by mosquitoes.

"Sit." Fisher pointed to the couch as he headed into the kitchen.

Danni sat. The couch was much nicer than Max's old one that sucked your body into the springs. Fisher went to the kitchen and poured them each a glass of iced tea before joining her on the couch.

"Thanks." Danni offered him a smile that was more like a twitch of nervous lips. "So, just to be sure, was I the one you guys were talking about, right? The perpetual problem in your life?"

"No, there's this other woman who makes me feel like I've lost my mind."

"Oh well, you might want to think long and hard about getting too serious. I mean, Tori is right, you do enjoy a good rescue."

"I'm not trying to rescue you." He set his glass on the table.

"Maybe not." She swallowed, took a deep breath, and tried

to explain without starting a fight or humiliating herself. "Fisher, you are the last person I would ever intentionally hurt. And I know you were disappointed in me last time, so I'm trying to do things smarter." Her lips were dry, so she paused for a sip of tea. "I don't want to do anything ever again that could ruin our friendship."

He took her hand and squeezed it. "Come on, Danni, I don't want to be your friend."

"You don't?"

"Of course not." He shook his head. His thumb traced circles on her palm. "Back then, when I thought we'd finally be together, that felt good."

"Then I—I messed it up, and I apologize for—"

He tugged on her hand. "Let's leave the past in the past. I think I was way ahead of you back then. I already knew I loved you."

"I've always loved you too."

"But different kinds of love. I don't think we were on the same page. Just like now—you're trying to save our friendship, and being friends with you is the last thing I want."

"So that means...." Bubbles of hope made her body feel light. But what if she was reading this wrong? Maybe tonight's dinner with Tori was a reconciliation, and he was about to cut her out of his life completely. "What does that mean?"

Fisher looked at her, brushing his thumb across her cheek. "It means I love you, Danni. I always have."

Her heart sped up, racing so fast she wasn't sure she could speak.

With gentle fingers under her chin, he positioned her face, so she had no choice but to look at him. "Are you all right?"

She nodded and took a deep breath. "It's just—I've always loved you too, but I was certain you hated me."

"I could never hate you."

She licked dried lips. Tears burned her eyes. Danni tried to blink them back, but they slipped out and rolled down her cheeks. Instantly embarrassed, she tried to brush them away.

"Don't cry, Danni. I'm sorry. I didn't mean to—"

"No." She licked dried lips. "I'm okay." Embarrassment made her cheeks burn. "I don't know why I'm crying."

He held her face in his hands and brushed away the tears with his thumbs before leaning in. This time when he kissed her, it was the most amazing feeling ever. He loved her. That confirmation moved through her veins like a drug. Her body tingled from her toes to her scalp.

He pulled her close, but no matter how tight she held onto him, he didn't feel close enough. He must have felt the same way because he said, "I want you, Danni."

"I want you too. But—"

"No buts. It's not complicated. Just love me, and the rest will work itself out."

She nodded and wrapped her hands in his hair, holding him tight as his lips made a hot trail of kisses down her neck to the tops of her breasts.

He paused a moment and pulled her hands free, kissing each one. "I don't have protection."

"It doesn't matter."

His hands moved across her skin as if he couldn't touch enough of her quickly enough to please him. She tugged at his shirt, finally getting it up and over his broad shoulders and his head.

He unbuttoned her pants, pushing them over her hips and down her legs. She watched as he stripped out of his, tossed them on the floor, and joined her on the couch. His body was warm and hard. She closed her eyes and settled her cheek against his shoulder.

Breathing in his scent, she tried to commit it to memory. He smelled like soap and fresh air. His skin was warm and smooth against her cheek. She wrapped her arms tight across his shoulders as he settled himself between her legs. She ran the inside of her calf up his leg, enjoying the different texture of him. His legs were hardened with muscles and sprinkled with dark, coarse hair.

He buried his face in her throat. "This is too good."

She kissed the muscles along his throat as her hands moved

over his ribs. She couldn't touch him enough to prove to herself this was real. "It's perfect."

"I'm trying to go slow, but you're killing me."

She shook her head. She didn't want to go slow. She wanted him. "I need you, Fisher."

"Damn it," he said as he lifted her hips and drove himself inside her. "I'm sorry, Danni. I can't wait."

A cry escaped her that was both pleasure and pain. Her body—hell, her soul—had waited a lifetime for this. "I love you," she whispered in his ear. "I missed you, Fisher. So much. I missed you so much."

Danni wrapped her arms across his shoulders and held on. His body made hers feel alive, every muscle, every nerve ending. Head thrust back, nails digging into his flesh, she found her release with a single, wonderful thought: for this moment, he belonged with her.

Chapter 30

Fisher pulled her body close. Happily, with a full, content heart, she leaned into him, resting her forehead against his chest. "I can't believe this is real."

"Is that a good thing or a bad thing?"

She gave him a squeeze. "It's a wonderful thing."

He kissed the top of her head, lips lingering, tickling her scalp with every warm breath. "I'm glad. I worry. When will you decide you don't want me around anymore?"

Danni looked up at him and shook her head. "How could you think that?"

He shrugged.

Danni snuggled back into him. Maybe his mother was to blame. She knew Fisher felt like Kitty abandoned him when she chose Bill's side in every argument and decision. One day she'd prove to him that she'd always be with him—even if it was as a friend. Having him in her life again felt too good. She'd never let go now. Leaning back, she looked up at him. "Come with me. Darby has a movie planned for tonight. You could watch it with us. And she could see you're not mad at her. She was so worried."

"I texted her."

"Is that a no to coming with me?"

Planting a kiss on top of her head, he released her. "No. But what if I prefer to stay here…with you…like this?" He feathered kisses across her cheeks. "Tell me you love me."

She wrapped her arms around his neck and kissed him. "What's it worth to you?"

"I'd give anything to hear it."

She ran her hands through his hair as she kissed him. His jaw was sharp with evening stubble. "I love you." She punctuated her words with a kiss. "I love you now. I loved you then." She brushed her thumbs across his eyelashes. "I'll love you forever. And one day."

"Just one?" he chuckled.

"Maybe two."

He hugged her close, squeezing the breath from her body. "If I squeeze and hold on really tight, can I get a few million extra days out of you?"

Her head tipped back with laughter. "Yes. That and forever if you kiss me too."

Rolling her back on the couch, he kissed her again.

Chapter 31

On his porch, he swept Danni off her feet and tossed her over his shoulder. "Come with me, Vixen."

Danni giggled as he carried her down the path to the hotel. "Put me down. You'll get a hernia. I swear you will."

He set her down by the garden gate. "Are you sure you don't want to go back to my place, where it's quiet, and you can be naked?"

Danni grabbed him by the waistband and pulled him to her, whispering in his ear, "I would like nothing better, but—"

"Damn, I hate the but part of your sentences." Danni pointed to a face peering out the kitchen window. Darby saw them looking and waved. Fisher sighed. "You're right. Let's go in."

Darby waved as they stepped into the kitchen. She was making popcorn and filling glasses with soda.

"I brought company," Danni said as she wrapped an arm around Fisher's waist.

"You came back." Darby ran to him and wrapped her arms around him for a bone-crushing hug. "I'm so sorry. I thought I'd screwed up big time."

"No, just me being a temperamental jerk. I texted you everything was fine."

"Yeah, adults always say everything is fine, even when life goes to shit—uh, I mean crap. And Danni was gone forever. I figured you two were fighting."

Danni blushed, but said smoothly, "I had to wait outside his door for Tori to leave."

"Oh." Darby gave Danni a look of sympathy.

"Tori is a friend, nothing more." He grabbed Danni's hand and pulled her into him. "Danni is too much of a distraction to think of anyone else."

"You two," Darby pointed to the pair. "You're officially a thing?"

Danni didn't answer, so Fisher said, "Hell, yes. Danni is officially my thing. I catch her kissing another guy, there will be hell to pay."

Darby rolled her eyes. "A simple yes would have been plenty." Darby grabbed her bowl of popcorn. "For the record, I called it. I should have put a money bet on it."

"I guess you should have," Danni said.

"What did you call?" Fisher asked.

"This. I told Danni on day one that she belonged with you."

"And she argued with you?" Fisher joked.

"No," Darby said. "She didn't think you'd ever choose a girl like her over someone like Tori. That's why I did her hair and—"

Heat pooled in Danni's cheeks. "Uh, don't you have a movie picked out? We better start it. You have school tomorrow."

"Darby," Fisher said. "Why don't you start that movie? We'll be right in."

"Sure thing." Darby gave Fisher a wink and headed for the living room.

Fisher wrapped his arms around Danni's waist and pulled her close. "Can I tell you something, and you not judge me for it?"

Danni nodded.

He leaned his forehead against hers. "I bought a suit for Max's funeral, just to impress you. And when you were in the hospital, passed out and sleeping, I kissed you."

"Really?" She smiled. "I thought I dreamed that."

He shook his head. "There's not been a day in my life that you weren't in my heart. I've missed you. I looked forward to a damned funeral because I knew you had to come back for it."

"You looked forward to a funeral?"

"Don't get me wrong. I didn't wish good old Max dead, but I did appreciate there was an upside to her passing. I knew she'd expect me to make the most of it, so I did."

Danni rubbed his shoulders, giving them a squeeze. "I have a feeling Max would not only have appreciated that but she'd have haunted you if you didn't."

He kissed her. It felt good to kiss her without hesitation or fear. "It's good to have my Loonie back."

They followed Darby to the living room for the movie, which he technically watched, but in reality, he paid attention to none of it. All he could think of was peeling Danni's clothes off and loving her again. This time slower. It had been mind blowing, but each time he'd had the chance to be with her, he'd been so damned eager, he rushed it.

He looked down at her, and she smiled up at him. His heart skipped a beat. He wrapped his arm around her waist and pulled her closer to him. It felt unreal. She was next to him, close enough to touch. Close enough to feel the heat from her body. Smell the wind in her hair. But it didn't feel real. It didn't feel sustainable. Not yet.

Chapter 32

At the end of the evening, he kissed her good night on the porch. She didn't want him to leave. What if this was a dream? If she went to sleep, would she be back to reality when she woke?

"I guess this is good night." He kissed her. "I suppose I'll be back in the morning."

"I'll be waiting," she sighed against his lips, her body relaxing into his.

"Aww, Danni, I don't want to go."

"I don't want you to go, but what would that teach Darby?"

"She's in high school. I bet she already knows."

Danni shook her head. "We can't. We're her role models."

He kissed her again as if this kiss had to last a lifetime. Her knees felt weak. If he asked her to do it there on the porch, she might agree. When he pulled back, he kept her face cradled in his hands. "You have no idea how long I've wanted this. To touch you, kiss you. Don't make me go."

Danni moaned, leaned close, and whispered in his ear, "I'll unlock my window, but you must be very quiet."

"You sneaky little minx. You're a genius. No wonder I love you."

"I'll go tell Darby goodnight. You wait for me in my room."

"You can bank on that."

Danni brushed a kiss across his cheek and rushed into the house. She went directly to her bedroom, unlocked the window, and pushed it open a crack. Then she hurried to the kitchen to straighten up.

Darby came in carrying popcorn bowls from the living room.

"You know what I was thinking tonight, Danni?"

"What's that, kiddo?"

"Good things can happen out of the blue, just like bad things do. The night Max died, I thought I was screwed. I mean, Max told me I'd love you, and you'd be awesome, but it was hard to believe. But when we ran away from Fisher's, it was like in a moment, we had each other." The sting of tears burned her eyes, but Danni blinked them away. While she concentrated on not bawling like a baby, Darby continued. "And tonight, when Fisher stormed out of here, I thought he'd never be back. I thought for sure he'd hate us both forever. Next thing you know, you're a couple."

Danni smiled. "I'm not sure I'd go that far. There are still things that will have to be considered. But yeah, for now, I'm going to keep him all for myself."

"More good things will happen, Danni. I can feel it. It's like we've dealt with our bad stuff, now we get the blessings."

Danni gave her a hug. "One thing is for sure—I love you. You are one amazing little lady, and I am so very blessed to get to call you family."

"You are pretty damned lucky to have me. You'd probably have blown it with Fisher on your own."

Danni laughed. "No doubt. Thanks for the help." Danni looked at the clock on the wall. It was after eleven. "Now, you better get to bed."

"Headed that way. Just stopped in for some cookies and to enlighten you. I was taking a shower, and the thought hit me. I figured you'd agree and could use a happy thought."

"Thank you. I appreciate it."

Darby grabbed a package of Oreos and a bottle of chocolate milk and headed for her room, Punkin, following on her heels. Danni wished them a good night, then resumed her speed clean of the kitchen. Once she was finished, she grabbed a quick shower—since that was her routine—and hurried to her room.

The window was closed, but there was no sign of Fisher. As she closed and locked her door, he popped his head out of the closet. "Is it safe?"

Danni jumped, holding her hand over her heart. "Yes, you're safe."

Fisher slipped out of the closet and wrapped his arms around her. "You taste so sweet," he said against her lips. "I won't ever be able to get enough of you."

Danni's heart raced as his hand trailed up her abdomen to her breast. She hadn't bothered to put her bra back on, so when his hand reached its goal, there was nothing between them but a thin veil of cotton.

He growled against her throat before scooping her up and carrying her to her bed. One tug of her pajama pants, and she was bare to him. Moonlight from the window reflected on her pale skin, making his hands look dark against her flesh as they moved over her body.

"You feel so silky, I swear, you don't feel real."

Her breasts rose and fell with her every breath. His breath was warm, teasing her flesh as he explored her body. His lips trailed down her throat as a roughened hand cupped her breast. The nipple hardened at his touch as if begging to be sucked. When he pulled its sweetness into his mouth, Danni's body arched against him.

He left her only long enough to strip off his clothes. She was ready for him, but he seemed to have lost the urgency to hurry. She reached for the blanket to cover her body, but he pulled it away. "No, Danni. I want to see you."

"Why?" she asked, reaching again for cover. The moonlight was too bright. He'd be able to see every lump and roll.

"Because you're beautiful. I want to know every inch of your body." He knelt before her and ran his hands down her thighs to her core. Her body twisted and arched toward him, and slowly the thoughts of how she looked no longer mattered. All that mattered was how he made her feel. He ran his tongue along the silky skin of her inner thigh, bringing a moan from her lips as her hands twisted into his hair.

Suddenly, his playful teasing ended. He moved up her body, his lips finding hers in a kiss that took her breath away. He pulled her body to his, lifting her hips off the bed as he drove his body into hers.

She clung to him, matching him stroke for stroke until she gasped, her body tensing until she could stand no more. She buried her face in his neck. Her voice was hoarse as she called his name. He held her tight as his body poured into hers.

Rolling away, he took her with him. She snuggled into his chest. He kissed her temple. "I can't imagine loving anything or anyone more than I do you, Loonie. You were made for me."

Danni kissed the area on his chest where his heart thudded under skin and muscle. She wanted to tell him everything would be perfect and wonderful, but she knew that was a lie.

"Do you realize…," he brushed the tangles from her hair, "That I can't think of a time where I wasn't either missing you or fantasizing about you?"

"Fantasizing? About me?"

"Hell, if I had a nickel for every time I've had sex with you in my mind, I'd be a damned millionaire."

She looked up at him with a grin. "Did reality hold up to fiction?"

He kissed her naked shoulder. "It's better. All that shit people tell you about sex feeling spiritual when you're in love is damned accurate."

She leaned on her elbow. She'd worry about reality tomorrow. Tonight was hers to enjoy. She smiled down at him. "Listen to you. I never realized you were such a romantic."

He grabbed her leg and pulled her on top of him. "Sweetheart, I assure you, I am full of surprises."

Chapter 33

Danni woke at dawn. Fisher lay beside her, arms tucked under his pillow, face soft with sleep. She kissed her finger then gently transplanted it to his forehead. He twitched in his sleep, offering her a sleeping smile. She sighed. For the first time in years, she felt happy.

Happy. A little word the world failed to fully appreciate. Euphoria and heart pounding elation, they were wonderful for short periods of time, but long term could wear out the heart. But happiness—that feeling of everything being right with the world—was the best. It was continual, strengthening the heart and emboldening the spirit.

As dawn brightened to morning, Danni gave his shoulder a shake. She hated to wake him, especially when it meant sending him home. But duty called. She needed to get Darby off to school without explaining why Fisher was sleeping in her bed.

The shoulder shake failed to roust him. She leaned closer and kissed him. He smiled but didn't open his eyes. She kissed him again and again until his eyes slowly opened, filled with desire and devotion.

Danni ran her hands across hard shoulders to the taut muscles of his back. "Time to wake, sleeping beauty."

"Now this," he said, "is how a man needs to be woken up. To think I've used a damned alarm clock all these years."

He pulled her to him, rolling her under him. His lips were hot against the skin on her neck as they seared a trail of kisses down her throat to the soft swell of her breasts, unbuttoning her pajama top as he moved lower. Danni took a deep suck of breath as he moved lower. When his tongue flicked across her belly button, she couldn't stop the moan, her back arching against him, forcing his body closer.

The sound of the shower running reminded Danni they weren't alone. Darby. As much as she wanted to strip him down, she couldn't, not with a teenage girl wandering the apartment.

Danni took a deep breath. "Stop, Fisher."

He shook his head against her belly, kissing his way to her hip.

"Darby."

The name made him groan, but he stopped. He rolled to his side, holding onto her hand. "Shit." He leaned up on his forearms. "She's in the shower. That buys me at least ten minutes—I'm up to that challenge."

Danni rolled out of bed and grabbed her robe. "No. It's too big of a risk."

"Marry me."

Danni gasped. He looked serious but had to be joking. "You're a funny guy. Now, come on. I've got to make breakfast."

Fisher sat up and reached for his pants. "She leaves for school at what, eight? I guess waiting an hour might not kill me."

"Might not?"

"I could have a stroke. There can't be any blood going to my brain, it's all pooled in the south."

"You poor guy." She kissed him. "Maybe," she traced her finger down the trail of fine, dark hairs from his abdomen to his groin, "if you're not busy for lunch...."

"Lunch? I'm coming back as soon as the school bus leaves."

"I have to meet with Max's attorney at nine."

"Well, hell," he groaned. "At least I know what I'm having for lunch."

"Now, you've got to go before it's fully light outside, and people see you climbing out my window."

"I'm not ashamed. Let them see."

Danni shook her head. "Don't be a problem, or I'll lock the window."

He stood, pulling her in and kissing her. "You don't have to be mean about it. I was going."

Danni combed his tousled hair with her fingers. "I love you."

"I love you, too," he said before crawling out the window.

Danni closed it, waving goodbye until he rounded the side of the hotel. She headed to the kitchen to send Darby off to school. After the girl was gone, she took Punkin for her walk, showered, dressed, and headed down Highway 12 to the little town of Avon.

She'd not traveled this far south in years. Danni smiled as she passed Dairy Queen. How many times had she and Fisher driven down here for ice cream? She thought of all the bonfires on the beach, four wheeling down to Cape Point…she'd blocked all those memories once she left. It hurt too much to remember.

But she could think of them now — the good times.

She turned into the parking lot. The attorney's office was just like the other stilted cottages on the beach. The only thing separating it from the other buildings was the sign — Claire Kramer, Attorney at Law. Danni was greeted by the receptionist, who took her to Claire's office.

Once she was settled in, the receptionist brought her a fresh cup of coffee. Danni set it on the table beside her and fussed with the buttons on her shirt. She didn't realize in her haste to dress and go that the buttons pulled a little between her breasts. Somehow that didn't seem like as much a problem as it had at the funeral. Fisher didn't seem to mind that her weight gain had pushed her from a B to a C cup.

Claire, the attorney, stepped in the room, and Danni blushed as if the woman could read her mind. Claire offered Danni her hand and her condolences. Danni shook it and mumbled a thank you. Danni's hands were suddenly clammy. But she took a deep breath and forced herself to be calm. Max always knew what was best.

Claire opened a file, read over the papers, and said, "Max has you pretty well set up. You're the sole beneficiary of the estate." She flipped the page. "And she has provided a financial contingency plan if need be, for Maureen to take custody of Darby, should you decide not to be her guardian."

"Max doubted I'd want her?"

Claire smiled. "Max was certain you'd stay and care for her, but I insisted she have a plan B, just in case."

Danni felt relief. Max did know she could depend on her.

"All of the financials are pretty much settled. There are some taxes to be paid, but Max has an accountant who will take care of all of that. As soon as the money is transferred to you, he will send you a check—at the hotel, I assume?"

"Yes, I'll be living there."

"The only thing left to consider is Darby's adoption petition. I filed the paperwork to have it transferred to you."

"She didn't already adopt her?"

"The final hearing would have been at the end of May. Given all the losses Darby has suffered over the last few years, I'll petition the court to expedite the process, so the girl is guaranteed a stable transition."

"What if they decide I'm not okay? I'm divorced."

"Being single won't matter. Social services will do a background check and interview you, and probably Darby. Fisher Cooper was granted temporary custody of her while Max was in the hospital without any hassles, and I assume they'll do the same for you. You will be her legal guardian until the adoption is granted."

Danni's throat went dry. She reached for the cup of coffee. She thought Darby was safely hers to care for. What if they decided she was a bad influence?

"It will be painless, I promise." Claire gave Danni a smile before diving into the stack of papers. "All righty, then, let's get down to the nitty-gritty. Max added you to her checking account, so you have immediate access to those funds. The rest will take four to six weeks to transfer. There is…," Claire looked over the paper, "Approximately $15,000 in that checking account. Is that enough to cover expenses until the rest is transferred?"

Danni's eyes widened. "That's plenty. Good lord, who keeps that much in checking?"

"Max moved it once she found out she was sick. She said you'd need some of it for her party."

Danni laughed. "Max must be wanting one hell of a party."

"The rest will transfer to you once we get the death certificate."

"Did she set any aside for Darby, for college?"

"I think she assumed you'd take care of that."

Danni nodded. "Of course, I will. Darby and I were thinking of renovating the hotel. We could probably do a lot with $15,000, then do more as we start to make money—"

"Danni," Claire said. "Max's estate is valued at well over ten million. Unless you're a fool, you will have plenty of income. She has the hotel and several other properties up and down the island. She even holds the lease on the land the shopping plaza sits on. That alone brings in five-thousand dollars a month."

"She what?" Danni's eyes popped open. Max was rich? Oh, hell, no.

"Max always was a smart cookie. A lot of old-timers on the island sold their family land; Max leased hers."

"That's—where did it all come from? From all accounts I've heard, my grandparents only owned the land their house sat on."

Claire shrugged. "I never asked—I just assumed she inherited it. As her attorney, my only concern was protecting her assets, not finding out how she got them"

Danni nodded, a bit stunned. She should be elated, but there was something about the news that didn't feel comfortable. Danni shook off the feeling. She was being ridiculous. Max had left her well taken care of, and she was over-analyzing it.

Claire handed Danni a heavy silver pen. "All you have to do is sign here swearing you will do as she asked, and it's all yours. Well, aside from a small sum for Fisher—oh, and the dog. The dog goes to Fisher." Claire chuckled. "I'm sure Fisher will be thrilled."

"He's more thrilled about it than you'd ever guess."

Claire gave her an odd look.

"He knows the dog is his," Danni explained. "He holds her over my head. Maybe with ten million, I can buy him off."

"I've got a mutt named Lucky; I'm open to negotiations if Fisher won't play ball."

"Punkin is special," Danni said with a smile. "It's amazing how much I like that stupid dog."

"It's the eyes. Dog eyes are like guilt incarnate. I spend thirty bucks a week on squeaky toys for my Lucky. How insane is that?"

Danni nodded. "I can see it. I walk Punkin two, three times a day, because she sits under her leash and stares at me."

Claire gathered up the stacks of papers and carried them to Danni. "You sign these, and I'll get you fixed up, and Darby too."

"Thanks."

Danni signed page after page, line after line, annoyed that she had everything she could hope for, and yet, as Max would say, she felt as nervous as a cat in a room full of rocking chairs.

Chapter 34

Danni arrived at the hotel before lunch. Standing in the humble living space, Danni felt like she was missing something. Her whole life, Max had lived like money was not so much scarce, but never to be squandered. From the threadbare rugs to the sagging furniture, why hadn't Max replaced a few things?

Her thoughts were interrupted with a "Hello" from the door. Danni turned, and her day turned with her. She took a deep breath. "Tori."

"I knocked. I don't think you heard me."

"No, I didn't. Why are you here?"

Tori puffed out her lower lip. "Now, Danni. Why are you being so mean to me?"

"I could ask you the same question."

Tori took a deep breath then let it out with a sigh. "Okay, full disclosure. I was jealous. I had...hopes of making things work with Fisher, and you were going to complicate that—which you totally did, by the way."

Danni relaxed and smiled. She did totally mess things up for Tori. "I can see why you didn't want to lose Fisher. He's worth fighting for."

Tori nodded and held a cake toward Danni. "A truce? It's chocolate."

Danni took the cake. "Truce."

"Do you have a minute? We could have a slice and catch up."

Danni looked at the clock on the wall. She wasn't sure what time Fisher considered lunchtime, but why did it matter? If she was going to have a relationship with him, there was no need to hide it.

"Sure," Danni said. "I'll make a pot of coffee."

Tori made herself at home in the kitchen, grabbing plates, mugs, forks, and a knife. While Danni let the coffee percolate, Tori cut the cake and set it on plates.

"So, aside from Fisher, have you done anything since being back?"

Danni's head snapped around to look at Tori. Fully expecting her to look like a smart ass, she was surprised to see Tori licking icing off her finger, seemingly oblivious to her innuendo. Danni took a deep breath. "Not much. I've been trying to get things sorted out here. I had thought Darby and I would need to hurry up and get this place up and running to have money to live on, but it seems Max has us pretty well set up."

"So I heard," Tori said, swiping her finger up the knife to get the rest of the frosting. "You know she owns property all over Salvo. I assume she used her blood money to buy all that real estate. That was a smart move. I wish my family had had a few million to buy up things during the '70s. People had no clue how much the property on this island would be worth in just a few decades."

"No, I'm sure they didn't," Danni mumbled. *Blood money?* She wanted to ask Tori what she was talking about, but couldn't. Danni knew too well that much of Tori's cryptic comments were baited traps. The cake was looking more and more like a Trojan horse.

Danni poured them each a cup of coffee and sat. Tori shoved a plate of cake at her. Danni took a bite. It was annoyingly delicious. It was like eating confectionery perfection. It was light and moist with a rich chocolate flavor that paired perfectly with a sip of coffee.

"Your coffee is good," Tori said. "If you want it to be better, you should run some vinegar through your coffee maker and then run a mix of vanilla and water through it. You'll appreciate the difference."

Danni nodded and took another bite. "Where did you learn to be so domestic? I never dreamed you were the type."

Tori sighed. "I did it for Fisher. I knew the one thing he wanted more than anything was the white picket fence and the big family, and I thought by having the skills to make a home the perfect place, he'd fall in love with me. But I think I knew—down deep—there was no replacing you. Now, you're back. You guys will get together, and pretty soon, you'll be getting married, having kids, and living happily ever after." Tori blinked back tears. "And I'm going to be happy with that. If I can't be mommy, maybe you guys will let me be Auntie Tori."

The mention of kids turned the delicious cake to cardboard in her mouth. Danni lost her appetite. She stood and carried her plate to the trashcan and scraped it into the garbage.

"I'm sorry," Tori said. "Was that too forward? I was just thinking we were all friends at one time...."

"It's not that."

"Then what? Was it that I suggested you guys would get married and have kids? Oh my God, you don't plan to stay around here long enough, do you?" Tori's mouth hung open. "Does Fisher know? Because I can guarantee you, he's thinking of having a family and kids and all that. It's all he ever talked about."

Danni poured herself a glass of water. Her throat was suddenly dry.

"Shoot, I think that's all I had going for me. He told me he was almost thirty and looking to settle down. We were so close to making it official, then damn." She took a deep breath. "I thought I'd won, or at least run down the clock." Tori poked at the icing on her cake. "But then Max died, and here you are."

Danni felt hollow. Tori was still talking, but she tuned her out after Tori said Fisher had offered to marry her so he could have a family. She gripped the edge of the counter. She felt a little dizzy.

The back door opened and closed. Fisher. He spotted Tori first and stopped in his tracks. "Tori," he said before turning to Danni. "We still on for lunch?"

Danni shrugged.

"Don't let me get in the way." Tori stood. "Just let me know when you finish that cake, and I'll come pick up the plate. Or drop it off at my office. I'm just up the road." Tori wrung her hands a few times before saying her goodbyes. Danni walked her to the door, gladly closing it behind the always-perfect blonde.

Back in the kitchen, Fisher was helping himself to the cake. "I will say, Tori can cook."

Danni frowned and took the platter from him. "Why didn't you cut off a slice, or do you plan to eat the whole thing at once?"

He set the cake on the table and grabbed her around the waist, pulling her onto his lap. "Are you jealous, or are you worried I'll enjoy my cake and eat it too?"

"I'm worried you'll piss me off, and I'll throw you out of my house."

Fisher laughed. "Don't be mad at me, Loonie." He tipped her chin until she was looking into warm brown eyes. "You know I love you."

She could see it in his eyes. He truly did love her. But was that enough? She could never give him a family. When she told him the truth, would it be over, or could they return to being friends?

"What's wrong, Danni? You look worried?"

It was the perfect opportunity to be honest with him, but when she opened her mouth to tell him, the words, *I can never have kids,* would not roll off her tongue. Instead, she said, "Max left me an estate worth more than ten million dollars."

"Seriously?" Fisher shook his head. "That's some serious cash. I'd think you'd be happy as hell."

"I am." Danni bit her lip. "But I wonder, where did the money come from? I always assumed the money my mother left me was from an insurance policy. But it seems Max had money too. And my grandparents were poor. I'm not even sure they owned their own house, much less a bunch of properties."

Fisher thought a minute. "Maybe there's a lot about them you don't know. Tori told me there was a third Lowry sister. Maybe you could find her and ask her about the parents."

Danni turned to him, her mouth hanging open. "No way. My mom and Max had another sister? How the hell did I not know that?"

Fisher shrugged. "After Tori told me, I asked my mom. She said there was another sister, but she couldn't remember her name or where she went."

"No way. Surely someone would have told me about that."

"I'd say there was a lot Max never told you."

It hurt that Max didn't trust her enough to be honest with her. First, there was the boyfriend, now a sister?

"You okay?"

Danni laid her cheek on his shoulder. "I feel like there is so much about my own family that I don't know. Is it that I never paid attention?"

"I don't think Max liked to think about the past. I think the people who know only know about it because they were around at the time."

"Tori wasn't around back then."

"Her mom was."

Danni stood and paced the kitchen. "How could Max have said nothing about another sister? There had to be something here...some clue about how to find her."

Danni left the kitchen and started going through closets, checking every box, bag, and envelope she could find. After thoroughly tossing the hall closet, living room, and office, she headed for the bedroom. She started by looking under the bed. Nothing but a few dust bunnies. She went through every dresser and the closet. Still, there was nothing.

Danni sat on the floor. "Nothing. Not even a picture of my mom or a guy...or a lost sister."

"Maybe Max wasn't sentimental?"

Danni shook her head. "Look at the walls." She pointed to the walls with her hands. "They're filled with mementos and pictures."

"Maybe she removed the pictures after the people died. Maybe she didn't like to be reminded."

Danni nodded slowly, then stopped. A thought crossed her mind. "There has to be more. Something she wants me to find. Why else was it so important for me to be the one who takes care of her personal effects? Why did it have to be me?"

Fisher shrugged. "Maybe she just wanted you here."

Danni shook her head. "She could have told you to make sure I stayed for Darby. Why did she specifically say she wanted me to take care of her personal effects?"

Fisher shook his head. "Does it really matter?"

Danni bit her lip. "You're right. It doesn't really matter."

He took her hand and pulled her in for a kiss. His hands moved down her waist as his lips moved from her mouth to her throat. Danni closed her eyes, enjoying the feel of his lips on her skin until she remembered intimacy with her could only ever be fun and games. It was hard to feel sexy when all she could think about was how Fisher would have been better off if she'd never told him how she felt.

When she pushed away from him, he looked hurt and confused. Danni grabbed at the only distraction she could think of— "The potting shed! Maybe Max left something there."

Fisher sighed and let her go.

Chapter 35

Fisher wrapped his arms around Danni's waist and nibbled on the smooth skin of her neck. "Are we done with the treasure hunt? Can we get back to more important things?" She turned into him, returning his kiss. Danni tried to lose herself in the kiss and relax, but the morning had been too full of snags. She should be happy she wouldn't ever be burdened by family, but she wasn't. The very thought of it hurt like hell.

She wrapped her arms around Fisher's neck and nestled into his warm strength. Wrapped tight in strong arms, she could almost forget all that was bothering her. Almost, but not quite.

"Is the family mystery bothering you this much?" Fisher asked.

Danni shook her head. "It's not just that. I don't get why Max wanted me to be the one to find nothing."

"Maybe to Max, it wasn't nothing. She was very private. Maybe she didn't even want anyone but you to know the balance of her bank account. That need for privacy doesn't necessarily mean she had something to hide."

"That's true. But still—it doesn't mean there isn't."

Fisher hugged her tighter. "That's not all that's bugging you. What is it?"

Danni thought of her infertility but couldn't bring herself to discuss that—especially after the visit from Tori. Losing him to some vague notion hurt, but the idea of losing him to Tori made her want to vomit.

"Come on, Danni. Talk to me."

Danni swallowed and said, "The visit with the attorney was

unsettling too. I thought Darby's adoption was complete, but it seems I still have to jump through some hoops to keep her."

Fisher sighed like he was relieved. "No wonder you're tense today." He kissed her cheek. "It'll be all right. And," he kissed her again, "no matter what, I'll be with you every step of the way."

Danni nodded, but her mind was still occupied with worries.

Fisher stood and offered her his hand. "Come on. Let's start planning this renovation. It will get your mind focused on something you can fix."

Danni took his offer and allowed him to pull her to her feet.

"Since you're rich, I'm calling in a work crew and some contractors. We can put your flip on steroids. I need to make sure you have a way to make an income fast, so you aren't tempted to leave me."

"But what if I get tired of sand?"

"Then I will follow you wherever you go."

Instantly, tears filled Danni's eyes. "You would leave here for me?"

He nodded. "I'm not losing you ever again."

Danni threw herself at him with such force she knocked the breath from his lungs. He wrapped his hands around her waist, taking a step back to steady himself.

"That's the sweetest thing you've ever said." She kissed him. She was so focused on him, she didn't hear the door open and close.

"Seriously guys, it's a hotel—plenty of rooms," Darby said from the doorway.

Danni released her grip on him and allowed her feet to return to the floor.

"Hey kid, how was school?"

Darby looked around the place. There were boxes of papers, books, and pictures scattered around the living room. Darby weaved past the boxes and dropped onto the couch and kicked off her shoes. "You guys have been busy today."

"Yeah, I know," Fisher said. "I missed the lunch that someone promised me because she wanted to toss closets like she was on an FBI raid." Fisher stared at Danni as he spoke. "Now, I'm starving."

Danni grinned.

"Me too," Darby said. "Chinese would be great tonight. Order me some take out, Danni, and I'll help you clean up your mess."

"I'll go," Fisher offered.

"Lo mein noodles and General Tso's with white rice...and an egg roll." Darby looked at Danni. "I skipped lunch too. I'm also starved."

"Get me whatever," Danni said. Fisher gave her a kiss before leaving.

"You guys look good together," Darby said once Fisher had gone.

"It feels good. I just wish—"

"I was thinking about that today. Let's say it was me—what would you say?"

"If what was you?" Danni was confused.

"If I couldn't have kids, would you tell me no man would ever want to marry me?"

Danni sighed. "Of course not. And it's not that—it's just complicated."

"Not really. You guys love each other."

Danni rubbed the back of her neck. "That's not what matters right now. There's also the information I got from Max's attorney."

Danni filled her in on the information about the money and the adoption.

"Max was a millionaire? Who knew?" Darby said.

"She definitely never acted like she had any money," Danni said.

"She was a special lady," Darby said. "I'm so lucky my mother wandered into this place. Can you imagine what would have happened to me if she'd have booked a room at a Holiday Inn? I'd ended up in social services instead of with Max."

"Max would say there is no luck, only providence," Danni said.

"We seriously need that wall of Maxisms," Darby suggested.

"And we will. Now that we know we can redecorate."

"Frugally. We can do it on the cheap — in Max's honor."

Danni smiled. "That would be a great idea."

"Do you think there will be any problems with the adoption? Is that why you're worried?"

Danni shook her head. She would never admit she was nervous about the situation. Instead, she took a deep breath and assured the girl things would be fine.

Fisher returned with the food, so they went to the kitchen to eat. During dinner, Darby got a text and asked if it would be all right if she hung out with friends. Danni agreed and sent her on her way, waving goodbye from the front porch.

When she stepped inside, Fisher was waiting on her. He pulled her to him, holding her as he planted kisses on her lips and undid the buttons on her blouse. "Can I have a bit of your time, Ms. Lowry, to ravish you before the next shoe drops?"

Chapter 36

Fisher was right. Focusing on the renovations took her mind off her past and her future. After a few weeks of painting and yard work, the place was beginning to look as picture-perfect as her mind remembered. She even devoted some energy to the back yard, planting both a flower and a vegetable garden.

Knowing how to plant what wasn't as simple as slapping paint on walls, so she called Maureen, who drove the twenty minutes up the island to help in person. Maureen sat on a lawn chair in the grass with a straw hat on her head and a glass of lemonade in her hand. "I'd help dig, Danni, but the hip...."

"Oh no, don't worry. It's nice to have the company and the direction. I kept planning to plant things in Oregon, but I never got around to it."

"I quit gardening a few years ago. Max never did. That girl did love to dig in the dirt."

"Yes, she did." Danni stuck the last tomato in the hole she'd dug in the sand and carefully lined the hole with potting soil and a bit of fertilizer. "Speaking of Max," Danni said, leaning back on her heels. "Did Max ever tell you she had another sister?"

Maureen looked at her, dumbfounded. "Now who told you that?"

"Tori."

Maureen shook her head. "Always the trouble stirrer, that one."

"I have to agree there." Danni pulled off her gloves and wiped the sweat from her brow. "But was she lying? Or is it true? Was there a third Lowry daughter?"

Maureen took a deep breath. "There was, but she was much younger than Max and Vi."

"Why did Max never mention her?"

Maureen shrugged. "I don't know that Max ever met the girl. You see, Max moved out of her parents' house and bought this hotel when she was in her twenties. Not long after that, her parents, your grandparents, decided to move to the mainland, and Vi moved in with Max."

"She didn't go with her parents?"

Maureen shook her head. "No. I assume Vi, being a teen at the time, probably didn't want to change schools and such."

"Don't you think it's odd that Max never mentioned having another sister?"

Maureen gave her a look—a mix of disappointment and concern. "Max never told you anything, did she?"

Danni shook her head.

Maureen frowned. "She probably never mentioned the girl because she never met her. She died in a house fire. They all died. Your grandparents and the daughter."

Danni covered her mouth with her hand. "That's awful."

Maureen nodded. "They weren't close. After your grandparents moved, it was like Max and Vi cut all ties with them. Maybe they had a row about something."

"Poor Max. What about the boyfriend? Fisher mentioned she had a boyfriend. Was she serious about him?"

Maureen sighed. "Oh yes, she loved him."

"Did they break up?"

Maureen shook her head. "No, he died in that same wreck that I got the bum hip. Afraid it was my husband who was driving. We were all headed to the beach. My George, big Fisher, and Daniel were all up front. Me, Max, and Kitty were in the back." Maureen stopped talking and licked her lips as tears pooled in her eyes. "There was a semi-truck. It crossed the center line and hit us head on." Maureen wiped away a stray tear. "None of the men...had a chance. Lord, was that a trial. There were days when I didn't think I'd ever get over it. But then there was my Jake. He was just a little boy. I came home from the hospital, ready to drink myself into oblivion, but my little boy met me on the porch and asked me where his daddy was. I knew then I didn't have the luxury of self-pity. I lost my husband, but my baby lost his father."

Danni gave her hand a pat. Maureen gave her a grateful smile. "And Max had Vi, and then you to get her through." Maureen took a deep breath. "Kitty, of course, found Bill." Maureen fiddled with her earring. "I suppose I shouldn't judge. Kitty was never strong...and little Fisher had Max. She was just a walk down the path away." Maureen gave her a smile. "That's probably how you and Fisher became as inseparable as you were as children. You two have been together since you were in diapers."

Danni laughed. "That's almost a little creepy. Like he's my brother."

Maureen was in the process of taking a sip of lemonade and choked on it. She laughed. "You're bad, Rodanthe Luna." Maureen gave her gray head a shake. "I will tell you one thing that boy never saw you as a sister. He'd always tell us that he was going to marry you."

"Seriously?"

Maureen nodded. "As a matter of fact, I was babysitting Fisher when he was—oh, I'd say five or six. He asked me why Jake didn't have to have a dad. Fisher wasn't too keen on Bill moving in and kept looking to get him out of the house. He just couldn't understand why his momma had to go and bring another man in when she had him. And me and Jake making it without a man added fuel to his fire." Maureen pressed the cool glass of lemonade to her cheek. "So anyhow, I thought of what I could say to this little boy—a little fella that was always a little too keen for his small britches—so I told him that George was my soulmate...that some people were put on earth with a single perfect match, and I had found and lost mine."

"Did he understand?"

Maureen nodded. "A little too well. He gave me that stare—you know the one—put his hands on his hips, and said, 'Then my soulmate is Danni. I'm gonna marry her.' Of course, we all thought it was the cutest thing...and we were all more than a little disappointed when you married Rick." Maureen smiled and held up her glass as if making a toast. "But Rick is gone, so here's to second chances." With the garden finished, Maureen struggled a bit to stand from her chair. "Seems like it's lunchtime. Why don't you get cleaned up, and I'll whip up some lunch?"

"You don't have to do that."

"Of course, I don't have to, but I'd like to. It feels be good to be here. I used to while away many hours in this old place; it's like being home."

Danni gave her a hug. "Then great. It looks like I'm going to finally get a good meal. I haven't had one of those in...years."

Maureen gave Danni's arm a playful slap. "Listen to you."

"It's total truth."

Danni set her loose in the kitchen and went to the bathroom to wash up. The front door opened and closed. It was too early to be Darby. Danni's heart raced. She ran from the bathroom. Standing in the doorway was Fisher.

"I knocked, but no one heard me."

Maureen was singing "Shall We Gather at the River" as she cooked. Danni smiled. "I was washing up. Maureen is making lunch."

"Aren't you one of the lucky ones?"

"You can be too." Danni grabbed his shirt and pulled him to her. Her heart felt near bursting. Could this perfect man truly love her enough to overcome anything? The warmth in his eyes told her yes. Her lips were so close to him; she could feel his breath. "To get lucky, all you have to do is stick around."

His smile brushed against her lips. "I've no intention of going anywhere."

Chapter 37

Fisher hated to leave her. She snuggled into her pillow, eyes heavy, her lips still full from his kisses. He brushed his thumb down her cheek, and she smiled drowsily. Darby had gone with Maureen to spend the night. Seems Maureen not only got WiFi, she got a television package she had no clue how to set up. Darby offered to go with her and help.

Fisher was just glad he didn't have to sneak off at the break of dawn. He'd like to curl up with her and sleep into the afternoon, but he had a work crew coming. He had a plan he was anxious to put in place, a plan that would put a permanent end to him having to sneak in and out.

He kissed her cheek, pulling the blankets up around her shoulders before heading to the shower. He lathered and rinsed with thoughts of his future. Their future. Their life together. Feeling refreshed and clean, he headed outside to meet with the four guys he had coming to help with the renovations.

As the men arrived, he gave them jobs to do. He hoped to get this place finished in another month. Danni had worked hard, getting everything stripped, cleared, and scrubbed. He was having the rest finished by his crew. The porches would only need a few more spindles and a few replacement boards on the floors. The biggest job was going to be busting up the concrete in the back and pouring a new pad around the pool. Then the outside would be complete, and they could work on the inside.

He and his men worked all morning. It was almost noon before Danni woke. She came outside freshly showered and dressed. "Hey," she walked up to him. "You should've woken me."

He wrapped a hand around her waist and pulled her closer. "I figured I better let you get some rest; I'd hate to wear you out."

"I've never felt more energized." She kissed his cheek.

"My supercharge worked for you, did it?"

"It was that or the nap." She gave him a kiss and a wink before turning to look over the hotel. "It's looking amazing. You guys fixed the spindles, and the roof no longer looks like horror movie wreckage."

"It just needed a few more spindles and some new boards. They're installing new gutter spouts. That will help keep that area from rotting out again." He took her by the hand and took her for a tour of what they had finished.

"It's looking good."

"It's coming along." He put his hands on her hips and turned her to face him. "I have an idea I want to run by you."

"All right."

"Come with me."

She followed him through the office to the private living space. "Okay, so what I was thinking was this. We could expand Darby's room by busting out the wall between her room and the hall closet. We close off the door to the closet and the door to the bathroom and add a door to her room, so she has an en suite. And turn that closet into a small study for her."

"I'm sure she'd love that, but we need the closet for storage. And we only have one bathroom. I'd have to go into her room to bathe."

"Then, in your room...," he led her down the hall to her room, "We make a door here, take one of the rooms to rent off the list, and turn it into your bedroom with your own en suite. Then we take your room and reconfigure it—make you a walk-in closet, add a powder room for the office, and then you'll still have enough space for an office that I could use as my own workspace."

Danni looked around the space. "I think Darby would love that, and I suppose losing one room wouldn't be such a big deal—wait, what did you say?"

"We could bust out—"

"No, the part about you having a workspace."

"I need a workspace. I thought about turning the apartment into a rentable space and asking you and Darby to come live with me, but then I figured that was stupid. When Darby becomes an adult, I'm sure she'll want to live here, so she can have my house. But until then, once you marry me, we'll need to make this space work for all of us until Darby is old enough to take it over."

"Marry you?"

"I'm assuming you want to marry me. You're seriously not just using me for my body, are you?"

Danni bit her lip. "Oh no, Fisher, we really need to talk about this—"

"Fisher," Luke yelled from the doorway. "We have a problem out here."

"Hell," Fisher looked down at her. "Hold the thought. We'll discuss this later."

Chapter 38

Danni was grateful for the reprieve. Things were going too well to start talking about the future. Right now was perfect bliss. She felt loved and desired...and happier than she had been in her life. Her world was in perfect harmony. But it wouldn't be as soon as Fisher knew that a life with her would mean the sacrifice of family. She bit her lip and blinked away the tears.

Fisher's voice carried through the open door, pulling her from her reverie. "You're kidding me, right? Damn bureaucrats. If it's not one damned thing, it's another."

Danni rushed to join him. He was talking to a uniformed city worker — Seth, according to his name tag.

"You know the rules, Fisher — probably better than anyone. You have to cease working until you have a permit."

"I applied for a permit, Seth. And I do know the rules. We're prepping the place for paint. I don't need a permit to paint an existing structure."

Seth looked around the hotel and nodded. "Can I look inside? Verify that you're not making any major structural changes? The complaint says you're doing interior renovations that exceed the $15,000 limit."

"Go to hell," Fisher said.

"Come on in," Danni said. She laid a hand on Fisher's arm. "He's just doing his job, Fish."

"Just let me have a look, and I'll verify that you're in compliance, and then I'll speed up your permit process, so you're not slowed down."

"Whatever. Danni, you can take him on a tour of the place. I have work to do."

"Come with me." Danni motioned to Seth.

"I appreciate this." Seth wiped away the sweat beading above his brow. "We drew straws in the office over who had to come and tell Fisher Cooper to halt work."

Danni took him through the private apartment and then on a quick tour of each room, opening each door one after the other. "You guys sure are diligent. Do you check every project so thoroughly?"

"Someone called in a complaint. If we didn't follow up, she'd have just kept rocking the boat until we had state inspectors nagging at us."

"She, huh?" Danni frowned. She knew the cake and friendly drop in was a ruse. "One guess who the hell that was," she said to Seth.

"They're confidential reports, but…." Seth paused to rub his ear. "I'd say if you guessed hot blonde, you guessed right."

Danni sighed and shook her head.

They finished their tour of the place.

"I'll put this in as a bogus report." Seth scribbled on the paper on his clipboard. "And I'll make sure you have your work permits by the end of the workday."

"I appreciate that." Danni breathed a sigh of relief. Seth appeared to be in his early forties with a soft gut and thinning hair, so she'd have guessed he'd have been at risk for falling for Tori's long legs and D cup. "Would you like a cold drink? Sandwich or anything?"

"I'd love a beer since this is no longer an official visit."

"Isn't that the island way?"

"Well, I will tell you island-friendly-like—it was a hell of a morning. A visit from Tori Smith, forcing us to shut down the worst tempered contractor on the island is not the best way to start a day."

"I totally understand. Let's get you that beer." Danni led him to the kitchen. "I have Bud Light and Weeping Radish dark brew."

"I'll take the dark brew. I'm a big supporter of local

businesses."

"And it's the best." Danni opened the fridge and pulled out a pint bottle and popped it open. She filled a glass and handed it to Seth.

He took a long drink and let out a relieved sigh.

"I'm so grateful you seem to be immune to Tori's charms." Danni poured the remainder of the beer into a glass for herself. "You could have made our lives miserable with red tape."

"Immune...yes, that's what I am." Seth pulled a hanky out of his pocket and wiped the sweat from his forehead again. "She tricked my cousin into marrying her years ago. She did that old, 'I'm pregnant,' trick."

"What happened to the baby?"

"There was no baby. It was a lie."

Danni shook her head. "Who does that?"

"A psychopath. Free piece of advice for ya, watch your back if she's out to get you."

Danni lifted her glass and tapped Seth's. "I hear ya. I take it she and your cousin are divorced?"

"She ditched him when Fisher got out of the navy."

Danni took a drink. "I suppose I can't blame her for that."

"I doubt you would." He drained the rest of his beer. "Much appreciated."

"I take it the inspection is over," Fisher said from the doorway.

"Yes," Seth answered, hands shaking a bit as he handed Danni his glass. "I best get going. Thank you for the libation, Ms. Lowry. I'll be in touch."

"Thank you." Danni walked Seth to the door.

After he left, she turned to Fisher. His arms were crossed over his chest, and he looked grim.

"Is something wrong?" she asked.

"I was just wondering if he came for business or pleasure."

"Business," Danni said. "Seems we have Tori to thank for the complaint."

Fisher's brow furrowed. "He said that?"

"Yep."

"To be honest, I'm not sure I trust the information gotten

from a guy who's willing to drink on the job. He was probably telling you what you wanted to hear."

"No, I asked him if they were always this diligent, and he said they had a complaint."

"And you assumed Tori?"

It was Danni's turn to cross her arms over her chest. "Are you taking up for her?"

"No, I'm not taking up for her, but I'm not going to trash her by accusing her without proof that she did it. She's been pretty understanding of everything."

"Oh, she's understanding, all right. She understands how to pull the wool over your eyes. Sugar wouldn't melt in her mouth, but I knew better than to believe she was anything but the conniving little—"

"Holy shit, Danni, ease up. She wants to be your friend."

Danni sneered at him. "My ass. If she wanted to be my friend, she wouldn't try to shut down my project."

"You don't know—"

"So, my word isn't good enough? Not to mention, who else would know you were even planning to renovate the inside of the hotel? Hell, Tori knew before I did. I assume she got that information from your little friend chats."

"You're changing the subject. We were talking about the guy who's supposed to be doing his job, but pauses for a cozy chat and a beer with a woman he barely knows—? I find his word and his motives to be questionable. Not to mention, everyone knows Seth hates Tori and blames her for divorcing his asshole cousin."

Danni bit her lip. It sure did sound like he was still firmly a Tori fan. Irritation and jealousy left her speechless, so she turned and left the room.

Fisher was right behind her. He grabbed her arm and pulled her to him. She shoved away from him.

"Don't be mad at me." Fisher wouldn't let go of her.

"Fine, who can I be mad at? Not Tori, oh no, she's perfect. She brings the cake that you can't resist."

"Okay, maybe she did it—"

"Don't patronize me, Fisher."

"I'm sorry. It's just—we have no proof she did anything wrong. She's been a good sport about all of this."

"Poor, poor Tori. Maybe you should go comfort her."

"Come on, don't be ridiculous."

Danni spun loose and left the room. There was nothing more she wanted to say or hear. She couldn't prove it, but she knew Tori was at the bottom of everything bad that had happened in her life. Fisher could act like she was crazy, but Danni knew. Just because something didn't sound rational didn't mean it was ridiculous.

Chapter 39

Fisher chased Danni to her room, closing the door behind him. "I'm going to talk; you're going to listen."

He regretted his words as soon as they flew out of his mouth. Danni turned on him, eyes wide, jaw clenched. "I'm not a child. I'm not crazy. If you want to be buddies with Tori, get the hell out of my house and go to it."

Fear and disappointment hit him like a wave. "Seriously, Danni? You're going to jeopardize everything we have over a disagreement?"

Her eyes filled with tears, and she turned away from him. "You should go. I need some time alone."

"No." He blocked the door. "We need to talk about this."

"Fine." Danni sat in the side chair by the bed.

"Fisher," a worker called from the door. "You need to come out here. We have a problem."

"Again?" he yelled back.

"Afraid so."

It sounded serious. Danni watched him leave. Part of her wanted to follow and see what the problem was; the other part wanted to run away and cry.

Fisher defended her enemy. Not to mention, he had to still be talking to her. There was no explanation for that other than he still had feelings for her. Maybe he didn't love Tori, but he could. If Danni was out of the way. If she had never returned to the island, Fisher would probably be planning a wedding and a future with Tori—one where he'd have kids.

Being inside was suffocating. She had to leave. She'd barely made it out of the parking lot before Fisher caught up with her. She heard his footsteps coming up behind her. Like a woman suddenly possessed with a pre-pubescent mind, she started to speed up.

It was no use. Fisher grabbed her around the waist and pulled her to him. "No more running from me. I love you. You're not just leaving me every time you get your nose bent out of shape."

"Nose bent out of shape? Excuse me, but—"

Her phone rang. She looked at the caller ID. It was the social worker assigned to Darby's case. They'd met with the caseworker twice and were assured the adoption was a done deal. Why the phone call? Danni turned away from him to talk.

"Ms. Lowry? This is Bev Johnston."

"Hi, Ms. Johnston. Is there a problem?"

The woman paused. "Let's call it a hitch. Is there any way you could come to my office this afternoon?"

"Of course, I can. What time?"

"Two-ish?"

"I'll be there. Should my attorney be there?"

Another pause. "It couldn't hurt."

Danni hung up the phone and covered her mouth with her hand. She suddenly felt nauseous.

Fisher stepped in front of her. "What's wrong?"

Danni's chest felt tight, and it was suddenly very hard to breathe.

"Who was on the phone?" Fisher asked.

Danni's voice was quiet. "The lady from social services. She said there is something wrong. I need to go in and meet with her."

"I'll go with you."

"I need to call Claire. She said an attorney might not be a bad idea." Danni walked back toward the hotel. "Oh my God, if I lose Darby…."

Danni's hands shook. Fisher grabbed them and held them. "Listen to me, it is probably some legal mumbo jumbo. We'll go and meet with her and get this all figured out."

Danni nodded. He was right. There was no need to panic. Not

yet. Her body started to shiver, which was ridiculous because the sun was shining, and the weather report said they would enjoy a high of sixty. It felt subzero to Danni.

"Come on, I'll drive." Fisher dragged her by her hand. "You okay? You're freezing."

"It's just a chill."

Fisher opened his truck door and handed Danni his jacket. She put it on, stuffing her hands in the pockets. Her hand bumped against a package. She pulled out a small bag with a velvet box inside.

Her heart skipped a beat. He'd bought a ring? That was so sweet. And awful. How was she going to tell him no?

"Danni, I can explain." He grabbed at the bag.

Curious, Danni pulled the box out of the bag and lifted the lid. It was a typical diamond ring—nothing special, but nothing to apologize for. There was a receipt in the bag. Fisher tried to grab it, but she turned from him as she read it. The ring was bought at the beginning of March—before they were a "thing," but after she'd returned to the island.

Slowly, it dawned on her. "This is for Tori."

He grabbed her by the arm as if he expected her to bolt on him again. "It was for Tori, but—"

"And you just carry it around in your pocket? Why? In case the perfect moment pops up?" Danni pulled her arm away. "God, I have been such an idiot."

"I was going to return it. That's why it was in my pocket."

Danni shrugged out of the coat. "Go home, Fisher. I don't want you here."

"It was stupid of me. I don't know why I bought it. I still thought you were married. I—"

"I don't want to hear it. Not now." Danni went back inside, grabbing her purse and the car keys off the desk. Her heart felt like it was being ripped in half, but she couldn't worry about that right now. She was too busy trying to think of what in the hell could've gone wrong with the adoption. Did a relative crawl out of the woodwork?

She turned to leave and bumped into Fisher. "Excuse me,"

she snapped.

"Danni."

"Don't Danni me. I've already told you I am not talking about this. Not right now. Maybe not ever. Maybe I'm just what's novel for the moment. This back-and-forth you have going on with Tori, maybe that's what you're meant for. You guys definitely have a connection I thought I could deal with, but I'm lying to myself."

"If you're saying it's you or her, I want you."

"I shouldn't have to ask you to choose. That should have been the natural choice for you—if you knew me. If you loved me like you claim."

Chapter 40

Fisher felt like a fool. He should have understood the extent of her fury and predicted she'd give him the slip.

"Go let Punkin in, Fisher," he said, mocking the words Danni used to sneak away from him. He made it outside in time to see her speed away, sending a spray of gravel across the parking lot.

Luke came up behind him and gave his shoulder a squeeze. "She'll calm down."

"Or kill herself with her goddamned temper."

"Meeting her head on won't help anything. You need to calm down and talk to her."

Fisher took a deep breath. "I need to catch her."

"You're not going to catch her. Traffic is too heavy. Where is she headed?"

"Social service office."

"Then you know where to find her. Come on, I'll drive."

"I can drive."

"Your truck is filled with everything the guys need to keep working. We'll take my car so they can stay on track."

Fisher nodded. He followed Luke to his car and climbed in the passenger seat. "I can't believe she gave me the slip. It's like I'm dating fucking Wonder Woman."

"She did move fast. I didn't see it coming."

"She had motivation—keep Darby and ditch me."

"What happened?"

"She found the ring I had for Tori in my coat pocket."

"You got Tori a ring?"

"It was before...when I thought Danni was getting back with

her husband."

"Why did you have it in your pocket?"

"I was going to return it and forgot."

Luke chuckled. "You dumb bastard. What the hell were you thinking?"

"I wasn't thinking. When Danni first came back...." Fisher looked out the window. How did he explain how much it hurt to have her close, but think he could never have her? Was it a reasonable explanation to say he hurt so bad, he'd have done whatever it took to make the pain stop? He sighed. "I can't explain it. I wasn't using my head."

Luke nodded. "You'll work it out. You're meant to be together."

Fisher scratched his head and nodded.

Luke pulled into the social services parking lot as Danni was getting out of her car. She looked at them over the hood of her car. As pissed as she was at him, she still seemed to be relieved to see him.

As Fisher got out, she said, "Claire can't make it."

"I'll go with you." He wrapped an arm across her shoulders. "It's going to be all right."

She nodded but said nothing.

Together they walked into the building and gave their name and the name of the worker to the receptionist. She escorted them to an office.

Bev Johnston was sitting at her desk and stood when they arrived. "You must be Danni. It's so nice to meet you. Max always spoke highly of you."

"Max was the best." Danni sat in a seat. She held onto her purse, but he could still see them shaking.

"Okay, so I can tell from the look on your face that you're worried."

"Yeah, is there a problem?"

Bev sighed. "Just another hurdle in the process."

"But, it's still in process?"

Bev smiled. "Most certainly. I interviewed Darby this morning at the school, and she is as eager as you are to get this done."

Danni breathed a sigh of relief. "So, what is it?"

Bev laid her hands on her desk and took a deep breath. "There has been a report filed that you suffered a psychotic episode recently — hallucinations, a possible suicide attempt?"

Danni looked at Fisher. If looks could kill, she'd have left him for dead. Fisher cleared his throat. "After Max's funeral, Danni was in a car wreck that caused her to have a head injury. She was treated at the hospital and released."

"I figured it was something like that, but I couldn't check it out and verify everything was kosher without getting Danni to sign a release for me to access her medical records."

Danni grabbed a pen from the cup holder on Bev's desk. "Of course, what do I sign?"

"Good. I figured you'd feel that way, but you never know. Some people get weird about releasing their medical records."

"No, no problem. I was really scared after you suggested I consult my attorney."

"It's always good to consult your attorney. I'll never suggest otherwise," Bev said.

"And as far as the suicide idea — that's absurd. I was upset after the funeral and failed to look both ways. Nothing more than stupidity. I'm sure whoever made this report mentioned my mother jumped off the Bonner Bridge?"

Bev nodded.

"Well, that's true, but that was my mother. She was a teenaged parent with mental issues. If you need more information on my mother's issues, you could call Maureen Privett. She is —"

"I know Maureen." Bev smiled at her. "Relax, Danni. I'll request your medical records and send them along to our psychologist, and I'm sure everything will be fine." Bev dug a paper out of a drawer and handed it to Danni. "Just fill out any places I could get medical records — like family doctor, places you've been treated. The more information I can get, the quicker he can make an assessment."

"Of course." Danni grabbed the paper and started filling it out.

Fisher watched her write. His heart sank when he realized Tori was right—second on her list was Summit Hill Fertility Clinic.

The idea of Danni trying to have a baby with her ex suddenly made her marriage seem too real. Until this moment, her marriage was just a mistake in his mind. Not two people sharing a life and trying for a family.

"Are you coming, Fish? Or are you staying here?"

Danni was standing, purse over her shoulder, ready to go. He stood. "Yeah, I'm coming. Nice to meet you, Ms. Johnston."

By the time they made it to the parking lot, Danni had pulled away from him. He didn't realize her short legs could move so fast, but his stride was longer, so he kept pace without a problem. When she stopped to unlock her car, he forced her to look at him. "We need to talk."

"I don't want to talk to you right now. There is only one way Tori knew about the hallucinations."

"You think I told Tori?"

Danni nodded. "No, Fisher, I don't think. I know you told her. Just like you obviously told her about the renovations. The only thing I don't know is why you're wasting your time with me."

"I think I've been pretty open about that—I love you. That's why I'm with you."

"Well, I'm not sure that's enough to make this work."

"Come on, Danni." He tried to hold her, but she shoved him. "Whatever is wrong, we can work it out."

"No, I don't think so," Danni hissed the words at him. "You obviously love Tori, and as much as it kills me to admit, you're better off with her."

"I love you. I don't know why I bought that ring—it was a momentary lack of sanity. You were telling me how Rick called and wanted you back, and I guess I felt lonely. But I never gave it to her. I knew it was a mistake. I knew she could never mean to me an iota of what you mean to me."

Danni shook her head. "It's over."

He grabbed her by the shoulders and made her look up at

him. "It is not. I love you. You love me. The rest is just details."

"I was never going to marry you," Danni whispered. "Never. This was always going to be temporary. Accept that and stop wasting our time."

Stunned, he let her go. She took advantage of the separation, hopped in her car, and drove away.

Fisher stood in the parking lot and looked for his truck, then cursed when he realized he didn't have a ride back. How could everything in his life go to hell in the blink of an eye?

"Mr. Cooper?"

Fisher turned to see Bev running out of the building toward him. "I was hoping to catch Danni," she said. "But maybe you can help me. This clinic she listed...." Bev handed him the paper. "It doesn't exist. I tried the number, and it was disconnected, so I called social services in Oregon, and they told me there is no Summit Hill Fertility Clinic."

Fisher looked it over. "That is curious. Maybe Danni made a mistake. I'll ask her and give you a call."

Chapter 41

Fortunately for Fisher, Luke had waited in the parking lot for him. He must have known the rift between him and Danni was going to take more than a simple apology.

"Was it bad?"

Fisher nodded. "Someone reported to the welfare worker that Danni was having some…emotional issues after the funeral."

"Tori?"

Fisher rubbed his head. "It's not anything Tori would know about."

Luke pulled out of the parking lot. "Still not seeing it, are you?"

"I'm not trying to protect her, I swear. But I can't blame her without some proof."

"Well, sewage lines are plugged too. Talked to Chris, and he guesses cat litter. He wants to know what you want him to do."

"Cat litter? Max didn't even own a cat."

"The lines were never a problem. They were fine this morning. The crew went to lunch, and when they got back, the toilets wouldn't flush."

"You think Tori put the cat litter down the sewage cleanout?"

Luke nodded. "She knows real estate. She knows we'll have to dig up that whole damned line and replace it. And Seth was probably telling the truth about it being Tori asking that our permits be checked. You know what they say about a woman scorned."

"She said she was fine with being friends. If you and Danni are right, Tori is deranged."

Luke gave him a look then concentrated on the road.

"Damn it, Luke. I'm not in the mood for games. What was that look for?"

Luke gripped the steering wheel. "You seriously don't realize that Tori is a huge game player? Seriously, I hate that bitch. The shit she does to my wife, the whole time pretending to be her friend. She's pure poison."

"And you've kept this opinion from me for how many years?"

Luke threw a hand in the air. "Hell, you liked her. I didn't want to piss you off. And I thought maybe she was just snarky to women. Like, after Tina had the baby, Tori would make comments about Tina's weight. Or how tired she looked. Or how the house looked. It was always these snide little remarks that made my wife a basket case."

"Why does Tina stay friends with her?"

"Because my wife, instead of realizing that Tori is nothing more than a shallow, jealous little bitch, lets it all depress her. Every time she'd think Tori was evil, here comes Tori with dinner in a basket or a trip to the spa. It's like watching the abuse cycle of friendship — you know how men will beat their wives and then be nice, just to be assholes again? That's Tori."

"I never saw that side of her."

"Of course not. She never trusted you enough to show her true colors. She knows — like we all know — that you love Danni."

Fisher took a deep breath. "That I do, but it doesn't seem to ever matter."

Luke slowed down as they approached his house.

"Why are you stopping? Take me home. I need to get my truck and find Danni."

"Maybe Tina can help. Maybe Danni will talk to her. I mean, no offense, buddy, but I don't think Danni is going to listen to a damn thing you have to say right now."

Fisher took a deep breath and nodded.

At the house, Luke gave his wife a kiss on the cheek.

"What's going on?" Tina asked, backing into the kitchen as the men came into the house.

"Tori is on a rampage. She tried to have our job site shut

down, poured cat litter down our sewage pipe—"

"So, flush it," Tina said.

"As it moves through the pipes, it turns to concrete. We'll have to dig the whole line up."

"Oh my, I didn't realize—"

"Most people don't. That's how we know it's Tori," Luke said.

Tina went to the fridge. "Can I get you guys a bottle of water or a soda?"

"Grab us those Mt. Dews. And that tray of sandwiches," Luke said, looking over her shoulder. Tina pulled them out and set them on the table. Luke grabbed one and started eating. "Now, someone told the welfare people that Danni is crazy and put a hitch in the adoption of Darby."

Tina sat in a chair, eyes wide, mouth dropped open. "You're shitting me. Poor little Darby? Tori went after Darby?"

Fisher brushed off the offer of food and held the soda without opening it. "We don't know that it was her. Danni thought she was being haunted by Max. She thinks I told Tori and Tori told social services. But I didn't say a word."

"How would Tori know?" Tina asked.

Fisher thought a minute. Slowly, it dawned on him. "I bet it was the nurse at the hospital," Fisher said. "What was her name, Lisa or something...?"

"Curvy chick? Bleached hair?"

Fisher nodded.

"Cindy Bettleman. Well, you can damn sure bet if Nurse Cindy knows, Tori knows, and she's not at all squeamish about using half-truths and misunderstandings to her benefit. Look at the trouble Tori caused telling you about Renzo. Whisper a bit of harmless truth in the right ear, and you have years of cold shoulders."

"You mean when Danni cheated on me? That's a harmless truth?"

Tina shook her head. "Oh my God, you seriously think Danni cheated on you?"

Fisher nodded.

"You're such an idiot. Danni never cheated on you. I mean, for one, she wasn't dating you. Two, she didn't do anything."

"She admitted it," Fisher said.

"She, as in Danni or Tori?" Tina asked.

"Tori told me Danni was with him; I confronted Danni, and she admitted it was true."

"Danni said she had sex with Renzo?"

"Yes, she said she was with him."

"With him, like making out at a party...or with him biblically?"

Fisher felt a headache coming on. "What the hell difference does it make?"

"The difference is in one circumstance—Danni never fucked Renzo. Damn, you're thick-skulled," Luke said.

"Listen, Fisher." Tina's words were calm. "I don't know what or why Danni confessed to something she didn't do, but I was there the night she was with Renzo." Tina gave his arm a squeeze. "She was with him, but she didn't have sex with him. She was supposed to, but she changed her mind and had me take her to your house."

"What about the next night? Did he get to finish what they started the night before?"

Tina shook her head. "Danni was very upset by it all. I doubt very seriously she went back for round two."

"But I asked her, and she admitted it."

"Think about it, Fisher. What exactly did she admit to?"

"She said she was with him."

"And who was it who equated time spent together with having sex? Tori?"

Fisher nodded. His palms were sweating.

"Tori's good, Fish. She put an idea in your head and probably counted on your temper to sink Danni."

"What do you mean, my temper?" Fisher tried not to sound pissed, but his question still made Tina lean away from him.

"Tori knows you both. She probably knew if she told you Danni messed up, you'd jump on Danni with both feet and Danni, feeling guilty and embarrassed, would look guilty. You probably confronted her like a pit bull, she probably said she could explain, and you probably stormed out. Is that about right?"

"If she had done nothing, she could have just answered no. It wasn't a tough question."

"Maybe. But that would have been a lie. You asked her if she was with Renzo. The answer to that was yes. But did she have sex with Renzo? No, she didn't. I know; I was there."

Fisher wasn't convinced, not that it mattered. They'd gotten past all of this.

Tina stomped her foot on the floor. "Nothing happened—for anyone. Danni was alone with Renzo for maybe ten minutes, tops, before she came rushing out, begging to leave. Look, I know, teenage boys are fast. But my date had barely made it to first base when Danni ended the party."

"Are you sure? Tori said—"

"Oh my God, no wonder Danni is pissed at you. How can you not see what happened? Tori wanted you. Danni was in her way."

"Then why did she admit to being with him?" Fisher wondered aloud.

"I don't know. It's Danni. Why did she take credit for that damn snake eating the rabbit for all those years?"

"You knew about that?"

"Of course. The three of us had been friends since kindergarten. I knew it wasn't Danni."

"I need to talk to Danni."

"Hell yeah, you do." Tina stood as Fisher stood. "If there's anything I can do to help."

"Thanks."

Luke put his hand on Fisher's shoulder. "Listen, buddy, until things have calmed down, promise me you'll stay away from Tori. I don't want you to do anything you'll regret."

"I'd never hurt her, but trust me, I'll gladly steer clear of her."

Luke loaned him his car, and Fisher left. How had he been so blind to Tori's games? If everyone was right, Tori was insane. What wouldn't she do to get her own way? Hell, if she was pushed, would she hurt Danni? He couldn't rule out any behavior. She suddenly seemed capable of anything. Fear made his neck stiff. Everything he thought he had was in jeopardy.

He drove to the hotel, but it was empty. Not a soul was there, not even Punkin.

Chapter 42

Fisher unlocked the hotel and checked every room. They were all gone. Even the dog. He sat on the front porch in a rocker and waited. It was all he could do. All his texts and calls were being ignored. At some point in time, someone would have to come back to the hotel for something.

The first to arrive was Darby. The girl crossed her arms over her chest and gave Fisher a head shake.

Fisher stood.

"She's not home and won't be home any time soon," Darby said.

"You talked to her?"

Darby nodded.

"Where is she?"

"She doesn't want to see you right now."

"Come on, Darby."

The girl put her hand on her hip and gave him a look that made him cringe. "You hurt her. You hurt us. I was interviewed at school today — asked if I thought I was safe with Danni."

"I'm sorry, Darby."

"Staying with Danni, staying here," Darby said, "that's all I've asked for. You and your girlfriend tried to ruin that." Darby's eyes filled with tears, and that seemed to add to her irritation. She took a slow breath. "Danni trusted you. How could you tell that...thing...that Danni was mentally unstable?"

Fisher looked Darby in the eyes. "I swear to God, I had nothing to do with that. I'm pretty sure it was a nurse at the hospital. A friend of Tori's."

"You weren't sharing secrets with your *fiancée*?"

"No, I'd never do that to Danni, or to you."

"So you say."

"Come on, Darby. You know me better than that. Would I ever do anything to hurt you?"

Darby shrugged. "I guess not on purpose."

"You've got to believe me. I had nothing to do with the call to social services. I haven't told Tori a damn thing about Danni. I love Danni. I even told Tori to stop dropping by my house."

"When was that?"

"Last weekend."

Darby nodded. "You've probably pissed her off."

Fisher thought of the permit hassle and the kitty litter—she was definitely pissed off. "I need to talk to Danni. Please, where is she?"

"I'm not telling. I backed you in this. I told Danni to trust you. That makes me a fool too, and I don't like that."

"Come on, Darby, you have to tell me where she is."

"No. I don't." Darby pulled her purse to her chest, marched into the hotel, and slammed the door.

Fisher knocked on the door. "I'm not leaving, Darby," he yelled through the door. "I love her. You know I do." He kept knocking and knocking until Darby finally swung the door open.

"She and I are leaving tomorrow for Oregon."

"Why? How? I thought she was worried about the adoption. Is now the best time to leave?"

"She called Ms. Maureen and Ms. Claire, and they fixed it. She has my temporary custody. My adoption hearing is next Friday. No thanks to you."

"I didn't do anything."

"Oh yeah, right, it was the evil nurse."

Fisher dropped his body in a chair, cradling a much aching head in his hands. "I love her. Goddamn it, I can't lose her. I need to know where she is."

"You probably should have thought of that before you were so stupid."

"You're right. I was stupid. I've been stupid for years." Fisher tried to hold himself together. He wasn't going to lose it and start crying in front of a kid.

Darby sighed. She leaned against the door jam, studying him. "Are you serious that you love her?"

"Yes. She's all that matters."

"You're done with Tori?"

"If I went near her now, I'd probably snap her damn neck, so yes, I'm done with Tori."

Darby chewed on her lip. "Fine. Danni will probably be mad at me, but she's at the store buying some things for the plane."

"She's really leaving?"

Darby nodded. "At first, we were just going to pick up her stuff, but with all that's happened, we're going to see if I like it out there."

Fisher's heart dropped. "That's not funny, Darby."

"I'm not joking. She's like my sister. I feel her pain. How could I ask her to stay here a few feet from the guy who keeps ripping her heart out?"

"She can't leave. I have to talk to her."

Fisher got up and headed for his truck. There weren't that many stores on the island. He'd find her eventually.

"I don't know if you want to talk to her in public. She is seriously hurt and soooo pissed right now. You might want to let her cool off. Maybe talk to her when we get back?"

The back of his eyes burned. That wouldn't do. He couldn't let her get on a plane hating him. "No, it has to be tonight."

"Fine. Take me to your house, leave your truck there, and you can sneak back over and wait on her. But you've got to get your truck out of here. She sees it, she won't come home."

"Thank you, kid. I swear, anything you need, I owe you."

He took Darby to his house then hurried back to the hotel. Night was falling, and he was beginning to wonder if Danni would ever come home. When he heard a key slide into the front door lock, his heart stopped, and he hid in a dark corner of the office. Danni flipped on the light and kicked off her shoes before walking through the apartment to the shower.

He went to her room and sat on her bed, waiting for the water to stop. Suddenly nervous, he stood. Standing felt awkward, so he sat. He was debating whether or not he should go meet her as she came out of the bathroom, but while he was thinking it over, she opened the bedroom door and let out a scream.

He hopped off the bed. His throat was dry, and he could hear his heartbeat pounding in his ears. "I need to talk to you."

"Where's Darby?"

"She's at my house."

"Right. She's so mad at you, she'd never go there."

"I explained things to her. I think she likes me again."

Danni gripped her towel tighter to her body. He was so upset, he hadn't even appreciated that she was naked until now. He tried to pull her in, to hold her, but she sidestepped him.

"Please, Danni, I'm sorry."

"Sorry, doesn't fix this."

"I never told Tori. Remember the nurse at the hospital? Tori's wedding obsessed buddy?"

Danni nodded.

"It was her. It had to be. Tina said she has no doubt it was this Cindy woman. Her and Tori are tight, and remember when you were in the hospital, how rude she was to you?" He grabbed her hand. "I can't prove it was her, but I swear to you, I never said a word to Tori or anyone about you seeing Max."

Her face softened, and he felt a surge of hope, but then she frowned.

"No, don't look like that. Come on, Loonie. I love you."

"You know, Fisher, I don't doubt that you love me." Danni sat on the bed. "But I'm not sure that's enough."

He squatted in front of her, forcing her to look at him. "It's everything."

Danni shook her head. "I don't think so. You see, I'm realizing that you also love Tori."

"Bullshit."

"You protected her."

"I admit, I didn't see what you saw, and I didn't want to hurt her. That doesn't mean I love her."

"You bought her a ring. After I got here. That's not the actions of a guy thrilled to have me home."

"You'd told me Rick was calling, and he wanted you back. I wasn't in a good place." He took her hand in his. "The truth is, I didn't want to love you. I was afraid we'd end up here—you threatening to leave, and me feeling like the world is collapsing."

She didn't answer. She sat there, twisting wet hair around her finger and chewing on her lip.

"I was afraid." He inched a little closer. "Afraid that if I allowed myself to be more than your friend, I'd lose you again. This time forever. I thought if I could keep you as a friend, no matter what happened, you'd always be in my life. People don't dump friends. But they do dump boyfriends."

A tear rolled down her cheek. "Maybe that's what we should do. Go back to being friends."

He shook his head. "I can't be your friend. Not now. Not loving you like I do."

"You obviously have feelings for Tori...."

"Do you seriously believe that? Even if you leave me, I will never trust her again." Fisher let out a disgusted sigh and stood, feeling caged. "I can never forgive Tori for what she's done to us."

"Putting Darby in jeopardy was pure evil, but thanks to Maureen and her connections to almost every person on this island, that's worked out."

"It's not just that—it's everything. The permits, the cat litter—"

"The cat litter?"

"It doesn't matter, just more Tori bullshit." He took a step toward her. "I realize she's been causing us problems since that asshole Renzo."

The color drained from her face. "What has Renzo got to do with anything?"

"That night you came to my house—did you go out with him after that?"

"Of course not." She stood and headed for the door. "I'm not doing this, Fisher. I'm not at all proud of what happened that night, but I was a kid, and I'm done beating myself up over it."

"Stay, please."

She looked at him, her arms hugging her near-naked body tight.

"Please?" he asked.

Danni leaned against the door jam. "What does the crap with Renzo have to do with anything? I was eighteen years old. I don't think I should constantly have to pay for that one mistake."

"Tori told me you were with Renzo after you were with me."

"She what?"

"She told me you and Renzo were together Saturday night."

"No, it was Friday. And I was *with* him, but I wasn't *with* him."

"Why, when I asked you, didn't you tell me that eight years ago?"

"As I recall, you woke me up in the middle of the night, dragged me down to the dock, and screamed at me. You said to me, and I quote, 'Danni, it's a yes or no question, were you with Renzo?' When I tried to explain, you said there was no explanation and stormed off."

"I was too furious and too jealous to think straight."

Danni sat on the bed with him but left several feet between them. "Wow, so you really thought I was a little tramp. Did you on Friday, Renzo on Saturday. Did Tori have anyone for Sunday for me, or was that my day of rest?"

He reached for her, but she stood. She went to her suitcase and grabbed a pair of panties, and pulled them on. "You know, Fisher, I think this is the proverbial last straw. I felt guilty for so many years because I made out with a guy at a party, and I thought you were upset about it." She grabbed a shirt and pulled it over her head before dropping her towel. "Little did I know, you honestly thought I'd screw you, then him the next day."

"You said —"

When Danni answered him, the veins in her neck bulged. "You screamed at me. I sure as hell didn't get the benefit of the doubt. Since I've gotten here, you've defended Tori. Tori wants to be my friend. Tori can't be underhanded, she bakes people cakes and has the perfect fake smile." Danni struggled with a pair of jeans, trying to slip them on as she yelled. Frustrated, she threw them to the floor and grabbed a pair of sweatpants. She shook them at him as she spoke. "Do I ever get the kid gloves? No. At every turn, you've thought the worst of me. You obviously thought I was a tramp then, and after accusing me of a tete a tete with Seth, you obviously still think I'm a tramp now."

"I'm sorry. I know it sounds ridiculous, but it's harder for me to be rational where you're concerned. And it wasn't just Tori—everyone was talking about you and Renzo."

Danni managed to pull on the sweats. "And your ditching my ass like a hot potato helped me look guilty."

"Why didn't you talk to me?" He realized, as soon as the words left his mouth, that they were a mistake.

Danni picked up a tray of perfumes from the dresser and threw them at him. "You son of a bitch. I called you. I came to your house. You refused to talk to me." She turned and strode from the room, slamming the door behind her. He was off the bed and ready to follow her when the door opened, slamming off the wall with such intensity, a picture fell and shattered on the floor. "If you remember correctly, not only did you ignore me, but I left for school, and you didn't even come and say goodbye."

He grabbed her before she could leave the room again or chuck anything else at his head.

She slapped at him. "I hate you."

"I know," he said as he held her. She tried to wriggle away, punching at him, hitting him, but he wouldn't let her go. He held her until she was still.

"I will never forgive you," she said before the tears started to fall.

He carried her to the bed and held her as she cried. He didn't know if she was listening to him, but she was no longer fighting him, so he tried to convince her he loved her. "Danni, baby, you are my everything. Even as kids, you were my friend, my escape when my family went nuts. I've always loved you. I've always needed you."

She hiccupped and tucked her head under his chin. He closed his eyes and prayed that meant she was forgiving him. "I don't remember a time when I wasn't in love with you. When we were headed to high school, I wanted to tell you, but I could never get the courage."

She was still silent, but he could tell from her breathing that she was awake, and if she was awake, she was listening. "That first day of school, you looked perfect. I told myself I'd better step up or some other guy would, but damn, you scared the hell out of me. I imagined whispering in your ear, 'I love you.' But I could never bring myself to say it."

Danni finally spoke. "Can you imagine how different our lives would have been if you'd said it?"

"Would you have been my girlfriend?"

"Of course. I always loved you."

He tipped her chin until she had to look at him. "I don't want to be your friend. I want to love you. I want to be in love with you. Please, tell me you love me."

"You know I do. But it's not enough."

Chapter 43

Danni laid her head against his shoulder. His body was warm and firm and fit hers perfectly. She'd never find this again, so she would savor the moment. Danni was never much of a dreamer. She was a realist. Today, he loved her, and his blood ran hot for her, but that wouldn't last a lifetime. He needed perfection, and she could never fit that description. "I need to get ready to go."

"No. Not until you promise me you won't leave me."

"I already promised Darby I'd stay until she graduates." She regretted the comment. The look of hurt on his face sliced through her.

"I no longer matter? How I feel, the promises you've made me don't matter?"

"I never made you any promises."

He looked down on her. "That's cold."

"It's the truth."

"Bullshit."

Danni shrugged. "Now, I have to get ready, or Darby and I will miss our plane."

He held onto her. "I'm not letting go until you promise me you'll come back."

"I promise I'll come back." Danni tried again to get up.

"Promise you'll come back to me."

Danni sighed. "Come on, Fish. I need a little space to think this through." She pulled away from him. "A lot happened today. My head is still spinning. I haven't quite decided how I feel about all of it."

"I'm sorry...about all of it."

She bit her lip. "I think the worst of it is that I feel like I've been someone's pawn my whole life. Manipulated by Tori, by Rick. You were the one person I trusted to never hurt me. And yet, here we are."

"I wish I could take it all back."

"But you can't. I need some space so I can make my own choices — think about my future and make a rational, reasonable decision. I can't do that here."

"I'll go with you. I told you I'd move, and I wasn't lying. I know you hate it here."

"No. To be honest, here — this place — was never the problem for me. It was you. You were what I was avoiding."

Fisher let go of her and stood. At the door, he turned to look at her. "You know, when you put it that way, just go."

"Fisher, wait."

"You win. I'm your problem. I'm the reason you left, I'm the reason you never came back. It was all on me. Go. I won't stop you."

~*~

Fisher scared the hell out of Darby when he swung the door open, and it banged off the wall.

Darby flew up off the couch. "Holy shit, you scared me."

"Sorry." He walked straight to the kitchen and poured himself a cup of coffee. It was cold, so he threw it in the sink, smashing plates and glasses that were laying there to be washed.

Darby leaned over the bar. "I take it didn't go well."

He shook his head. "It's over."

"Whoa, what the hell happened? I thought you loved her?"

"I do, but the shit of it is, love isn't always enough."

"What happened?"

Fisher grabbed a beer out of the fridge. "Go on home, Darby. You guys need to get ready, or you're going to miss your plane."

"I can talk to her." Darby looked worried.

Fisher took a deep breath. "Don't worry about it. Things will be fine. While you guys are out there, I'll finish fixing the hotel. I promised I would, and I will. And when you guys get back, I'll be on my best friend-zone behavior, so Danni doesn't feel awkward here."

"I thought for sure—"

Fisher flashed her a smile. "Go. Get out of here."

Darby paused at the door. "I'm sorry, Fisher."

He shrugged. "That's life, kid—a real kick in the balls."

Chapter 44

Danni stood behind Darby in the crowded check-in line. Guilt beat on her. There was the legitimate, inescapable guilt — if she had bothered to fly in an airplane a month ago, she'd have been able to say goodbye to Max. Then there was the illogical guilt. She'd hurt the one person she loved more than anything in the world.

But she had every right to be mad. Hadn't Fisher judged her harshly time and time again? With everyone else, he offered some explanation for their behavior. But not her. She was held double accountable for everything, even things she didn't do.

Wasn't that reason enough to end things? He obviously didn't know her well enough to know when Tori was lying about her. And how do you love someone when you don't really know who they are?

But then there was the look on Fisher's face when she told him he was her problem — she'd never seen him look so crushed. That look would haunt her for a lifetime. Her goal wasn't to hurt him, it was to....

What the hell was her goal?

She rubbed the back of her neck. Did she really want it to be over? Return to a life where Fisher was a stranger? Maybe, after her time away, they could be friends again. She pulled her phone out of her pocket and looked at his number. If she called him, what would she say? "It's still over, and that may be good for you in the long run, but I still miss you."

Nothing like mixed messages to rub salt in the wounds. It was best if he found comfort elsewhere. A bead of sweat rolled down her back as she realized she'd also left him completely vulnerable to Tori. But wasn't that better? With her, he could at least have a family.

The thought made her want to vomit.

Darby snapped her fingers in Danni's face. "Are the tickets paid for, Danni? Is this where you pay? Are you worried your card will be declined?"

Danni shook her head. "The tickets are paid for."

"Whew. When I was little, my mom could barely afford gas for the car. One time, she paid for groceries in pennies. The guy at the counter was so pissed, and my mom was embarrassed, but I told the guy money was money, count it. What a jerk. Like my mom wasn't embarrassed enough to pay for bread and milk with a sock full of pennies."

Darby was an excellent reminder that there was a difference in life between real problems and bullshit. Worrying about Fisher falling out of love with her and in love with someone else was a bullshit problem, one that she was totally responsible for creating. Danni's mouth felt sour and watery—she might really vomit. She took a deep breath and tried to shake off the feeling.

"I never thought I'd get to fly," Darby continued. "Ever. That's a rich people kind of thing. Are we rich, Danni?"

Danni swallowed the nauseous feeling and focused on the girl. "No, we're not rich. But we don't have to worry about money. Not anymore."

"You afraid we're going to crash?"

Danni pointed, silently directing the girl to move forward in line. Darby never bothered to turn around, she walked backward. Danni had to stop her before she bumped into a man talking on his phone.

"No. I don't think we're going to crash."

"Then why do you look like you're going to puke?"

Danni shook her head. "It's nothing."

"Come on, tell me."

Tears filled her eyes. She couldn't talk about it here; she shook her head.

"Is it Fisher?" Darby whispered.

Danni nodded.

"So, call him. I guarantee you he feels just as bad."

"No. He needs to move on. It's for the best."

"Whatever," Darby said. "Did you hear Tori got fired from her job? So did the nurse. Someone turned them in for calling in false reports."

"How would that get Tori fired?"

"I guess her boss started watching her like a hawk and found out that being crooked is like her hobby. A friend of mine said she will probably lose her real estate license too for overcharging fees to clients."

Danni sighed. "She'll probably be all pathetic and run to Fisher."

"I can see that. That would be a smart play."

"Thanks, Darby."

"So, call him." Darby's raised voice made everyone in line turn and stare at them.

Danni turned her by the shoulders and whispered, "Hush, before we get tackled by Homeland Security or something."

"Well, I just don't see what the problem is. He's miserable; you're miserable. You guys make zero sense."

Chapter 45

When his phone buzzed, Fisher peeled off his work gloves and answered. It was Darby.

"Hey kid, what's up?"

"I snuck off to the bathroom to call you. Danni is miserable. She cried in the ticket line at the airport."

"What's wrong?"

"I think she's realizing she screwed the pooch ditching you."

"I could call her —"

"No, that's dumb. Let her suffer a little."

Fisher didn't like hurting Danni, even as an end game. "I don't know...."

"I won't tell you anything else if you tell her I told. If I wanted Danni in the loop, I'd have called from the waiting area with her next to me."

"All right. Could I at least text her to have a safe flight?"

"That I will allow. But don't you dare tell her I'm conspiring for her."

"For her?"

"I'm not exactly conspiring against her. This is for her own good."

Fisher smiled. Darby had her own wonderful logic. As soon as he hung up, he texted Danni a simple, be safe. C U guys when you get back. Her response was an immediate thank you. Then a minute later, miss you.

With renewed energy, he put his gloves back on and grabbed his sledgehammer and knocked the first hole through Danni's wall. He knew he'd not get to live here, but still, these changes, the extra room, would be good for them. And he wanted to surprise Danni in a big way. He'd even hired another construction company in addition to his own to make sure they could get it all done in five days.

He hoped to get the demo done today. As soon as he had all the walls torn out, he was going to head down to see the sign design Maureen's daughter-in-law had made for the hotel. He hoped while he was there, he could get Jenna's husband and his crew from Coulter Construction to jump on board and help him out. They were the leading company on rehabs in the area. If anyone could give this place the art deco magic, it was them. And if he could get Jenna Coulter to do the design and decorating, this place would knock Danni out.

If he could get to work inside, his men could focus on the hotel rooms and give them a quick makeover. Nothing fancy — new carpet, fresh paint, and bathrooms with updated fixtures. He could also hire a landscape crew to fix up the grounds and paint the fences.

It was past noon when he finished the demo. Using a snow shovel, he scooped old drywall pieces and dust into a garbage can he had strapped to a dolly. Once it was filled, he rolled it out to the dumpster in the yard.

When he opened the door, there was a red sports car with Oregon plates. Curious, he took a few steps toward the car. There was a lone driver. Fisher guessed it was a man, but he couldn't be certain because the light in the parking lot was shadowed. But he was certain he saw the driver look over his shoulder then peel out, spitting gravel and dust toward Fisher.

Chapter 46

Maureen's daughter-in-law, Jenna, showed Fisher her design for the hotel sign. Danni was going to love it. It had the art-deco look that Danni wanted, but the icing on the cake, so to speak, was the smiling sun wearing Max's iconic fishing hat. On seeing it, Fisher had to take a full suck of breath and swallow past the lump in his throat. He cleared it away and said, "Danni is going to love this."

Jenna smiled. "It's the way I remember Max. Warmth of the sun and that damned old hat."

"Max would get a chuckle out of this," Maureen said from the doorway. "I swear, my Jenna has a special muse. Isn't that just perfect?"

"It truly is," Fisher said. He took a deep breath. "You ladies seem to know what's best in all things."

Maureen shuffled over and joined them at the table. "I have to say, that sounded more like a plea for help than a compliment. Are things okay?"

Fisher shook his head. "Not at all, but there's nothing that will fix it."

"Maybe not, but I do love to put my two cents in—tell me what's going on, and maybe I can help."

Fisher rubbed his chin. "Danni broke up with me and headed back to Oregon with Darby."

Maureen's eyes bulged, and her mouth dropped open. "What?" She shook her head so hard, her chin waddle shuddered. "I declare, if ever I was to start using the F word, now would be the time. Has the girl gone mad?"

"Oh, she's mad all right. Mad at me."

"But to leave?"

He shrugged. "Isn't that what Danni does?"

"Is she coming back?"

"She says she will, but who knows." Fisher rubbed his face with his hands. "I messed up. I let Tori come between us."

"Contrary to Maureen's excellent display of shock, we've heard about Tori's meddling," Jenna said with a frown. "When Tres and I had our problems, my insecurities made it all worse. Of course, there were the misunderstandings and lies, but the deeper issue was my insecurity. Until I got it through my head that I was what was best for Tres, we were like a dog chasing its tail—round and round pointlessly. But I kept telling myself he was better off without me. If there was a prize for martyr of the year, I'd have cinched the award. But, listen to me, Fisher, my resistance had nothing to do with me not loving him. Be patient. Fix what you broke while reminding her you love her. You don't know how grateful I am Tres didn't give up on me."

"As I recall," Maureen said, "he was leaving town when I told you to go talk to him."

Jenna blushed. "That's true. So now I'm passing along that good advice to you, Fisher. Keep telling her you love her. Don't let her go."

"Pride goeth before the fall," Maureen added. "Grovel, Fisher. Grovel like you have never grovelled before. Life is too short not to live it with the people you love. I've buried two husbands and my only child. But God saw fit to leave me with a daughter. And now," Maureen smiled at Jenna, "because her and Tres worked out their issues, we have the big wonderful family we have today."

Fisher nodded.

"And remember," Jenna said, "insecurity can come from anywhere. For me, it was my past...my family. Maybe it's the same for Danni. She is a bit haunted by her mother's death, isn't she?"

Fisher nodded. "She's always been embarrassed by it. I can't imagine it would be enough to make her feel ashamed." *I'm the only one to make her feel ashamed.* Fisher didn't mention this revelation. These women were kind, but even they might want to take his head off if he told them how he'd hurt her. He cleared his throat. "It's on me. I lose my temper with her and...it's all my fault. Maybe if I make it up to her. Apologize but also show her I mean it."

Jenna and Maureen nodded.

"She wanted to flip the hotel. The outside is done. I busted out the walls in the living quarters. I'd like to make it look so beautiful it takes her breath away. That will show her I'm sorry and that I love her, right?"

Jenna bit her lip. Maureen was quiet a minute.

"Women like surprises, right?"

"Wow," Jenna said. The notoriously shy woman's cheeks turned a little pink. "That is a bold plan. I'm not sure. What if Danni gets mad that you changed her home without her permission? You seriously already did the demolition?"

Fisher nodded. "I did the living room wall and the bedrooms. I'm going to rip out the kitchen cabinets when I'm done here."

"That's...bold."

"It's romantic," Maureen said. "Remember, Jen, Tres dragged you to the top of the lighthouse to propose and make you finally listen to him."

"But that wasn't permanent."

"He also said he was moving to the island, whether you liked it or not."

"Threatening to move here and demolishing someone's home are—"

Maureen slapped the table. "Now that's just silly, Jen. What woman wouldn't want to come back to find her home made over?"

Jenna shrugged and bit her lip.

"They do it all the time on TV, and the people are always thrilled." Maureen smiled. "I like the idea. I'll help. Danni would never be mad at me."

Jenna nodded slowly. "Fine. I suppose if you guys are committed to this, I'll help too. I think, between Maureen and me, we can help come up with a design that suits Danni's personality. And to get done in time, I'll talk to Tres. I'm sure he'd help."

"Of course, he will," Maureen said. Then with a gasp, she added, "And I'll record all the changes, so Danni can see it later. Oh! Fisher, we could make a video proposal for the end. We could make it part of the Big Reveal. Or," Maureen's voice squeaked with excitement, "we could make a banner...or you could hide a ring in a fancy new appliance, like a dishwasher. Or—"

Jenna patted Maureen's hand. "Slow down, Cupid. Maybe we should see how Danni likes the first surprise before Fisher hits her with more."

Maureen sighed. "You already admitted I was the fixer for you and Tres. I know what I'm doin'. Oh, and Fish, it wouldn't hurt to buy another ring to keep in your pocket. So that way, if she finds another one, it's for her."

Fisher's heart sank. What the hell had he been thinking buying that ring? "I think I'll listen to Jenna on this one and go low key. I might have to accept that I've hurt her too deep to ever fix it, but I still want her to have something nice to come home to. I want Danni to be happy—with me or without me."

"Oh, darlin', it will be all right."

"I better get going. I have a lot of work to do."

"Before you go," Maureen hurried to the back door, "I think you need to take a friend home with you. Come on, little Punkin, Fisher needs someone to give him some love."

Chapter 47

Danni tried not to cry in the crowded airport. She wished Darby hadn't gone to the bathroom, or that she'd have gone with her—though Darby was right, she needed to keep an eye on their carry-on bags. Once alone with her own thoughts, Danni immediately missed Fisher—and Punkin, and the run-down hotel that had become more of a comfort to her than she realized. Sitting in the cold plastic chair watching strangers be happily together, she felt out of place, lost and alone.

Her phone buzzed. A text arrived from Fisher wishing her safe travels. God, she missed him. Tears rolled down her cheeks, and the feeling of homesickness tripled, which was totally irrational. It was her idea to leave. This was what she wanted.

No, not what she wanted. What she needed.

Darby plopped down in the seat next to Danni. "We don't have to go."

"Yes, we do." Danni dug a tissue out of her purse. "I need some space from him, so I can think clearly."

"What is there to be clear about? You love him. He loves you. I don't get why there's a problem."

"He didn't believe in me. He never has, even when we were teens."

"Seriously? You're going to hold that against him? It was years ago, and honestly, from what you've told me, you hardly defended yourself when he asked you about that guy."

"I was only eighteen—"

"And so was he. Both of you were still idiots."

Danni stuffed the tissues back in her purse. "There's still

other problems."

"Like what?"

Danni took a deep breath. "Evidently, his feelings for Tori were deeper than he ever let on. He bought her a ring. After I was home. Probably after he knew I was divorced."

"But you were hardly giving him any hope. I mean, even when we talked, you were dead set against being anything more than friends."

"So, you can't get what you want, so you marry someone else?"

"Hello pot, meet kettle." Darby pretended to introduce her right hand to her left. "Duh. Isn't that what you did? With Rick?"

Danni bit her lip.

"Uh huh, tell me I'm right," Darby challenged.

Danni shrugged but said nothing.

"You never loved Rick. You said it yourself. You were hurt and lonely, and he was fun to be around. Trust me, for a guy, Tori is fun."

Danni glared at the girl.

Darby laughed. "I mean, she is everything a guy thinks he wants—it's all phony, mind you—but she cooks, she cleans, she knows all about baseball, football—hell, she even knows soccer."

"Then maybe he should be with her. It sounds like she'd be perfect, and with her, he could have a family." Danni opened her purse, rummaging blindly for a tissue. Tears clouded her vision.

Darby pulled the small pack of tissues out of the purse and handed them to Danni. "You of all people should know you don't have to give birth to a child to raise it and love it. You guys could adopt. Where would either of us be without Max being willing to raise children other women gave birth to?"

Danni couldn't answer. It took her several long minutes to compose herself enough to answer. "All good points."

"I know. Now, listen to me and call him."

Danni nodded. She silently gathered her purse and phone and headed to the bathroom. She washed away the tears and mascara. She took a deep breath and dialed his number. It went straight to voicemail.

She imagined him with Tori rejecting her calls. Maybe he was mad at her for blaming him for everything. She'd shoved a knife through his heart and twisted it. How could he forgive her for that?

In the midst of her mental turmoil, she got a text from Darby. Their plane was loading. Danni took a deep breath. No more rash decisions. She'd go to Oregon and pack up her life like an adult. The rest she'd take one step at a time.

Chapter 48

Fisher had to chase the damn dog across the parking lot again. Punkin was making a habit of bolting through the front door when he opened it. He managed to grab the dog before she made it to the road. He carried her back, chastising her like a wayward adolescent. "You trying to get me hated for sure, Punkin? What the hell's gotten into you? Get yourself killed, and Danni will never forgive me." The gravel crunched under his feet. "She loves you, you stupid mutt. She'd get smashed by a car to save your furry hide, so knock it off."

A horn blew behind him. He turned. Tori. He shook his head and turned toward the hotel.

Her car door opened. "Don't walk away, Fisher. I just wanted to apologize."

"I'm not the one you need to apologize to."

"I…." Her gaze dropped to her feet. "I'll apologize to Danni too. Is she here?"

"No." He didn't offer her any more explanation. She didn't need to know Danni had left him. That all of her lies and bullshit worked. "Now's not the time. Leave her alone."

"I truly am sorry. I got scared. I knew I was losing you."

He felt like his head would pop off his shoulders. "Are you delusional or what? You never had me. We weren't even together."

"But we could have been if she hadn't come back."

"Get the hell out of here, Tori. I'd never hurt a woman, but I'll be damned if you don't make me want to."

Tori nodded. "I know. And I understand, really I do. That's

why I'm here — I want to help." Tori took a deep breath. "I'll call her. I'll —"

"Just get the hell out. Just go away and never come back." He turned and started for the hotel.

"I suppose I better go," Tori said to his back. "I hope we can still be —"

Fisher didn't hear the rest of her sentence as he closed the door. He needed a beer. He set Punkin on the floor and headed to the kitchen, where he found beer in the fridge. One beer, then he had a date with his sledgehammer. The wall between the kitchen and the living room was his last hurdle.

Maureen was right. He'd make this place so perfect, she'd be like the women on TV who break down in happy tears. There'd be hugs and laughter, and in the midst of all that good feeling, she'd forget she was ever mad at him.

He drained his beer, tossed it in the trash, grabbed his sledgehammer and headed for the living room. The first swing smashed through the drywall with ease. From his vantage point, he could now see through the kitchen, out the window to the sun sparkling on the sound. Just the one-foot hole in the wall not only added a million-dollar view to the living space, it brightened up the dark room considerably. This was a good idea.

Fisher went to the kitchen. He needed to remove all of the cabinets and move the fridge to another wall. He'd wait for Jenna to decide on the exact design of the new space. Right now, he'd focus on getting this wall demolished. He grabbed a garbage bag and started tossing in food items from the cupboards. Up above the fridge, he found Max's junk food stash. Cookies, cakes, and chips all concentrated in the uppermost cabinet in the room. Fisher had to grin. Max surely had to get a chair to reach her stash of goodies.

Cleared of food, Fisher noticed a box in the back of the cupboard. Reaching above his head, he pulled the box down and set it on the table. Danni's name was written on the top, and the box was duct taped closed.

"Is this what you wanted Danni to find, Max?" Fisher asked the empty room. There was no response, but he knew this was what Danni was looking for.

Fisher pulled his phone out of his pocket and cursed. He'd missed a call from Danni. Over an hour ago — probably while he was talking to Tori. "Damn it."

He tried to call her back, but she didn't answer.

She needed this box. He'd mail it to her...but he didn't have her address. He called Maureen and told her about the box and the hole in the wall.

Maureen laughed. "You're not wasting any time, are you?"

"It was that or sit around and think."

"Oh, sweetie, it will be all right. I have a good feeling."

"I don't know, Ms. Maureen. We have a lot to work out."

"She'll calm down. I think the ring shocked her, but she'll realize it didn't mean anything. She knows you love her. And she loves you, so much."

"I think she does, but I worry that won't be enough to get past the hurt and.... Well, Tori told me something a few weeks ago that bugs me, especially after Jenna said what she did about her not feeling like she was good enough for Tres.."

"What did Tori say, dear?"

Fisher leaned on the box and stared out the window. "She told me that Danni couldn't have kids."

"Oh." Maureen was quiet a minute. "Do you think there's any truth to that?"

Fisher sighed. "Let's say it wouldn't shock me."

"Oh my, poor Danni."

"I know, and I think it's part of the reason she left me. Tearing shit up has given me a lot of time to think, and I was thinking... Danni told me she wasn't ever planning on anything permanent with me, that she was going to refuse to marry me all along, no matter what. I know she loves me, so there has to be some other reason she planned to say no all along, and infertility makes sense."

"I suppose I can see where she thinks refusing to marry you might be doing you a favor."

"Why would that be doing me a favor?"

"Oh, I don't know, Fisher. I suppose to some men having

children would matter."

"I guess if she just didn't want kids, it would matter...because who wouldn't want kids? But if it's a problem of biology, who gives a damn? I love her, and I want her with me. It's not like I'm looking for an incubator."

Maureen laughed. "You have a way of putting things, son. Maybe Tori did do you a favor. Now that you know, you can question Danni directly about it. Force her to see reason."

"Not back down."

"That's right, son. Hold your ground."

"That's exactly what I'll do." Fisher looked at the clock on the wall. He had about a half an hour to get this box in the mail. "Maureen, I hate to run, but I need to get this box in the mail. Would you have Danni's address in Oregon?"

"I do. Hold on." Fisher could hear drawers open and close. "Here you go."

Fisher wrote down the address.

"Would you mind if Jenna and I came up in a bit? Jenna wants to measure the rooms so she can get started."

"Of course. If I'm not back from the post office, do you have a key?"

"I do. I'll see you in a bit. Oh, and Fisher?"

"Yeah?"

"Try to relax, dear. True love always wins in the end."

"You sure about that?"

"Pretty sure."

Chapter 49

After delays and layovers, Danni and Darby arrived in Oregon a full day after they left North Carolina. Danni was exhausted, so she rented them a hotel rather than making the drive to Eugene the first day. She'd hoped a night's rest would make her feel better, but she woke up feeling as sick as the day before. Not to mention the sick feeling of missing yet another call from Fisher. She couldn't believe she slept through the buzz of her ringer.

Darby was up and ready to go. Danni tried to be excited, but she didn't have the energy. Unlike Darby. Darby was enamored with everything—even the name of the city, Eugene. During the drive, or at least during the times when Danni's face wasn't shoved in one of the extra airsick bags she'd gotten from the flight attendant, Darby teased her about living in Eugene.

"Hi, I'm Rodanthe," Darby said. "Rodanthe from Eugene. I'm from Eugene, Oregon. Isn't that a weird name, Danni? Eugene." Darby repeated the name over and over.

Danni smiled apologetically at the driver, who kept turning around and looking at Danni as if trying to send her a mental message to shut Darby up.

"Danni, when we get home, can I get a cat so I can name him Eugene?"

"Sure," Danni said with her head leaning against the cab window, appreciative of the coolness against her forehead. She felt bad that she felt so awful. She was ruining Darby's trip.

"Eugene is prettier than I imagined," Darby said. "Very green. Kind of like mainland North Carolina on a rainy day."

"It rains a lot here," Danni said.

"So, what is there to do?"

Danni shrugged. "I'm sure there are museums and stuff. Maybe a movie theater."

"How many years did you live here? Did you do nothing?"

"I worked a lot. We went to a lot of clubs because Rick loves the underground music scene."

"Of course he does," Darby said with an eye roll.

The cab pulled up to the apartment. It was in the basement level of a restored Victorian. Darby's first thought was that Danni owned the whole thing.

"You live here? It's amazing."

"It is beautiful, isn't it?" Danni pulled her keys out of her purse and walked toward the basement door.

"So, you live in the basement?"

"Yeah, the whole place has been divided into apartments."

When the door swung open, the place looked just like Danni had left it—bare. She had a couch, a small TV that sat on a microwave stand instead of a table...and that was pretty much it for the living room and dining area.

"This is the living area. Bathroom and bedroom are down this hallway." Danni walked her down the hall. "You can take the bed; I'll take the couch."

"I'm good with the couch. You don't have a TV in your room."

"No, but I have a lamp and books."

Darby looked the space over. "You were sad here, weren't you, Danni?"

Danni looked around her home. It was void of personality and warmth. Nothing like the apartment on the island. "I wasn't exactly happy, but I don't know about being sad." A knock on the door made her jump. "Who could that be?"

Darby gave her a nudge with her elbow. "Maybe Rick's been stalking your house."

Danni took a deep breath and went to the door and opened it. "Mrs. Bennet." She was relieved to see her landlady.

The woman offered a box to Danni. "This arrived this

morning. Seems someone paid a pretty penny to send it here in the overnight mail."

Danni took the box. It was from Fisher. Danni's heart did a flip flop.

"Is everything all right?" Mrs. Bennet asked.

"Everything is fine. I just have a flu bug."

"Oh, well, for heaven's sake, get yourself some rest." Mrs. Bennet took a few steps back. "I'll leave you be. If you need anything, let me know."

Danni took the box and sat on the floor. She had played phone tag with Fisher all day yesterday. Maybe the box was to make up for that? Maybe it was filled with helium balloons that would float out when she opened the box with a note that said I'm sorry, or I love you. Danni shook her head. That was ridiculous. The damn thing was too heavy. Maybe it was a box of sand to remind her to come home?

Darby sat on the couch. "Who's the box from?"

"Fisher."

"Open it."

"I am.

"Like, open it faster."

"Don't rush me." Danni touched the box gently. "Why don't you watch TV? The remote is on the stand."

"I want to see what's in the box. Open the box."

Danni touched the box gently. A thought crossed her mind — what if he shipped her the stuff she left behind and told her to stay in Oregon?

"Are you ever going to open the box?"

Danni nodded. She peeled off the layer of paper. Taped to the top of the box was a note from Fisher. *I found this in the kitchen cabinet. It must have been what Max wanted only you to find. Love you and miss you. Please hurry back, Fisher.*

Danni held the note to her chest for a second.

"What is it, Danni?"

"It's a box from Max."

Danni unwrapped the duct tape from around the shoe box. Danni lifted the lid. There was no note, just a childish journal, the kind with the little brass lock on it. Under the journal were stacks of drawings, each one signed, Vi.

"This is my mom's stuff," Danni said.

Darby picked up a handful of papers. "She was really into crosses." Darby laid down page after page of painted crosses. "They're beautiful, but why so many?"

Danni shook her head. "I didn't even know she could paint."

"How old was she when she died?"

"Nineteen."

"Wow, so young."

"She was crazy. She tried to kill me when I was a baby."

"And then jumped off the bridge?"

Danni nodded.

The key to the journal was at the bottom of the box. Danni unlocked it. The writing looked large and childlike. She read through the first few pages, and they were typical kid stuff— what she had for dinner, things she found on the beach. Midway in, the print became smaller, more mature. Vi started adding drawings to the pages when she was in the third grade. Juvenile sketches of birds and seashells.

By the fifth grade, her work was becoming more mature, impressive for a young kid. By the summer of the same year, the journal went very dark. Vi's entries were no longer happy posts. And the first cross appeared.

"Read this." Danni handed the journal to Darby.

Darby read several pages. "Danni? Was your mom being molested?"

"It sure sounds like it, doesn't it?" Danni took the journal back and started reading. As she read, a very sad, very tragic picture of Violet Lowry came to life. "The cross obsession was her trying to stop evil. She says Mr. George is a bad man. Makes her play the tickle game."

"That's horrible. That poor kid."

"She writes she's going to run away to Max and Danny's." Danni paused.

"Who the hell was Danny?" Darby asked.

"Daniel, Max's boyfriend. Him, Fisher's dad, and Maureen's

husband all died in the same car wreck."

"That's awful." Darby leaned toward Danni. "Did Vi run away?"

"It doesn't say. There are just more crosses, no more story." Danni laid the journal down and went through the paintings. "Here's a good one." Danni showed Darby a painting of a huge black dog. He was solid black except for a moon shaped crescent of white on his chest. Danni sat back. "Why would Max not leave a note? This raises more questions than it answers."

"Call Ms. Maureen. Her and Max were friends, she should know something."

Danni pulled out her phone and called.

"Put it on speaker."

Danni hit the speaker button when Maureen answered.

"Ms. Maureen, this is Danni. Hey, I'm here in Oregon, and Fisher mailed me this box of my mother's things. It's kind of disturbing, and I wondered if you knew anything about it."

"I knew Fisher was mailing a box, but I didn't know what was in it. Honestly, I didn't know Max saved any of Vi's things. I'm glad she did. I told her to, a long time ago."

"I hate to ask this, but there are entries in my mother's journal that are pretty creepy—about a friend of her mother's, a guy named George? He'd force her to play tickle games. Was my mother molested?"

"Oh, dear lord, I never thought of that. But you know, that makes a lot of Vi's behaviors make sense. George was George Vasquez. He was one of your grandfather's friends—a very rich man. He'd rent a room off your grandparents to go duck hunting every fall."

"She writes some very disturbing stuff about him. And his arrival seems to correspond with her cross obsession."

"She drew crosses anywhere and everywhere. She told me once they were to stop the demons. I always thought it was the voices in her head. I never thought about it being a person. George was on the creepy side. I never cared for him. Max and I were much older than Vi. Max had moved out of her parents' house when she bought the hotel. Come to think of it, Danny never liked George at all, but I always assumed it was because George was always inappropriate. He'd say very suggestive things to us, but we were of age. I never dreamed he'd touch a child."

"Did Max ever say anything?"

"Nothing like that. When your grandparents had the new baby, they decided to move to the mainland. Max insisted that Vi be allowed to live with her and Danny. I remember Danny saying one night that if Max's parents refused, he'd go to the police. He was very close to Vi, you know. His threat must have worked because they let Vi stay with Max and Danny. The parents moved to the mainland, and a few months later, they all died in a house fire. You know, when Danny died, poor Vi might have taken it harder than Max. She swore she killed him. Poor, poor girl. Kids can think the oddest things."

"In her journal, she wrote that the demon said he'd burn anyone she told. You think she told Danny what was happening to her?"

"That makes sense. To be honest, Max was in her early twenties and not at all ready to raise a child, much less her own sister, a troubled adolescent we all assumed was showing signs of schizophrenia. But Danny insisted. He probably knew what was going on. He was a good man...somewhat like your Fisher."

Danni smiled at the name drop. Maureen was lovably predictable.

"One more question and I'll quit bugging you—did my mother have a dog?"

"Oh, yes, Luna. What a dog!" Maureen laughed. "Danny gave your mother that dog. She was an amazing animal. She was a Newfoundland. Huge black thing. She was your mother's shadow. No one got near Vi unless Vi told Luna to heel."

"Thanks, Maureen."

Danni hung up.

Darby gave her a look. "Oh my God, Danni. It all makes sense. The rich guy probably paid off everyone in the family for what he did to Vi. Then, all the people who knew what happened died tragically. Your mom had to think this guy really was a demon, or in the very least, that she was cursed."

Danni ran her fingers over one of the crosses, tears blurring her vision. She'd never considered what might be haunting her mother. She was always too angry with her for leaving her to consider it.

"Now we know how you got the odd name, Rodanthe 'Danni' Luna," Darby said. "You were named after a dog and a dude."

"I always assumed the 'Danni' was named for the town of Rodanthe. An idea I always hated—almost as much as the name Danni. But maybe it was for both. I suppose I'll never know. What I do know is my name was my mother's blessing to me."

Chapter 50

It was well after midnight by the time Fisher showered and settled himself on the couch with a beer. They'd gotten a good day of work in. Between his crew and the Coulter crew, the demolition was done. He had a bit of dust and debris to clean up in the bedroom, but the smell of Maureen's homemade pulled pork sandwiches and hand cut French fries had encouraged him to take a break before finishing the clean-up. Maureen cooked the whole time they worked, making a bagged lunch for the men to take home.

Fisher carried his to the living room. He decided he'd watch some *Sport's Center* while he ate. Food this good needed to be appreciated, not gulped standing over a counter. Punkin lay down beside him. She loved him most when he had bread crust to share.

Before digging in, he checked his phone. Still no call from Danni. After he missed her call, he called and left her a message. He thought about calling her again. But he worried that would annoy her.

He put his phone back in his pocket.

Punkin's ears twitched. Head cocked, she listened, as if waiting to see if she'd identified a sound that was worth leaving a snack over. Fisher muted the TV. A creak of the floorboards on the porch of the hotel sent Punkin off the couch like a brown streak. Barking all the way, she headed straight for her perch—the front office window. Fisher glanced out the window on his way to the door. The red sports car was back.

Fisher grabbed his shirt he'd hung on a coat peg in the hall and pulled it over his head. When he opened the door, standing before him was none other than Rick Cee.

I'll be damned. The little son of a bitch is even smaller looking in real life than he is in pictures. Darby's description of him as a mangy, old Justin Bieber was perfect.

"Hey, I'm looking for my wife—Danni? I think this is her hotel. Is she here?"

The word wife made the hair rise on the back of Fisher's neck. Suddenly, Fisher imagined himself in the middle of a cheesy soap opera where Danni thinks she's divorced and then the husband shows up to admit he never filed the papers. Fisher decided it was best to play dumb. He opened the door in welcome. "This is her place. She went out of town for a few days. I'm here doing some construction while she's gone."

Rick rubbed his beard. He looked worried. "Do you have her number?"

"You don't have your wife's number?"

Nervous laughter. The tiny man stuffed his hands in his pocket. *Stupid move,* Fisher thought. *A man can't defend a punch with his hands stuffed in his pockets.* "Funny story, really. I lost my phone and had to get a new one. That was when I realized I don't know Danni's number. She was in my contacts—I never needed to know the number."

Fisher nodded. "Damn shame. I don't know it either. I suppose we're both waiting for her to call us."

"Yeah," Rick said. He turned like he was about to leave but then turned back to Fisher. "Look, I assume you have the keys to this place. Would you mind letting me into a room? I have been on the road for three days to get here. I'm whipped."

"Place isn't open yet. Most of the rooms are wrecks."

"Honestly, I don't give a shit. I'm too tired to care. I came here earlier, but I didn't see Danni's car. I went to a friend's house and don't you know, with my bad luck streak, she's not home either." Rick shook his head. "And don't you know, I lost my wallet when I lost my phone."

"Seems you aren't very lucky."

"I know, right? Damndest thing. I was showering in one of

those truck stop showers and thought the door was locked, but it wasn't. Someone emptied out my pockets. The night clerk at the truck stop was nice enough to let me get a full tank of gas and a burner phone to get me to here."

Fisher nodded. The story seemed plausible enough. He supposed he could give mangy old Bieber a room. As a practical thinking man, if Rick was here waiting on Danni, then he wasn't in Oregon, complicating her decision on whether to live on the west coast or east. And it might give him an opportunity to better know his enemy.

Chapter 51

Never in his wildest dreams did Fisher think he'd be in Danni's kitchen, making her ex-husband a sandwich while Rick sat at the kitchen table and whined. The guy bitched about everything, starting with the drive across the country. The food was bad, the roads sucked — hell, even the lumbar support in the driver's seat wasn't sufficient. Fisher handed the man a beer just to shut him up.

Fisher piled roast beef on rye bread and handed the plate to Rick, along with a jar of horseradish. He had a tub of Maureen's pulled pork, but he wasn't about to share anything he treasured with someone unworthy of the sacrifice. "You want any chips with that?"

"Sure, if you have some. I'm starved. When I lost my wallet and everything, the lady at the truck stop gave me this frozen pot pie thing that you microwave — god-awful slop. Barely edible, so I tossed it. Twelve hours later, I was starting to regret that."

"Well, hopefully, the sandwich is all right."

Rick tore off a big bite. "It's not a meal for a king, but at least it's edible."

Fisher pulled a bag of chips out of the cupboard and tossed them on the table. "Perfect then, seeing as how you're not royalty."

"Indeed, I am not. Just a man trying to save his marriage."

Fisher grabbed the entire carton of beer and set it on the table before he sat down. He pulled one out and opened it as he asked, "I thought Danni mentioned she was divorced — uh, when I asked her if her husband was around for me to discuss the renovations."

Rick took another bite. "Technically, yes, we are divorced. But as soon as Danni realizes I came all this way, I think she'll see things differently."

"Really? Is she one of those types who demand heroic efforts and big gestures?"

"No, not usually. It's just that lately, she's been ignoring my calls. I think my magic is wearing off."

"You're divorced, right? That's a pretty good sign the magic is gone."

"I know she only divorced me to teach me a lesson, for being a bad boy." Rick winked at him.

Fisher took a long drink and did his best to hold his temper. As "the help" staying in her house, Fisher had to play neutral observer, and a neutral observer wouldn't punch Rick in the face. Fisher tipped his beer to the man. "Bad boy, huh?"

Rick's grin widened. "I've always had a way with the ladies."

"Imagine that." Fisher dropped his empty bottle back in the carton and pulled out another.

"Trust me. When I turn on the charm, I've never been denied."

Fisher's eyes narrowed. He'd probably learned enough—time to punch him in the face. Rick must have taken his silence for doubt because he offered Fisher proof that he was the ultimate Don Juan.

"Seriously," Rick said. "Everyone who knows me knows I know how to charm the coldest heart. I will admit, Danni was my toughest challenge. When my friend called me and told me Danni was the perfect catch, I was, of course, certain I could meet the challenge. But then I met Danni, and at first, she had zero interest. Not that it was me she wasn't interested in, but in any guy."

"You obviously married her, so how did you manage to change that?"

"I'll let you in on a little secret." Rick grabbed a napkin and wiped his fingers before grabbing himself another beer. "When you're dealing with a woman who's been hurt, under the anger and the defiance are some deep-rooted insecurities. All you have to do is heal the wounded heart by reminding her she's desirable."

Rick chuckled. "And it helps to be the polar opposite of the jerk who hurt her."

"Basically, take advantage of them while they're weak."

Rick chuckled and took a long drink. "That's a bit of a crude synopsis, but yeah...heal their pain, and they will love you for it. In Danni's case, once I was allowed into the friend zone, it was a piece of cake. Danni was bleeding out. I applied the tourniquet. Boom. I was the hero."

His words felt like a knife to Fisher's gut. He'd made Danni vulnerable. Isn't that what she'd told him? Of all the people who had hurt her, he'd hurt her more than anyone else. "She told you she had a broken heart?"

Rick finished his beer and shook his head. "Hell no. To this day, she denies she ever loved this guy, her *friend*."

"So, how did you know?"

"Tori, my friend, told me," he said. "Not that I couldn't have figured it out after knowing Danni a month or two—"

"Tori told you? You knew Tori before you met Danni?"

"Do you know Tori?" Rick looked alarmed like he'd just said too much.

"I'm acquainted with her. She's a real estate agent, and I do construction, so I've bumped into her a time or two. And let's be honest, no man with a pulse could not notice a gal who looks like Tori." Fisher gave him a wink and a sly smile.

Rick relaxed and nodded. "She *was* a real estate agent. She's not anymore. Danni dicked her...got her license suspended. They were going to make her clean houses, but she told them to go screw themselves."

"Is she the friend you said you were going to stay with?"

"Yeah, but she hasn't been home all day. And don't you know, I don't have her number either. You wouldn't—?"

"Nope. Sorry."

Rick shrugged. "No harm asking." He took another bite of his sandwich. "I'll try her again tomorrow, but not tonight. I'm too damned tired. And a little pissed. She knew I'd be here tonight. She could have left me a key to get in."

"Danni was expecting you?"

"No, Tori. She's the one who told me to come. I drive three days straight, and she's nowhere to be found."

"You guys are pretty good friends, huh?"

"Actually," he said as he leaned toward Fisher and grinned. "We're far more than friends. Tori is begging me to move to Florida with her and set up our own real estate company."

"You're a lucky man. Tori is a gorgeous woman."

Rick shrugged and grabbed another beer. "She is. But I'm coming to realize that she can be a drain. Ever since I trashed my marriage for her, she's blown through most of my money, and I swear to God, she calls me twenty goddamned times a day telling me what to do."

"My guess is a gal who looks like Tori is used to getting her way."

"Exactly. But lately, I've had to ask myself — is she worth it? I bought her a car and new boobs. You'd think that was enough, but no, she wants Botox injections, a house on the water. Honest to God? I'm going broke with this girl."

"I guess high-end models have big price tags."

"Then Tori tells me Danni inherited more money, so while I'm busting my ass trying to earn enough to keep her happy, she tells me I also need to woo Danni into reconciling for a cut of that money. Being with Tori is like being forced to run a marathon. Marry Danni. Divorce Danni. Make up with Danni. I'm telling you, it's damned exhausting trying to please this chick."

Fisher gripped the bottle in his hand. He should call the sheriff, find out if this could be a conspiracy to defraud Danni. As Fisher considered the option, Rick chattered on about his plans.

"But I've been thinking, Danni might not be the obvious looker that Tori is, but she's cute. And she sure as hell was easier to deal with. Lately, I've been thinking I made a mistake. Now that Tori is a daily reality, I think I'd be happier with my wife."

Fisher rubbed the stubble on his chin. "So, here you are."

Rick leaned back in his chair and smiled. "Here I am."

Danni is not stupid. She won't fall for this. Fisher tried to remain confident, but his shoulders felt tight, and his neck muscles were tense. After Fisher hurt her last time, Rick won by picking up the pieces. Fisher really had to fix things with Danni before it was too late.

Fisher took a handful of chips from the bag. "Have you dumped Tori yet?"

"No, and I'm not sure I will. I don't want to be too hasty and make a wrong move."

"You've got some major-league-sized balls, that's for damned sure. Tori will know you're on the island. It's too small of a place to hide for long. What will she think of you chasing your ex right under her nose?"

Rick grinned. "That's the beauty of it. Weren't you listening? Tori wants me to reconcile with Danni."

"That's right. To get access to her assets. Isn't that illegal?"

Rick shook his head. "I don't plan to steal it. I'll invest it. In the long run, Danni will make money. Trust me, it's a sound investment."

"The real estate business in Florida?"

Rick nodded.

"As much as she's putting into this hotel, I assumed she planned to run it," Fisher said.

"Maybe for a while. In the end, she'll sell it. Once we're remarried...maybe have a kid or two...she'll go where I go, just to keep her family together."

Chapter 52

Fisher escorted Rick to a room, opened the door, and handed him a key. Thoughts of murdering him and dumping his body in the ocean crossed his mind. He'd be doing the world, or at least his world, a favor.

Trust Danni. The thought crossed his mind loud and clear as if screamed at him through a megaphone. *Besides, murder is murder, you dumb ass, even if the guy is a moron.*

Fisher took a deep breath as he reminded himself to stay calm. Nothing good would come of him maiming, killing, or even bruising the man. Danni would never fall for his bullshit twice. And he'd be there this time to tell her about Rick and Tori's plan.

"I'll put towels outside the door. You might want to flip on the heat. At least for a bit to get rid of the damp smell. Or open a window."

"Thanks, man." Rick held out his hand. "I never did catch your name."

"It's...Todd."

"Well, I thank you, Todd. If you hadn't been here, I'd have been up a creek."

"I'm glad I was here too."

Rick stepped into the room, then popped his head back out. "Remember, if Danni calls, tell her to call me. Tell her I'm here, waiting for her."

"Sure." Fisher turned and walked away.

Back in the apartment, he felt restless. He snapped the leash on Punkin and set off for the beach. Maybe some fresh air would help.

He barely made it across the asphalt road when his phone buzzed. Darby. He answered, "Hey, kid, what's up?"

"I wanted to give you a head's up. Danni is talking about coming home early. She's sicker than a dog with the flu, and her landlady suggested she ship her boxes of stuff home instead of renting a car and driving back. And since Danni owns next to nothing, it won't take us long to pack and ship this stuff."

"Shit."

"I thought you'd be happy to see us."

"I am happy, but Rick's here. And the place is upside down."

"Wait. Go back. Bieber Rick?"

"Yes, ex-husband, asshole Rick. He showed up tonight. He's here to win Danni back."

Darby was quiet a second. "It won't matter. She loves you. She's miserable and no fun at all."

"I really wanted to surprise her. As it stands, all I've done was tear the hell out of her house without her permission. If she was mad at me before, she'll want to kill me now. What if this gives that little Bieber-looking bastard the upper hand? You have to stall her."

"I can try. But she's been so weepy and sick feeling, this has been a horrible trip. I can maybe buy one full day. We will have to pack and mail tomorrow. All she's keeping is her clothes. She's leaving the furniture and everything in the kitchen for the landlady to rent the place as furnished."

"Son of a bitch."

"I'm really sorry. I can try to talk her into—"

Fisher took a deep breath. "It's all right. Let her do what makes her happy. I'll get as much done as I can. If she's sick, maybe she'll sleep tomorrow."

Darby laughed. "I'll forget to set my alarm, but I'm not making any promises."

Fisher hurried back to the hotel. He could fix up as much as he could in the few hours he had before she came home. Maybe, if he was lucky, he could at least make it presentable. But before he did that, he had to break a promise and make one phone call.

Chapter 53

Danni lay in bed, listening to Darby's television show through the closed door. She tried hard to get to sleep, but her mind was crowded with everything from Fisher to family. And as a bonus to her torture, the pizza they ate for dinner was giving her heartburn. All the stress of late was playing havoc with her stomach.

Her phone buzzed. She flipped onto her back and fumbled around in the dark for her cell phone. Fisher. She couldn't help but smile as she answered.

"Hey," she said.

"Danni," he sounded relieved. "I wasn't sure you'd answer. I was beginning to think you were dodging my calls."

She sat up, pulling her knees to her chest. "No, I just kept missing them. The first time we were on the plane, then we had to land because there was an issue with the engine and we had to wait on another flight, and then—"

"You were on a faulty plane?"

Danni smiled. He sounded so alarmed. If she'd have crashed and burned, he'd have been crushed. Was she a horrible person for that to please her? "The plane was fine, but it took us a full twenty-four hours to make it to Portland. I was beat, so we got a hotel. Then I slept through your next call."

"It's all right. Even if you were hating on me and icing me out, I understand."

Was she wrong to not be mad at him anymore? Was she a welcome mat? For now, it didn't matter. She wasn't going to be miserable to prove a point. "I don't hate you. I could never hate you."

She could hear the relief in his voice when he said, "Thank God."

There was an awkward pause. There was so much Danni wanted to talk to him about, but at the same time, she wasn't sure how to bridge the gulf she helped create.

"How's your flu?" he asked.

"No better."

"Really?"

"No, honestly, it's been awful. Poor Darby, her first time flying, and I had my head in the vomit bag the whole flight. How'd you know?"

"Promise not to tell?"

"Let me guess — Darby?"

"Yeah, she's keeping me updated."

"That rotten kid. Where is her loyalty?"

"I told you she liked me again."

Danni lay down, running her hand over the empty space next to her, wishing he was there with her. She took a deep breath. "I like you too, Fish."

He was quiet a moment. "You know, Danni, I hate myself for hurting you. For not trusting you. You don't know how damned bad I'd like to have a do-over."

"I could use a few of those myself."

"Will you come back?"

"Of course. I was never going to stay here. I only said that to be mean."

"Good. I suppose I deserved your spite." Fisher was quiet a second before he said, "You guys should have some fun out there. Take your time. No need to hurry back."

"Really? You don't miss me?"

"I miss you like crazy. The truth is, your ex is here. I'm jealous enough to be sure you miss his visit."

"Rick? He's in Salvo?" Danni moved the phone to her other ear as if the one she was using was defective and hearing wrong.

"I gave him a room at the hotel. He's waiting on you."

"Why? Why is he there?"

"He came to win you back."

"Seriously?"

"That's what he said."

Danni shook her head.

"Did you tell him I was here?"

"No. If I said that, he'd run out there. My goal is to keep him here while you're there. When you're at the airport to come back, I'll tell him you're in Oregon."

Danni laughed. "You're awful. That's mean."

"You want me to tell him where you are?"

"No, I don't want to deal with him. You enjoy your time with him. Maybe you two will bond."

"He is a chatty little thing."

Danni snickered. She had no idea what sort of things Rick might say. His filter was pretty much non-existent. "What did he say?"

"Remember when you told me he bought a car for his mistress and ran up a high tab at the plastic surgeon?"

"Yeah."

"Guess who he was spending your money on?"

Danni didn't have a clue, so she took a wild guess, "His secretary?"

"No. Think about it, Danni. Who drives a shiny new Ford Mustang and has a big set of fake boobs?"

"Tori?" Danni nearly yelled the name, then she thought of Darby, covered her mouth with her hand, and whispered, "You're kidding me?"

"Nope. They've been meeting in Florida for the last few years."

Danni smiled. She was awful to think it, but reality was unavoidable and sometimes a pleasure. "Fisher," she taunted. "Your perfect little Tori was cheating on you."

"She's not my Tori."

"Oh, now—"

"Fine. You were right. Tori is the devil, and you knew it all along. I'm a moron and—"

"All right, stop. Just as long as you never question me again."

"Never."

Danni smiled into the darkness. Fisher would never get over this. Tori made him look like a fool—he hated that above all else. "That is so bizarre." Danni scratched the back of her head. "It explains how she knew so much about my marriage. I wonder how they met."

"She probably hunted him up to make your life crazy. She seems to hate you quite a lot."

"And here I always thought she was jealous I had you."

"I'm sure she is. I am a helluva catch."

Danni laughed. "Darby calls you the big Fish."

Fisher laughed. "What was my mother thinking when she named me? Fisher— what a dumbass name."

"I like it." She smiled. "Speaking of dumb names, guess what I found out tonight from that box of stuff you sent—thank you, by the way. That was sweet of you."

"I figured it was important. Max had hidden it in the kitchen."

"I never dreamed to look there." Danni told him what she learned about her mother.

He listened quietly. When she finished, he said, "That explains a lot."

"It does. Can you imagine being a little girl and thinking someone who's hurting you is a demon, and then people start dying? My guess is she trusted this Danny fellow and told him. He dies. That had to scare the hell out of her. That on top of her parents dying in a house fire. Honestly? I'm a little creeped out myself. My mother painted all of these pictures of crosses. Oh, and a beautiful portrait of my doggy namesake. Or so Darby says. The dog's name was Luna, so Darby thinks that's where Mom got my middle name."

Fisher laughed. "Nothing gets by that girl. Maureen said the dog watched out for her, right?"

"Mmm hmm."

"She must have thought she was giving you a name that would protect you. She was obviously grasping at talismans and protection. In some cultures, names give blessings and power."

"My poor, crazy, broken momma."

"It's good to hear you say her name like that."

"Like what?"

"Without the hurt. I wonder why Max kept this from you. She could have cleared up a lot of misunderstanding just by sharing that box of stuff."

"I'm beginning to realize Max had a hard time being open and vulnerable. Same pattern of behavior as with the cancer. Who hides having cancer? The same lady who hid child abuse and insanity in her family."

"I'm shocked she didn't throw it all away."

"I thought about that, but it's Max — she never threw anything away."

"It was hidden in the top cabinet. Hard to tell how long it would have taken you to find it, shorty."

"Good thing you're tall, right?"

"Tall and looking for chips."

Danni laughed. "Thanks for mailing it to me."

"Anything for you; you know that."

"I do. I'm sorry for saying you were to blame for everything. And that you were what I was avoiding. That was really mean of me."

"It was the truth. You don't have to apologize for that. I was raised by a volatile jerk. I guess some of his personality rubbed off."

"You're nothing like Bill. Don't even say that."

"I was pissed, and I let my temper get the best of me. I don't blame you for feeling like you did. I don't want you to feel bad for standing up for yourself."

She bit her lip and wished he was there so she could kiss him.

"You okay?" he asked.

"I'm fine. I'm glad you called."

"I am too. Sleep well, Loonie."

"Sleep well, Fish."

Chapter 54

Danni fastened her seatbelt as the hum of the airplane engines grew louder. It was almost time. Time to go home. "Don't forget your seatbelt," she said to Darby. The girl was on her phone, typing furiously as if trying to get her messages sent before she had to shut it off.

"Yeah, getting it." Darby never looked up from her phone.

The flight attendant approached. The woman gave Darby a light tap on the shoulder and a smile. "Phone off. Buckle up."

Darby hit send and shut it down with a sigh. The flight attendant stood in the aisle, staring at Darby until Darby snapped the belt, pulling it tight against her tiny waist.

"Thank you." The flight attendant's smile was all teeth. "Enjoy your flight."

"I tried to warn you," Danni said with a grin. "You got in trouble."

"I bet you were a brown-noser in school."

"I wouldn't say I was a brown-noser, but I did follow the rules."

Darby rubbed her nose with her closed fist.

Danni stuck out her tongue at the girl and leaned her head against the seat. The plane was moving, but her stomach wanted to stay put. Whatever bug she'd picked up wasn't going away. Nothing helped. She'd tried sleep, nausea medicine, Alka Seltzer... nothing helped. Feeling as bad as she did, she just wanted to be at home. A good night's sleep in her own bed was what she needed. Maybe a dose of salt air.

And she wanted Fisher. Maybe she was being a fool. Perhaps

a savvier person would hold a grudge longer. And maybe she was being selfish, robbing him of the chance to have a family, but she was too tired and too homesick to care about either dilemma.

The plane took off, making Danni's stomach feel like it slammed against her spine. Nausea washed over her. Darby handed her airsickness pills, and Danni took two more, then ran to the bathroom to throw them back up. She gripped the sink until most of the queasiness passed.

She washed her face, patting it dry with the coarse brown paper towel. She felt better. Maybe she should just stop fighting it. An empty stomach seemed to be the answer. What was the worst that could happen? She could finally lose that last ten pounds?

She made her way to her seat.

Darby handed her a navy blue blanket. "I asked the stewardess for a blanket. I figured you'd want to sleep."

"You're a sweetheart." Danni took the blanket and snuggled in for the flight. She yawned and said, "And it's flight attendant. I don't think they go by stewardess anymore."

"Meh. She can get over it."

Danni chuckled. Darby wasn't one to quibble or waste time with guilt or details. But she was a good sport. When Danni said she'd rather take a bullet than drive across the country in a rented car, Darby was agreeable. She said she liked flying because it made her feel like she was worldly. All the girl asked for was that Danni see a doctor if she didn't shake the flu within three days of returning home. Darby's mother had thought she had the flu, and it turned out to be cancer.

Danni promised she'd go the first full day back. That softened the worry lines on Darby's face. Danni didn't think she needed a doctor, but she knew Darby didn't need to worry about losing more people.

~*~

Danni and Darby arrived on the island a little before dinner time. They'd made good time, not even bothering to stop for food. Skipping meals didn't break Danni's heart. She'd tried to eat lunch, but it didn't stay down. To avoid the humiliation of vomiting in the parking lot like a drunken co-ed, she made her way to the nearest garbage can, the memory of which still made her feel queasy all over.

She stopped at a small bait and tackle/grocery/gas station to pick up a fresh gallon of milk and something easy for dinner. The car dinged as she opened her door. "Did you want anything?" she asked Darby.

"Get me some Dr. Pepper. And maybe some Twinkies. And chips."

As Danni was getting Darby's list, Tori's yellow Mustang pulled into the lot. Danni frowned and shook her head.

Darby scowled. "I say we bust her up."

Danni looked at Darby with wide eyes. "Darby!"

"What? You weren't thinking it?"

"No." Danni would never *bust her up*, but maybe she would key that fancy car Danni paid for. Repossess her knockers. Other than that, she wasn't the overly temperamental or violent type.

"I swear, if I wasn't reformed and civilized, I'd make that bitch bleed."

"Ignore her," Danni said as she climbed out of the car. She popped her head in the window. "I'm serious; ignore her."

Darby nodded. Danni grabbed her purse and headed for the store.

The gravel crunched under her feet, and shaking legs made the walk to the store more stressful than it needed to be. Before she made it up the wide wooden steps, Tori grabbed her arm.

"Excuse me?" she said to Tori.

Tori's blood red nails dug into Danni's arm. "You know, Danni, I always knew you weren't the sweetheart everyone makes you out to be."

"Let go of my arm. I've got nothing to say to you."

"Well," she said, "I have something you need to hear."

Danni jerked her arm away. "Save it, Tori. I don't give a damn what you have to say."

"You callous little bitch. Fisher and I were happy before you came along."

"Then why were you screwing Rick?"

"That is a damned lie, and you know it."

"Rick is on the island, hanging out with Fisher and telling him everything."

Tori let go of Danni's arm. She looked nervous — eyes big, lip twitchy. "There's...nothing to tell."

"Seriously? You're sticking with that story? Seems Rick is way more honest than you are. Tell me, are you enjoying the boobs I bought you? Love the car."

"Screw you, Danni." Tori took a step back. Danni imagined she needed to get hold of Rick and find out how deep he was digging them.

"I wonder, if I contacted the police, would this count as criminal embezzlement, or just another stupid woman who trusted the wrong man?" Danni took a step toward her. She wasn't allowing Tori to retreat so easily. "But I'm done wasting time with the wrong guy. You can let Rick know, this attempt at a reconciliation is a waste of time. You're not getting Fisher, and Rick sure as hell isn't getting any more of my money."

"Enjoy Fisher while it lasts. Once he realizes you won't ever, ever be able to give him the family he's always wanted, we'll see how perfect you are to him and how long he stays with you."

Danni took a sharp breath.

"Or maybe he won't leave you. Then you can grow old knowing you robbed him of the one thing he always wanted most. You know him better than anyone, don't you, Danni? You know how this will hurt him. Maybe not now, but one day."

Tori smiled at her, a slow, smug smile as she stepped off the porch of the store. She walked backward across the lot to her car, taunting Danni as she took each step. "You know I'm right. I can see it on your face. Hurt him now or hurt him later; the choice is yours."

Danni couldn't even formulate a response. In her shock, she didn't see Darby get out of the car until it was too late. "Darby, no. Get back in the car."

But it was too late. Darby was quick. She looked like a real stuntman sliding over the hood of the car, grabbing Tori by the shoulder, spinning her toward her, and punching her in the face. Tori hit the ground with one hit. Darby looked up at Tori and grinned. "That's what they call a glass jaw."

Danni ran down the steps and grabbed Darby by the arm. "What are you thinking?"

"You're no mother, Danni," Tori said, holding her hand to her bloodied lip. "You shouldn't be trusted with a kid. Social services should take her away and put her in a good home."

Danni kept a firm grip on Darby's arm. "Go ahead and call them. If it takes every last dime I own to keep her, I'll gladly pay it. I've spent millions on dumber things, so don't think that money means a damn thing to me." She held onto Darby's arm. "Come on, kiddo. Let's go home."

In the car, Danni had to remind Darby to buckle up. Darby was nervous and shaking. Danni reached across her and grabbed the buckle, snapping it in for her.

"I messed up, didn't I, Danni?"

Danni patted the girl's hand. "It will be fine. We have Ms. Maureen on our side, and I swear, I will hire every attorney I can find. And if she really wants to push me, I will hire someone to find out what her and Rick did with my money." Danni hit the steering wheel. "God, I am such an idiot. I should have known."

Darby rubbed her knuckles. They were red and swelling. "Fisher evidently never caught on either. She was cheating on him. You know what makes no sense to me," Darby said. "Why would Tori talk Rick into divorcing you? She had to know if she wanted Fisher, if you were single, you'd be a problem."

Danni shook her head. "Tori is very conceited. She probably thought she could keep them both. She also didn't know Max would die and force me to come home. Or that I'd pull out in front of a truck." Danni reached across the console and grabbed Darby's hand. "And she never counted on you. Tori expected me to run away from this island hours after the funeral. She failed to realize I'd never leave my little sister."

Darby swiped at tears. "I don't cry. Damned allergies."

Danni laughed and turned on the radio.

When they arrived at the hotel, Fisher's truck was in the lot. Danni felt instant relief. He would know what they should do about Darby. Sure, she told the kid not to worry, but there was probably cause for worry.

Danni hopped out of the car and headed for the hotel. She was so focused on finding Fisher, she didn't notice Rick approaching her. It seemed like he came out of nowhere like a swarm of mosquitoes wrapping her up in a hug.

"Rick?" she asked.

"I came to surprise you. Are you surprised?" He smiled down at her as he crushed her body to his.

"I'm stunned."

"My beautiful girl. I missed you."

Fisher hadn't been lying. Danni's mind reeled. The moment felt like a dream. One of those bizarre kinds where zoo animals wore pants and drove cars. It wasn't until his lips met hers that she woke up and pushed him away.

Rick took a step back but didn't release his grip on her. "I've missed you. Life is nothing without you. I realized I needed you, so here I am."

"Here you are," Danni repeated. "When are you leaving?"

"I'm staying, babe. Todd, your maintenance man, let me have a room, and I'm here for the long haul. I know we can work this out."

She pulled herself free. "Todd, my maintenance man, huh? Rick, you've been hanging out with Fisher. Telling my very best friend in the world all the lousy shit you've been doing to me, so let's quit pretending there is a snowball's chance in hell of there ever being an us ever again."

"He—" Rick closed his mouth and shook his head as if he realized he was wasting his breath.

"And your girlfriend, the one with the fake boobs I bought her, is bleeding in a parking lot about a mile up the road."

"What?" Rick's eyes opened wide. "Tori is hurt?"

Danni nodded. "If I were you, I'd cut my losses here and head up the road."

Rick looked genuinely concerned. "Bleeding? What happened?"

"She ran her mouth. Do her a favor. Tell her to forget about me and forget about Fisher, because I swear to all that is holy, if you two cause me any more headaches, I will hire a forensic accountant to comb over every business deal you've ever put your signature on."

"Danni, I—"

"Get the hell off my property before I have you arrested for trespassing."

"Can I get my stuff?"

"Five minutes."

Rick hurried to the hotel room, gathered his bags, and took off without saying goodbye.

Her and Darby stood on the porch and watched him take off. Danni had to chuckle. "You know, Darby, worst case, I could probably cut Tori a check for a few thousand, and she'd forget you ever knocked her out. Those two are the greediest."

"I'd hate for her to get anything good from any of this."

Danni gave Darby's ear a tug. "Defiant little thing, aren't you?"

"Well, it's just wrong. Screw her. I'll gladly go to juvie first."

"Let's go find Fisher."

Danni opened the door of the hotel, and her eyes popped open. It looked like they'd been robbed. Everything, including the walls, was gone.

"What the hell?" Danni looked left and right. The place was stripped bare. No kitchen. No bedrooms. No living area. It was just one big empty space.

Darby stepped in front of Danni and did a little two-step with jazz hands. "Surprise."

"What the hell is going on? Where is Fisher?"

"We came back too soon, Danni. Fisher is doing a total flip, but he needed us gone a week or so to finish."

"Fisher," Danni yelled.

Fisher stepped into the room from the back porch.

Danni waved her hands across the empty space. "Gee, *Todd*, you've been a busy guy while I was gone."

"I wanted to do something nice for you—to make up for what I did. Come look." He dragged her to a table made of sawhorses and plywood. "These are the designs. Coulter Construction is doing the interior. Jenna is doing the designs, see?"

He flipped through page after page of rooms so perfect, Danni couldn't help but feel like Christmas came early. "These are beautiful," she said.

"Jenna calls it cottage style. I told her you'd want something homey, but soft and feminine, and comfortable—and something that includes some of Max's paintings and that ugly-ass owl lamp."

After years and years of ultra-modern design that Rick had insisted on, these designs were perfect. "You helped pick these?"

"I tried to pick things you'd like. I hope I got it right."

"It's perfect. How much—?"

"I'm paying for it."

"You don't have to do that."

"I want to. It's my way of making up for how bad I screwed shit up. And," he grabbed Danni by the waist and pulled her into him. "I'm hoping you'll let me live here. Not in sin, because I know, I know—be a role model. But after I marry you." He kissed her hand. "Marry me. Then this is just an investment in my new home."

She touched his face, placing her hands on his cheeks. "You know I love you, but there are things we have to talk about."

"Come on, Danni, no buts. You love me, and I love you. It's that simple."

"I'm afraid there is nothing in life that is that simple."

Chapter 55

Danni led Fisher out onto the back porch where there was still somewhere to sit, and they could have a conversation.

Once seated on the swing with the sun shining so bright and the squeak of the chains joining the chirps of crickets and tweets of birds, it seemed unfair that there were still problems in her life.

Fisher took her hand and gave it a squeeze. "If it's the infertility, I don't care."

Danni almost suffered whiplash looking at him. "How did you—?"

"It doesn't matter how I know; I just know."

Danni shook her head. Fisher had just spent two days with Rick, and Rick did love to talk.

Fisher put a hand under her chin and turned her toward him. "It's not a big deal."

"You say that now, but one day—"

"If I have a change of heart, I'll knock up a stripper."

Danni rolled her eyes. "You're not taking this seriously."

"You're right, I'm not. It's a non-issue. Hell, we have Darby. Do you seriously think she's not going to be a handful?"

Danni thought of Darby punching Tori and shrugged.

He cradled her face in his hands, forcing her to maintain eye contact. The pressure of his hands on her cheeks, the look of desperation in his eyes, and the smell of fresh cut lumber that clung to his clothes made her want to think that everything could just be as easy as saying I do.

"I do love you an awful lot," she whispered.

His lips felt perfect. A natural fit. He moved closer, pulling her into him.

The door slammed behind them. Both of them turned to the sound. It was Darby, hand on her hip, head shaking like a pissed rooster. She threw a package at Fisher with enough velocity that it bounced off his chest and hit the floor.

"What the hell?" Darby asked. "Is that why the miserable bitch attacked Danni at the store?"

Fisher looked at Darby. "What do you mean, attacked Danni?"

"Tori grabbed Danni in the parking lot and was threatening her. I had to punch her in the face to back her off.

Danni bent over and grabbed the pink and purple box off the porch floor. She closed her eyes and shook her head. Was life ever going to cut her a break?

Danni handed the box to Fisher. "A pregnancy test? Oh my God Fisher, did you get Tori pregnant?"

Chapter 56

It was Danni's worst nightmare — Tori getting to have Fisher's baby. Every insecurity and inadequacy she'd ever felt ripped through her, making it nearly impossible to take a breath. Fisher held her, his arms tight around her. She tried to get away, to stand up so she could get enough space to take a breath. Getting free wasn't an option. His grip pressed her against him.

Once she stopped fighting, he brushed her hair away from her face. "I bought that for you."

"For me?" Tears burned her eyes. "Are you joking or just being cruel?"

Cradling her face in his hands, he explained. "He lied to you, Danni."

"Who?"

"Rick. He lied to you about the infertility. Did you ever actually go to the Summit Hill Fertility Clinic? Like physically go into a building or an office?"

Danni shook her head. "I went to my gynecologist, and the fertility clinic reviewed my tests and charts."

"No, they didn't. The place doesn't exist. Bev was the first to figure it out, and she asked me to have you verify the name of the place for your health report."

"That's ridiculous."

"Check it out. Try to find a phone number or a website. Summit Hill Fertility Clinic doesn't exist anywhere."

"He's right," Darby said behind her. "The place doesn't exist."

"But they sent me the reports."

Fisher took a deep breath. "Rick must have sent you those reports."

"That's insane," Danni said. "Rick can be a selfish jerk, but that's...that's maniacal. What would be the point?"

"I don't know exactly what his motives were—maybe preempting you wanting a baby."

"I never suggested we have a baby. I thought it was a bad idea. He's the one who wanted the baby. This is ridiculous. If something has happened with Tori, just man up and tell me about it."

"Nothing happened with Tori. I haven't had sex with her in months."

"TMI," Darby said behind them.

"Darby, can I please talk to Danni alone?"

"No," Darby said, arms crossed over her chest, foot tapping on the porch.

"Darby, go in the house," Danni said.

"Fine." The girl slammed the door on her way into the house.

"Here's the honest to God truth. The clinic you got the report from is a hoax, and Rick told me a family would tie you to him, so he obviously knows the fertility issue is bullshit. Add in the fatigue and nausea you're having, and it only makes sense."

Danni shook her head. "The only thing it proves is how desperate you are to deny the truth."

Chapter 57

Fisher envied his ancestors. A couple hundred years ago, he could have killed her husband in battle, traded her family a few horses, and secured her hand in marriage.

Okay, so maybe it wasn't at all like that, contrary to what Danni thought—he wasn't obsessed like his mother with lineage and ancestry. He didn't know the first damn thing about the Hatterask Indians or their customs. But for his comfort musings, that's how he imagined this could have played out before white men and all their damn rules showed up to ruin things.

He rubbed the stubble on his chin and tried to sound calm. "I love you. I don't see why it's so difficult to see we belong together. Unless you're still mad at me for being an ass about Renzo—"

"Of course not. I told you I'm over that."

"Then there's nothing. Nothing should be standing between us."

"Infertility isn't a *'no biggie.'* It's huge. And your far-fetched hope that Rick created this massive conspiracy to fake me into thinking I can't have kids is not only insane, but it shows that at your very core, you're desperate to believe it's not true."

Fisher sighed. When he'd bought the test, he knew he couldn't just ask her to take it. He wasn't sure how the hell he planned to trick her into giving him a urine sample, but he had never planned to tell her what he was thinking. He'd feared she'd react like this. Doggone Darby for being so aware of every damn thing around her.

Fisher took the box from her and stuffed it in his pocket. "You're right. Don't bother with it. Rick's too stupid to carry off a plan like that anyhow."

"He's not completely stupid," Danni mumbled.

"Well, he sure can't keep his mouth shut. If he'd have faked medical reports and contacts at fictitious fertility clinics, he'd have bragged about it."

"So, you admit it was just wishful thinking?"

Danni's eyes sparkled with tears. He kissed her forehead. "Yeah. I was wishing I could trap you into marrying me. Now, I'm just going to have to hope I can appeal to your love for me — if you really do love me."

"Fisher...I do love you; it's just — "

"If you mean that, then fine. Whether you marry me or not, I'm moving in. I've already started building myself a room."

She laughed. She evidently thought he was joking. She'd figure it out when he refused to go home tonight. Or tomorrow night. She'd either have to call the police to have him dragged away or give in.

"Hey, Darby," he yelled.

"What?" the girl answered from behind the screen door.

"Google how long someone has to live with someone before it's declared common law marriage in North Carolina."

"What are you...?" Danni looked confused.

"I'm finding a loophole to your no. I'm not leaving. After — Did you find out how many years it takes, Darby?"

Danni stood. Head shaking, she gave him a look. "You're not taking any of this seriously."

He stood. Toe to toe, eye to eye, he locked horns with her. "You're right. I'm not. It's ridiculous. I'm asking you to be my wife and my partner. Not my incubator. Whether or not I have kids doesn't matter to me."

Tears spilled over her eyelashes and down her cheeks. Her body trembled. "It matters to me."

The look on her face sent a pain through his chest. It physically hurt to see her in pain. He pulled her in and held her. After a few minutes, her body relaxed, and her breathing calmed. "I'll make you a deal," he whispered in her ear. "You marry me, and if I ever change my mind about kids, you can give me permission to have a girlfriend."

She chuckled. He felt a ray of hope. Wrapping his hands in her hair, he held her close.

"You win," she said.

"Not the romantic, yes, I imagined, but I'll take it." He yelled over his shoulder, "You hear that, Darby, I win."

Danni wrapped her arms around his waist and held him tight. "I love you, you crazy goon of a man. I was trying to do the noble thing. But while I was away, I realized two things." She held up a finger. "Number one, I am miserable without you. Second, I am not noble. I'm pretty damned selfish because the worse I felt, the more homesick I became, and all I wanted was you. If one day you have regrets, then tough shit. You don't get any sort of pass."

"You could take the test," Darby yelled from the other side of the door.

"Eavesdropping is rude, young lady," Danni yelled back.

"Seriously, Danni," Darby said. "What could it hurt?"

"Take the test, I'll give you Punkin."

Danni grabbed the box from Fisher's back pocket and stepped away. "I want that in writing."

"Sure thing."

Danni stared at the white and purple box. "This is insanity, but since it's here...."

Fisher grinned and followed her into the house.

Danni grabbed a notebook and handed it to him. "Give me Punkin."

Fisher nodded. Darby handed him a pen, and he bent over the table, scribbled a few lines, ripped off the paper, and handed it to Danni.

Danni read it. "It says if I marry you, I get the dog. I said I'd take the test to get the dog."

"I don't give a shit if you take the test or not. I want you to marry me."

"I want you to take the damn test," Darby said. "Think about it...the nausea, the fatigue, the mood swings."

"I'm not moody," Danni snapped.

"Excuse me, queen of serenity, I was mistaken," Darby said. "But think about it, Danni. The place is nowhere on the net. And you have the flu no one else is catching. I'm thinking it's not that insane an idea, especially considering all the other lies Rick and Tori cooked up."

Danni looked at the box in her hand. Worst case scenario, it was negative. She still had Fisher. A crazy lunatic of a man. And Darby. A temperamental, quick-fisted lunatic of a girl. A home. A ripped-up shell of a place. And she finally would get her dog. Ugly as she was.

Wasn't that the kind of life every girl dreamed of?

As if reading her mind, Fisher whispered, "No matter what, I love you."

Danni ripped open the box and headed toward the far wall where the bathroom used to be. "Do we still have a bathroom?"

"Through the eastern wall that used to be your room. The hotel bath is still intact."

Danni walked through the skeletal walls to the old hotel room. She went in alone and closed the door. With shaking hands, she read the instructions. She tried to calm herself, but she was too nervous. If she dropped the damned thing in the toilet, she wasn't rescuing it. She'd consider that a fated no.

There was a knock on the door. "You okay, Danni? You need me to help?" Darby asked.

"No, I got it."

Danni did her business, wrapped the plastic stick in toilet paper, and set it on the back of the toilet. She washed her hands and left the room. Her hands still shook so badly, she had to squeeze them together to still them. A wave of queasiness washed over her, making her run back to the bathroom and drop to her knees over the toilet bowl. Fisher came in behind her and closed the door.

"I'm sorry to put you through this. I thought of every way I could do the test without you knowing. Would you have believed me if I'd told you I need a piss sample to order furniture?"

Danni sat on the floor and smiled. "Not likely." She leaned her head against the vanity. "What if it's negative?"

He took her hand and kissed it. "It doesn't matter. We still have Darby to raise, and she's a teen. There's at least a 35% chance she'll have an unwanted pregnancy, and we can buy the baby from her."

Danni kicked his foot. "That's awful." She rolled her head against the wall. "But you are right. She needs a family. She was so worried I might have cancer. If something would happen to me, you have to be there for her."

"Nothing will happen to you."

"I'm not saying anything would, but if it did. Would you be willing to add your name to her adoption papers? She'd need someone. She has such a temper. She punched Tori in the face in the mini-mart parking lot today."

Fisher grinned. "She did? Damn, I love that girl."

"I don't think we should encourage her."

"Is she in trouble?"

Danni shrugged. "I called Claire. I'm going to meet with her tomorrow."

He gave her hand a squeeze. "I'll go with you."

She nodded.

He grinned. "Look at that, Loonie. We're parents."

She smiled at him. "I love you, Fish."

He pulled her close and kissed her. "I have been waiting to hear that."

"You are an amazing guy, Todd, the handyman."

Fisher chuckled. "I like to think that was me being an amazing genius and not him being a total moron, but...."

"I still can't believe he came here. He must know I have more money."

Fisher took a deep breath. "The guy's a dick, and I would think you were a total fool, but I think you should know that he really does regret divorcing you."

"Really?"

Fisher's jaw tensed, and his cheeks flushed. "You want me to call him and have him come back?"

Danni smiled and took his hand. "Of course not. You know I'm crazy about you."

"Then marry me."

"Shouldn't we see —?"

"No. Promise me right now that you'll marry me, no matter what. Simply because you love me."

She rubbed her nose against his. "You know I love you. But if you never get to have a family, you might regret marrying, and then what?"

"You could just check the stick," Darby yelled from the other side of the door.

"Are you eavesdropping, young lady?" Danni yelled back.

Fisher grinned and leaned his head against the door.

"Of course. Would you two stop messing around and just check that damn stick before I break down the door and do it myself?"

Danni took a deep breath and looked at Fisher. "We have really got to do something about that girl's potty mouth. I don't know where the hell she gets it."

"No shit," Fisher said.

"I'm listening, you know. If you were worried about being good role models, you'd have been using condoms," Darby yelled.

Danni blushed but yelled back. "Maybe I was shooting for a tragic life lesson."

"Would one of you please look at the damned stick?" Darby turned the handle, but the door was locked. "I promise you, I won't be having any kids you can buy."

Danni laughed and grabbed the stick. She handed it to Fisher. "You look."

Fisher stood. Danni stayed seated on the floor with her knees tucked to her chest. He unwrapped the paper from the stick.

"Two lines. Is that good or bad?"

"Two lines are positive," Darby yelled. Danni could hear her jumping up and down. Fisher unlocked the door to show her. Darby looked at the stick in his hands and squealed, "Oh my God, you're gonna have a baby. That's so awesome. A little creepy that you're holding a stick Danni peed on, but awesome."

Fisher turned to Danni. She never moved from her spot on

the floor. "You okay, Loonie?"

Grabbing the hand towel by the sink, she buried her face in it and cried. "I'm so happy," she said after blowing her nose.

Chapter 58

It took three months, both for the hotel renovations to be finished and for the forensic accountant to find enough dirt on Rick and Tori to make them plead guilty.

Strangely, it wasn't illegal to steal money from your spouse to give it to your lover. But if you're foolish enough to set up a company and make your mistress your VP, you can both go to jail for embezzlement when you use company funds for things like sports cars and boob jobs. Sadly, the lying lovers were only getting six months each in a federal prison, but when Danni found out that Tori would be denied all cosmetics, even deodorant, that somehow pleased her more than imagining her behind bars. A stinky Tori with dark roots made Danni grin.

Not to mention, it helped Darby's assault and battery case. Once it was proven that Tori was such an openly awful, manipulative person, the judge dropped the charges. When Tori threw a fit about it in the courtroom, the judge was kind enough to give her twenty-four hours in jail for contempt to both calm down and to get acquainted with confinement. Darby predicted Tori would end up racking up extra time in prison because ever since she was busted, she seemed absolutely incapable of maintaining her temper. Darby tried to get Danni to bet twenty dollars on Tori punching a guard within a month. Danni refused to take the bet on principle.

Her life was going so great, to gloat over Tori's downfall seemed petty. Danni had everything she wanted. The day after Rick and Tori surrendered themselves to the sheriff, Fisher and Danni married in a small service at the same church Max haunted.

Darby, now Darby Lowry Cooper, was the maid of honor. They were a family. Danni rubbed her belly. And that family was growing.

There was only one thing left. It was time to lay Max to rest. Maureen's party plans started with the hotel's big reveal. The new neon sign would be lit up for the first time tonight, and it would be the first homage to Max. After the sign would come the fish, fresh off a boat at Manteo. Then there would be a toast at sunset while Maureen and Kitty, Max's best gal pals, rowed out into the sound and scattered the ashes of their friend.

Then they would tap the keg, and a band from Kitty Hawk would play, and everyone would dance. Just the sort of party Max would want.

First order of business was the sign. Danni hadn't gotten to see it yet. Jenna designed it and had it made as her family's tribute and memorial gift to Max. Fisher and Luke mounted the sign the morning of the party but left it draped in tarps.

Once everyone arrived and stood along the road, waiting for the canvas to drop, Fisher yelled to Darby, "Flip the switch, kid."

Darby ran to the hotel office, flipped the switch, and ran back. She stood next to Danni, looking eager and anxious to have the place open for business.

When they dropped the canvas, Danni gasped. It was perfect. It was the art-deco style she requested. The words Sun Shiner Inn Hotel stayed lit as blinking lights pointed the way to the beach. At the top of the sign was a smiling sun wearing Max's fishing hat. Tears clouded her eyes.

Maureen wrapped an arm around her. "It's right perfect, isn't it, darlin'?"

"It's better than I imagined." As Danni looked up at the sign, she felt a flutter. She wrapped her hands around her belly and gasped.

"Everything okay?" Fisher yelled from his spot next to the sign.

"I think I just felt it move." Danni refused to call the baby he or she, for fear that when the baby was born, it would think she had a preference one way or another.

"A fluttery feeling, like butterflies in your belly?"

Danni nodded.

"I want to feel it." Fisher hurried over.

"Oh, wait your turn. You've got another month before you can feel it," Maureen chuckled. "It's the quickening. And only the momma can feel it. Now, let's go see those renovations."

"Hey Fisher, remember when you thought you could get this done in ten days?" Darby asked.

"I could have." He wrapped an arm around Danni's waist. "But someone came back and was a distraction."

"Well, it was better not to rush perfection, and this place looks perfect," Maureen said. "I don't think I've ever seen it look any better."

It was looking top notch. Everything was rehabbed, from the exterior to the apartment to the hotel rooms. Danni did slow down the work when she and Darby came up with the genius idea of turning every hotel room into an efficiency. That took switching around the floor plan of the entire hotel, but the result was worth it. Each room was more like a studio apartment pulled from the 1950s than a hotel room.

Maureen lifted a wooden box out of her gigantic purse. "All right, Max, you've been patient, but this is your night." Maureen looked over the hotel. "Time for you to rest in peace, my friend."

~*~

The party was in full swing, a crowd there to celebrate the life of Max Lowry. The cove was filled, as was most every inch of the public porches. Danni was looking for a quiet place to get away from the crowd for just a bit. In the office window, Punkin stood on her hind legs and scratched.

"Hey, little lady," Danni said through the window. "You need a break too?" She opened the door and grabbed the leash. Punkin hopped around and whined. To Punkin, a walk was as good as chocolate or crack. Danni enjoyed a walk on the beach, but she'd never jump up and down for one. Punkin would run circles around the office, half out of her mind with excitement.

When Danni bent over to snap the leash on Punkin, the baby fluttered again. Danni stood, and it stopped, so she bent over again. More flutters. Each time Danni bent over, the baby would move. Obviously, it wasn't a fan of being tipped on its head.

Eugene, a big black Tom, sat high above on a file cabinet watching them both with a flick of his tail like he was embarrassed to be associated with the likes of them. "Don't give me that look, Eug. I could have left you in the weeds as snake food. Trash eating cat giving me attitude." Eugene yawned and closed his eyes, but the judgmental tail kept flicking.

Off they went, the fur ball full of energy and the slower-moving pregnant chick. This walk to the beach was one of Danni's favorite parts of the day. The beach was an ever-changing constant. Some days the shore would be nothing but smooth sand and calm water. Other days, the landscape would be changed by turbulent waters. It was on these days the shore was most interesting. Tidal pools formed by shifting currents and channels of water on the beach. Even as a young girl, the beach after a good storm was her favorite place. As Max would say, *the greatest treasures are found after the storms have passed.*

Danni couldn't agree more. If she'd have clung to her safe life and never faced the challenges of coming home, she'd have missed out on so much.

The beach was empty as far as her eye could see, so Danni unclipped the dog from her leash and let her run after the pale shelled ghost crabs that thought they owned the beach at night. Punkin taught them that the canine still ruled, barking and chasing crabs until they retreated to their holes.

Danni sat in the sand and closed her eyes. The crashing of the waves relaxed her. Resting her cheek on her knees, she felt her body grow heavy, and the world grew dark. In that darkness, there was comfort. A warmth in the wind and the smell of vanilla and brown sugar enveloped her. Danni lifted her head. It was no longer evening, but the bright of day. The sun shined so bright, she had to squint to see through the glare.

Coming from the mist, dressed in white, was Max. She stopped first to scratch Punkin's ears, then she made her way to Danni and sat beside her, digging her toes into the sand.

"Danni girl, you done good. I'm proud of you."

Danni smiled. "I miss you."

"Of course you do. Who wouldn't?" Max gave her a smug look.

Danni smiled. "My mom, is she all right?"

Max wrapped her arm in Danni's. "She is. The pains we have on earth don't follow us here, though she worried about you. It was her love for you that forced me through the veil if you want to call it that."

"I read her diary."

"So, you know?"

"I think I have it figured out."

Max looked in her eyes as if she could read her thoughts. She nodded. "You know."

"Is that why you never spent the money? It was bought with her shame?"

"She was the most delightful child, my little sister. Happy and full of dreams. He robbed her of all of it. I was her sister but couldn't see. If not for Daniel, I may never have helped her."

"Daniel sounds like a good man."

"The best." Max smiled.

"Is that where I got my name?"

Max nodded. "Vi took her most loyal loves and handed your care to them."

"My blessing?"

"Your blessing. You got my Danny's intuitive heart, or you'd have never noticed I was hanging around, pushing as much as I could. No one else noticed."

"Maureen did."

Max laughed. "The old gal is plumb crazy. I ain't no bird."

"I'll never tell her."

"No, you shouldn't." Max took a deep breath. "But I'll tell you a secret...angels gather when we mourn — little signs, like Maureen's flowers. And when angels walk the earth, they're most often movin' on four paws. I always knew I was right about that. I'm one smart cookie, little girl."

"So that's what Maureen was saying about Punkin being a guardian angel."

Max nodded. "I knew you weren't listening to her."

Danni shrugged.

"It's all right. You had a lot on your mind, getting haunted by your dear auntie and all."

"I thought I was going insane."

"Sorry about that, but it had to be done. Vi wouldn't have rested knowing her daughter was headed for misery."

"I was?"

"Fisher is your soul mate. Denying it would have ruined you both."

Danni reached out to hug her aunt, but as she leaned toward her, she disappeared, and Danni was falling, falling toward the sand.

"Danni."

Danni opened her eyes. Punkin was nestled against her hip, asleep. Her cheek hurt where her knee pressed into it as she slept. She lifted her head and rubbed her eyes.

"Fisher."

"You were gone a long time. I started to worry."

"I fell asleep."

"I see that. We should go home and get you to bed."

"I'm not tired anymore." She leaned her head against Fisher's shoulder as she watched the moon dance off the water. "Fish, if this baby is a girl, can we name her Violet?"

He kissed the top of her head. "I can't think of anything more perfect."

"And if it's a boy—"

Fisher shook his head. "She's a girl."

Danni smiled. "Is that your guess?"

"Not at all. You think you're the only one Max bosses around from the beyond?"

Elizabeth divides her time between her beach cottage and her scrupulously clean house in the hills of West Virginia.

Ooops. That's fantasy Elizabeth. The real Elizabeth spends her days schlepping after her four boys (five if you count their father) and the assortment of pets they swore they'd take care of.

She does live in West Virginia; the house is clean when the mother-in-law visits, and she does have serious dreams of living at the beach.

Elizabeth is a Marshall University graduate with a degree in counseling. This has proven very beneficial when dealing with the make-believe friends she hangs out with all day (she calls this 'writing').

Follow her blog at: http://www.eseckman.blogspot.com

www.ingramcontent.com/pod-product-compliance
Lightning Source LLC
Chambersburg PA
CBHW071851220626
47052CB00002B/62